THE
BONE
FIELD

**The Dark Paradise Mysteries
by Debra Bokur**

The Fire Thief

The Bone Field

THE
BONE
FIELD

DEBRA
BOKUR

KENSINGTON
PUBLISHING CORP.

www.kensingtonbooks.com

KENSINGTON BOOKS are published by

Kensington Publishing Corp.
119 West 40th Street
New York, NY 10018

All Kensington titles, imprints, and distributed lines are available at special quantity discounts for bulk purchases for sales promotion, premiums, fund-raising, educational, or institutional use. Special book excerpts or customized printings can also be created to fit specific needs. For details, write or phone the office of the Kensington Special Sales Manager: Attn. Special Sales Department. Kensington Publishing Corp, 119 West 40th Street, New York, NY 10018. Phone: 1-800-221-2647.

Library of Congress Card Catalogue Number: 2020952451

ISBN-13: 978-1-4967-2775-6
ISBN-10: 1-4967-2775-4
First Kensington Hardcover Edition: June 2021

ISBN-13: 978-1-4967-2777-0 (ebook)
ISBN-10: 1-4967-2777-0 (ebook)

10 9 8 7 6 5 4 3 2 1

Printed in the United States of America

To my son, James Walker McDaniel:
Thank you for inspiring and delighting me each and every
day of your life, and for filling my own with awe and joy.

ACKNOWLEDGMENTS

With my appreciation and deep gratitude to T. Kuʻuipo Alana for her generous assistance and invaluable insight on the spelling and pronunciation of the Hawaiian words, phrases, names, and places that appear in this book, and also in *The Fire Thief.* My thanks, too, to my family at Kensington, and to my readers—and to the islands of Hawaiʻi for providing endless inspiration.

CHAPTER 1

The midmorning sun hammered down on the old pineapple field's rutted surface, imparting a relentless, blazing glare. The ocean breeze had failed, on a colossal scale, to deliver a cooler version of tropical air over the lip of the coastal cliffs and down into the Palawai Basin plains of Lānaʻi Island's central region. It was hot, and it was early, and it was going to get hotter.

Detective Kali Māhoe peered once again into the recesses of the freshly dug trench at her feet. She'd been in, out, and around the hole for most of the morning, and her sleeveless green T-shirt, tied in a messy knot just below her breasts, was soaked with sweat. Streaks of dirt partially obscured a tattoo encircling her upper left arm, depicting a stylized, slightly geometric interpretation of a thrusting spear.

At the bottom of the hole in front of her was an old refrigerator, its door flung open and partially resting on the mound of red-tinged dirt that had been created during its excavation. There was a small backhoe parked close by, on loan from the island's community cemetery. It was close enough that she could feel the additional heat radiating from the surface of its recently used engine.

The area around the open ground had been enclosed by crime scene tape, while a makeshift tarp on poles covered the hole, tenting it from the unlikely possibility of wind interference on this unusually still morning, and fending off the sun's glare for the benefit of the police photographer. In place of the abundant natural island light, bright, artificial lights had been set up around the perimeter, angled to illuminate the depths of the hole.

The tarp had proven completely ineffective at providing any semblance of shade. In the trench, Maui medical examiner Mona Stitchard—commonly known as "Stitches," but only behind her back—was kneeling beside the refrigerator, taking measurements and making notes in a small book. Her hooded, sterile white plastic jumpsuit clung to her arms and the sides of her face, held in place against her skin by a layer of perspiration. Kali could see that her narrow eyeglasses were sliding down her nose.

Kali studied the peculiar contents of the open refrigerator, then took a long swig of water from a bottle hooked onto her belt, leaning her head back as a few drops trickled down off the edge of her chin.

Police Captain Walter Alaka'i walked up and stood beside her. He regarded the refrigerator with curiosity, his frown giving way to a row of creases in his wide brow. "Well, I gotta say this is definitely a new one. Any brilliant initial thoughts you're not sharing?"

Kali shook her head, considering the question. "Sorry. Nothing yet, beyond the obvious, slightly bizarre component."

She looked away, across the field, and then back down into the hole. What she didn't say was that she was keenly aware of a residual sadness and loss still clinging to this space, filling the molecules of earth around her feet, newly disturbed after untold years.

Stitches glanced up at Kali and Walter.

"Well, I suppose we all like a challenge." She waved her arm at a fly buzzing by her face. "And this should certainly be interesting."

The three of them regarded the derelict refrigerator. It was an older General Electric model, with a single, large main compartment and a smaller freezer door on the top. The shelves from the main compartment were missing.

"My mother had a refrigerator like this one," said Walter, pointing at it with the opened bottle of water he was holding. "And a matching stove. She was crazy proud of them. Horrible shade of yellow, if you ask me."

"Technically, the color is harvest gold," said Stitches. "Hugely popular from the 1960s all the way through the '70s."

Walter frowned at her.

"You think it's been here that long?"

"Hard to say," she answered, shrugging. "Though it doesn't seem likely someone would bury a new one."

She stood up, passing her medical bag to Kali with one hand and stretching out the other toward Walter, which he grabbed and pulled. Emerging from the depths of the trench with impressive composure, she tugged the plastic hood away from her face and hair, now plastered wet against her head. She peeled off her jumpsuit with relief, and stood beside them, taking off her glasses to clean them. Walter passed her the bottle of water he'd been holding for her. She replaced her glasses and took the bottle, drinking from it gratefully.

There were a number of people milling about the area surrounding the trench, each involved in either further securing the scene or attending to some detail: Tomas Alva, Lānaʻi's only full-time cop, officially part of the Maui County Police Department; a police photographer busily loading equipment into the back of his car; the crime scene team from the main station in Wailuku on Maui; Burial Council officials who were required to attend the scene of any uncovered grave that might have a cultural tie; and a terrified-looking young couple who were clearly tourists, huddled by a rocky outcropping at the edge of the field. They were dressed in matching brightly patterned Hawaiian shirts, and on the ground beside them were two metal detectors, their long, narrow handles clearly visible.

Looking over at the couple, Kali sighed. "I guess I should go and talk to them one more time before the woman passes out or starts wailing again," she said.

The offer sounded half-hearted, even to her own ears. Stitches glanced at her. Walter regarded her with a raised eyebrow.

Kali glared at them. "Seriously? Surely both of you can see she's one wrong word away from another bout of hysteria," she said in a defensive tone. "And yes—before anyone points it out, I'm fully aware I'm not at my best with over-excited twenty-somethings."

Both Stitches and Walter turned toward the young couple, considering.

"Probably put a big dent in her day, right?" said Walter, his smile lopsided. "They're just kids on vacation. Not every day you go looking for buried treasure and turn up something like this."

Kali exhaled. "Okay, okay. Point made."

Walter's grin widened. "One of these days, you'll realize I'm always right."

Kali snorted. "Playing the uncle card?"

He reached out and patted her lightly on the shoulder. "I can safely say that not only are you my *only* niece, you're absolutely, without doubt, my favorite one."

He turned to Stitches, who had begun to wad her used jumpsuit into a ball.

"You all through here?"

She nodded. "For now. I'll know more, of course, once we've moved everything back to the morgue and I can do a proper examination." She surveyed the long-abandoned appliance in the hole. "Meanwhile, good luck with the search. Hopefully you can find something that will be useful in ascertaining an identification."

"Well, we've searched as much as we can with the fridge still there," said Walter. "Maybe there's something still hidden beneath it. We'll see, I guess." He wiped a few drops of sweat from his brow with the back of his hand. "I'm going to head back to Maui after we get the body and fridge loaded up on the launch."

Stitches had already walked off, making her way toward a waiting car that would take her to the harbor for the roughly nine-mile boat crossing back to Maui across the 'Au'au Channel. Walter strode toward the backhoe, gesturing to the driver. The engine turned over. Parked beside it, a truck fitted with a flatbed also roared to life. The drivers of both vehicles made their way slowly toward the open hole, guided by Walter.

Kali peered once more into the depths of the trench. Lying inside the no-longer-gleaming harvest-gold refrigerator, dressed in a pair of rotting overalls, was a skeleton, its bony hands folded neatly across the chest. It was lying on its side, both legs bent at the knees, feet pressed together. She had the impression it had been placed there with great care—even reverence, perhaps. She looked more closely. Her initial feeling suggested to her that whoever had performed this strange burial had possibly cared about the dead person in some way.

She supposed it looked like a small man, but it was difficult to tell. Resting on the corpse's narrow shoulders, in lieu of a skull, was a large, ornately carved wooden pineapple, a macabre adornment that gave no sense at all of who the long-dead figure might have been—or how he'd come to be resting here, in a dormant field of fruit, bereft, headless, and utterly alone.

CHAPTER 2

It was well after noon by the time Kali had compiled her notes with details about the burial setting and finished her final interview with Brad and Jan, the tourist couple. As she'd predicted, the woman had broken down into a fit of wild crying midway through her account of the morning's events.

Brad had been more pragmatic, even a little excited.

"We thought maybe we could find some old coins, you know? Something to take home as a souvenir that didn't come from a gift shop."

Kali refrained from pointing out that removing a historic artifact from the islands wasn't likely to be looked upon kindly by the authorities. She watched his face, fascinated by the difference between his reaction to the discovery of a body, and that of his girlfriend.

"When the metal detector starting going off, we dug around the spot and kept hitting metal. Jan thought it might be a treasure chest, but I figured it was probably some old piece of harvesting equipment that got covered up." He patted the girl on her leg, as if consoling her for the loss of an imaginary fortune.

Kali frowned. "And when you realized it was an old refrigerator, why did you keep digging?"

He grinned. "Well, why would someone bury a refrigerator? I mean, maybe something important had been stashed inside of it. You know, valuable—not just a pile of old bones."

He fumbled as he saw the expression on Kali's face. "I mean . . ."

"You mean that the body of some long-dead human being, perhaps a local person, is of no possible concern, or any value." She watched as he squirmed. "Correct?"

"Well, no, of course not. It's just that . . ." He looked from Kali to Jan, and back to Kali. "Jan called 911 right away, you know? I mean, a body, right?"

"Yes, a body. Exactly right."

Jan made a fresh sobbing noise. "I didn't want to open it," she said, making an effort to keep her voice from breaking. "In the movies, opening the box buried in the remote field never turns out to be a good thing. I knew there was something bad in there. I just knew it."

"The skeleton belonged to an actual person, you know," said Kali. "A living human being who probably had a family and friends."

"And at least one enemy," Brad joked.

Kali swallowed her irritation at his shallow response, doing her best to temper her character assessment with some degree of kindness. She turned to the woman, ignoring Brad.

"You could look at it this way: Thanks to you, maybe someone will finally find some peace and closure knowing that their loved one has been found."

The woman grasped at the thought gratefully.

"Well, glad to have helped, of course. I mean, anything we can do . . ."

"You're absolutely sure you didn't find anything else?"

Exchanging glances, Brad and Jan shook their heads. They looked directly at her with no apparent subterfuge.

"No," said Jan. "Nothing at all."

Kali waited, but they just sat there, disheveled and sweaty. The woman's shoulders sagged. Kali noticed a small tear in her shirt, as well as soil stains on her beige sneakers. "I'd appreciate a call if anything occurs to you."

Again the couple looked at one another, before Jan spoke.

"So, it's okay if we go back to Maui tonight? We have a flight home to California the day after tomorrow. Should we cancel it? Will you need to hold us for more questioning or anything like that?"

Kali suppressed a smile. There were, she thought, simply too many police shows on television these days.

"I don't think that will be necessary, but we'd appreciate it if you could keep all of this to yourselves until we've been in touch," she said, keeping her voice even. She could tell they were more than ready for cold showers and the hotel bar, where they'd most likely retell their story over and over, no matter how many times she might ask them not to. "Just make sure Officer Alva has all of your contact information before you leave." She lent them a more serious gaze. "Just in case."

The refrigerator, still holding the body, was carefully lifted from the ground and loaded onto the flatbed truck. To give them space to work, a command center for the police and crime scene crew had been set up near the parking area. The surrounding area was searched diligently, the soil sifted for any small item that might shed some light on the moment when the refrigerator had been covered and abandoned. As the day lent itself toward dusk, more lights were set up around the now-empty hole. Armed with a bucket, sieve, and small shovel, Kali helped turn over the loose earth meticulously.

She could see the undulating landscape of the pineapple field rolling off into the distance, shrouded by the growing shadows. Tomas Alva stood just outside the line of light, waiting patiently. Like Kali, he was covered in dirt.

"We're going to shut this down for the night," he said wearily. "Probably take forever, but we've got a team using ground-penetrating radar coming in the morning, and a crew to start digging up the rest of the field if necessary . . . in case the head's nearby."

It won't be, Kali told herself. The pineapple suggested that the burial had had some sort of ritual significance, and it was unlikely that a head had been relegated to a separate box and conveniently planted somewhere in the vicinity. She kept her thoughts to herself. It wouldn't hurt the SOC crew to spend a few days with backhoes and shovels. The last thing she wanted to do was keep anyone from feeling useful.

She felt Tomas's eyes on her. They'd known one another for years, and she suspected that he'd likely read the gist of her thoughts. He said nothing, only grinned tiredly.

"I'll give you a ride into town when you're ready," he said.

She brushed herself off, succeeding only in making her hands dirtier than they already were.

"I'm going to make a mess of your car seat," she said, somewhat apologetically.

"Can't get any dirtier than my seat will be," he said. "Come on. Let's get you settled, and I'll go and see if there's any supper left for me at home."

They walked to the car and climbed inside. For a moment, Tomas sat with his head back against his headrest. He reached forward slowly, turning the key that had been left in the ignition. As the car's engine rumbled softly, he backed out of the makeshift parking spot and pulled onto the narrow track leading to the two-lane main road.

They rode in silence for a minute. Then Tomas turned to Kali. "Can you think of any reason someone would replace a head with a wooden *hala kahiki*?"

She considered his question. "Well . . . it's an obvious way to conceal the victim's identity, at least in the short term," she offered. "But I think it's more likely there was something significant about the choice. Why not a real *hala kahiki*? It's not as though there's a pineapple shortage here. Market shelves are full of them."

"That's what I was thinking. Seems like someone went through considerable effort to find a wooden one."

Not if the person's death had been planned in advance, and the carved pineapple had been conveniently at hand, she thought. That scenario suggested a premeditation that might somehow tie to the image of this particular fruit. "I don't love these cold cases," she said instead. "It's bad enough when we know who the victim is to begin with, but when we have to figure out who it is before we can hunt for a reason, I start losing sleep."

"Maybe," Tomas responded, his voice thoughtful, "it was a natural death, or an accidental one, and the pineapple was an afterthought."

She looked at him sideways. "Natural death by decapitation?"

Tomas shrugged. "Yeah, it does sound a little crazy, doesn't it? What about an accident, maybe with some of the equipment, and someone wanted to hide it?"

It was Kali's turn to shrug. "I'm sure stranger things have happened. But in all likelihood this wasn't just an accident."

They drove the rest of the short distance in silence. Darkness had almost completely fallen as Tomas pulled the car up in front of the entrance of the Hotel Lāna'i in Lāna'i City.

She unclipped her seat belt and opened the car door, already anticipating the magic of a long shower and late dinner.

"Mahalo for the ride," she said, climbing out. "I'm heading back to Maui early, but I'll be in touch before I leave."

"*Pomaika'i*," called Tomas, using the Hawaiian word for "good luck." He gave a wave as he pulled back out into the street, taillights fading as the road curved away into the night.

Kali turned, gazing at the small plantation-style building that housed the hotel. It was painted a soft yellow and surrounded by blooming foliage. She climbed the front steps, stopping halfway with her hand on the rail, scanning the tranquil setting in appreciation. The designation of "city" was stretching things more than a little bit, she thought. The tiny town was hardly more than a pretty square bordered by a few shops and restaurants, with beautiful residential neighborhoods spreading out beyond.

Never the tourist magnet that continuously drew hordes of visitors to Maui and O'ahu, the island of Lāna'i had become identified with the sweet, prickly crops of fruit growing in orderly rows across its face. The small hotel had once served as private lodging, and was modest in comparison to the two enormous resorts located in other parts of the island.

While the nickname Pineapple Island had eventually become popular, promoted in newspapers, magazines, movies, and television, Kali knew that the island's dark history had little to offer in the way of sweetness. Lāna'i, so green and peaceful, was steeped in dark myth and violent legends that whispered of man-eating spirits that stalked the living.

"I wonder how many of the tourists who make their way across the channel know about the Lāna'i monsters?" murmured Kali, half to herself.

"Probably none of them," answered a male voice.

Kali started, surprised that anyone had heard her. A very old man was standing on the porch above her, partly in the shadows near the rail, looking out toward the dangling moon, which was surrounded by faint, glittering stars. She halted her ascent up the stairs just before the stranger.

"Do you think it would make a difference to them if they did know?" she asked.

The old man shrugged. "I doubt it," he said. "Just fodder for T-shirt slogans, I would think. No one believes in anything anymore unless they can see or taste it."

She mused over his words, and the abundant truth in them. "Or unless it touches their own life directly," she added.

"Exactly so," he said. He bowed slightly in her direction, then turned back to the rail, resuming his observance of the moon's widening glow. "You must excuse me. I have an agreement with Hina, you see, that I will, whenever possible, greet her as she arrives to light the night."

Kali was surprised to hear him speak the name of Hina. *The Hawaiian goddess of the moon.*

"That's quite an honorable agreement," she said, her voice carrying a genuine respect. "I'm sure, Grandfather, that she looks forward to seeing you each evening."

The man smiled broadly, evidently finding her use of the title *grandfather* friendly. They stood together in companionable silence for several minutes, looking at the sky as the cool night breeze whispered across their faces. As she turned toward the door, she noticed the deep lines around his eyes; there was old grief written there, but laugh lines as well, deep crevices that came from a lifetime of many smiles. For a fleeting moment she wondered what her own face revealed, and if others might someday look at her and see nothing but regret or the disillusionment that regularly arose from constantly dealing with the results of the cruelty and selfishness of her fellow humans.

"*Aloha ahiahi*," she said softly to the man, nodding her head. As he returned the gesture, she opened the door quietly and passed into the hotel foyer, imagining the imminent comfort of climbing beneath the fresh, cool sheets of her temporary bed, where she might dream, all the while bathed in Hina's silvery light.

CHAPTER 3

In the morning after coffee, Kali checked with Tomas by phone to see if anything useful had been uncovered at the pineapple field. Nothing had, so she climbed into a golf cart taxi waiting by the hotel's front steps, ready to transport her to the dock at Manele Harbor. The police launch was already there, waiting in a slip, and the trip across the channel—a short, pleasant journey—delivered her to the parking lot at the port in Lahaina on Maui, where she'd left her ragged, army-issue Jeep in the parking lot.

The Jeep was a relic from the years following the attack on Pearl Harbor, when squadrons of US military had been stationed throughout the islands, and the sturdy workhorse vehicle became ubiquitous on the tropical landscape. While the deteriorating condition of Kali's Jeep had become an increasing concern, she wasn't yet ready to part with it. A newer model would serve the same purpose of negotiating the rough, uneven back roads found on the island's southeast coast where she lived, but a new vehicle would be devoid of the memories carried in the patched seats and scratched paint of her current car.

She inserted the key into the ignition, but before she

turned it, she patted the dashboard superstitiously as she'd recently begun to do whenever it had been left untended for any notable length of time. The tension in her face dissipated when the engine turned over. She eased out slowly from her parking space and drove to the lot exit. Instead of joining the flow of traffic heading south on Highway 30, she turned north, then followed the road along the coast until it joined Highway 340, eventually crossing the narrow isthmus connecting Maui's two sides.

From here, she chose the inland road that allowed her to avoid the unpredictable, bumper-to-bumper tourist traffic along the legendary Hana Highway. The roads she followed had no coastal views, but she loved driving through the island's lush interior landscape, where every possible shade of green could be discerned among the trees and foliage. This route option was exactly why her Jeep was so necessary— the paved road devolved at the far end into a rough track that was unlikely to be tolerated by a fancy sports car.

By the time she pulled into the driveway of her small house near the village of Nu'u, not far from Hana, she was ready for something to eat. She cut the engine, and the silence was filled almost immediately with the sound of mournful howling. The deep, resonant sound emanated from the property next door, and was soon followed by the noise of galloping feet. An enormous gray dog was making a beeline for the Jeep, hurtling through the opening of a pathway in the thick forest that began at the edge of Kali's overgrown lawn. She slipped from her seat to the ground, and was met by the dog, who threw himself onto the grass at her feet in a frenzy of unfiltered joy.

Then Kali heard a series of heavy footfalls. As she knelt to rub the dog's belly, a tall, muscled man appeared on the same pathway at the edge of the lawn. He was also heading for the Jeep, but unlike the dog, he was moving in a steady, athletic lope, his long blond hair caught up in an untidy ponytail that swung against his shoulders as he ran. Cheeks creased in a wide smile, he waved.

"Welcome home!" he called, slowing his pace as he drew near. He gestured to the dog. "Hilo missed you. He seemed to think you might never come back."

She smiled in return.

"Thanks for watching him, Elvar." She braced herself as the 130-pound animal—a cross between a Weimaraner and a Great Dane—climbed to his feet, leaning his considerable weight against her thigh. His long tail thumped against her leg. She stroked his head affectionately as she turned to Elvar. "I don't know why he has to be so dramatic about everything, but I hope you know how much I appreciate the babysitting."

"It's no problem. He's good company. He's been supervising me while I repair my forge."

She noticed the faint "vee" sound when he said the word *forge*; a subtle reminder that Icelandic was his native language, though his English was nearly flawless.

"Did something happen?" she asked, curious. Elvar Ellinsson was a highly regarded bladesmith, and she knew that forge trouble would pose a significant hindrance to his knife-making business.

Elvar looked rueful. "Well, it got knocked over."

Kali felt her heart sink.

"By a giant dog?"

Elvar threw back his head, laughing. "No, Hilo is completely innocent. It was Birta. She was moving some furniture from the terrace into the storage shed, and she accidentally swung a lounge chair into it. The chair leg caught the edge of the forge just at the right angle and tipped it over."

Kali felt a mixture of relief and mild horror. Elvar's older sister, Birta Ellinsdóttir, wasn't the sort of person who was prone to accidents. Overly sensible, at least in Kali's opinion, Birta ran a tight ship. The house she and her brother shared was always spotless and tidy. Nothing was out of the way, and a mishap resulting from furniture reorganizing had likely sent her into a tailspin.

"Oh dear," she said. "Is Birta okay?"

"Oh sure, she's fine. Berating herself, of course. And annoyed at the mess. But I've just finished cleaning it up. I'll have the forge back up and running in no time."

"You're lucky nothing caught on fire."

"The forge was cold. But it would have been safe. The reason I extended the brick terrace as far as I did is so that the forge and any hot tools would always be resting on a surface impervious to the heat."

Kali looked up at the sky. The mares' tails above drifted in wisps through the wide blue expanse, shifted by air currents moving far beyond them. Fixed on the clouds, she felt a profound stillness sweep over her.

"Anyway," said Elvar, watching her, "I suppose I should get back to work." He paused almost long enough for her to intervene with an alternative suggestion.

Kali felt it, but hesitated too long, searching for something to say. As the moment passed unfulfilled, Elvar turned and headed for the path leading to his house through the trees and shrubs that separated Kali's home from his own. He waved, a friendly gesture, uncomplicated.

"Well," he said, stopping under the trees. "Glad to know you're home safe and sound."

Then he was gone, his figure blending into the shadows. Hilo stirred, whimpering softly. Kali reached down, stroking the dog's head. She exhaled, the sigh laden with regret.

"What's wrong with me, Hilo?" She looked again toward the spot where Elvar had disappeared. "The least I could have done was invite him in for something cold to drink." She tugged at one of Hilo's floppy ears. "I'll bet he earned it."

* * *

That night, Kali slept deeply, grateful to be home. She'd slept in her bed instead of the sofa where she usually fell asleep, and admitted to herself that her back was the better for it, despite the fact that Hilo was taking up an inordinate amount of the available space at the foot of the mattress.

She woke as the sun's beams stretched through the open window of her room and across her pillow. A glance at the clock on the small wooden table beside her bed showed that it was far too early to call Walter, so she got up and walked into the living room, retrieving her worn blue yoga mat from the corner behind the sofa. Hilo followed her as she went outside, across the lanai, and down the steps that led to a wide, flat lawn. She spread her mat on the grass and stepped onto it. Bending down, she turned first to the left, then to the right, loosening her muscles.

Her mind was racing. She lowered herself to the mat and made herself sit still, breathing in and out deeply, savoring the salt-laced air, counting each inhalation and exhalation in an effort to concentrate. But it was no good. Instead of rising to test her thigh muscles in warrior pose, she found herself slumping slightly on the mat, staring blindly ahead to where the land sloped gradually down toward the sea in one direction, and abruptly to a deep cove in the other. Walter's ramshackle fishing boat, the *Gingerfish*, was moored there, rocking slightly with the current. She drew her knees up to her chest, wrapping her arms around them, letting her eyes follow the movement of the boat.

Hilo flopped down on the ground beside her. She stroked his head absently, her thoughts filled with images of the small, forlorn skeleton in the abandoned refrigerator, left to face eternity from the dubious vantage point of a pineapple field long starved of fruit. *Why is his head missing, and where on earth is it? Who was he? Who placed his body in a kitchen appliance, and why?*

The questions ran in an endless loop through her mind. "I think this is pointless, big guy," she finally said aloud. Hilo whined softly in response, his tail thumping against the ground. "Let's go make some coffee."

She got up, rolling the mat and tucking it under her arm. Hilo padded along beside her and up the steps. She opened the screen door and let him in, leaving the mat next to the door. Her small kitchen was flooded with sunlight, which played against the cream-and-dark-green-patterned ceramic backsplash behind the countertop. Every other tile was decorated with the familiar Hawaiian motif of a *honu*, or sea turtle. Some of the tiles were cracked, and the grout had begun to wear away between them, but she loved the design, remembering fondly how pleased her grandmother, who'd lived in this house for most of her life, had been to have the tiles installed. Kali smiled to herself. That memory alone was enough to keep her from ever replacing them.

She made herself a carafe of coffee in the glass press that had been so treasured by her late fiancé, Mike Shirai. This small morning ritual of measuring the coffee beans into the heavy steel grinder, transferring them to the press, heating water in the electric kettle, and pouring the steaming water over the ground beans evoked a different set of memories than the ceramic tiles; memories that still carried a sense of grief—and a silent fury that Mike's life had been cut short during a police raid and a frenzied volley of gunfire directed at him by a crew of meth dealers.

As she finished making the coffee, she poured herself a large mug, carrying it to the kitchen table where her computer was set up. Mike would have laced his coffee with a flavored cream, but she preferred hers unadorned, except for an occasional spoonful of sugar. For the next two hours and over the course of two more mugs, she did Internet searches on pineapples and what they represented, looking up what she could find about the pineapple industry on Lānaʻi Island.

By the time her phone rang just before eight thirty, the pad beside her keyboard was covered with notes, many followed by question marks. She glanced at the phone screen before she answered.

"Aloha, Walter. You calling to share any good news?"

"I am not." His voice sounded weary. "Stitches wants us to take a road trip to her office in Wailuku. I'll pick you up in about twenty minutes. I missed breakfast. If you make me a sandwich, I'll leave you something in my will."

"You don't have anything I need. Actually, you don't have anything at all, do you?"

He grunted. "Boat."

She laughed. "Yeah. Threatening me with your creaky old fishing boat isn't going to motivate me to make you a sandwich."

"How about this, then: Bring me something to eat, pretty please, or I'll *definitely* leave her to you."

He rang off before she could respond. She went to the table and collected her notes, stuffing them into her day bag, and checked Hilo's bowls for food and water. The dog, recognizing all of the signs of Kali's imminent departure, parked himself across the floorboards at the threshold of the front door.

By the time the police cruiser pulled into her driveway, she was already waiting on the steps of her lanai, holding a fried egg and Spam sandwich, topped with a slice of Maui onion and slathered with sweet mustard.

Walter parked in the limited shade offered by a stand of tall palms. He got out to join her, carrying an insulated travel mug. His face lit up when he saw the sandwich.

"I knew you'd do the right thing," he said, reaching for it.

Kali raised her eyebrows. "I was only looking out for myself. The last thing I need is to be trapped in a car for however long it takes us to get to the morgue with you grumbling the whole way about how hungry you are."

"Fair enough," he said. He shook the travel mug. "Got any coffee made?"

She sighed and rose from the steps. "Aren't we expected somewhere?"

From inside the house, the sound of whining and scratching could be heard.

"Yeah, but you're driving, and some fresh coffee would be great with this sandwich." He gestured toward the house with his mug. "Plus it sounds like your horse is trying to break down the barn door."

They pushed their way past Hilo and entered the kitchen. She watched Walter as he transferred the cold, leftover coffee in the press into a glass measuring cup and placed it in the microwave, pressing the numbers on the timer's keypad.

"Did Stitches give you any idea why we need to make a trip all the way over to her, instead of just telling you over the phone what she's found?"

The microwave pinged. Walter removed the measuring cup, carefully pouring the hot contents into his insulated mug waiting on the counter. He tore a paper towel off the roll next to the sink and wiped down a few drops that had spilled onto the counter's surface.

"Just that the skeleton is male, as you suspected. Said she'd fill us in when we got there. I thought we'd make better time if we took the back roads in your Jeep."

She regarded him with a small measure of surprise. "Sure. Happy to accommodate. I'm not sure I actually remember the last time you rode in the Jeep without complaining about it the whole time, though. You know—like a little kid covered in mud, bitching about having to take a bath."

"Yeah, funny," he said as they left the house. Kali wrestled with the door, which was being pushed from the other side by a newly distressed Hilo, now absolutely convinced that he was, indeed, being abandoned. Walter and Kali made their way down the steps and across the yard. Once they climbed into the Jeep, Kali slipped the keys into the ignition. She revved the engine, and as it warmed up, she pulled her notes from her bag and passed them to Walter.

"You can take a look at what I found regarding pine-apples." She looked at him meaningfully. "And don't get mustard all over the pages."

Walter took a bite from his sandwich as Kali pulled out of the driveway and onto the road. She headed south, retracing part of the route she'd taken on her return home from the harbor. He shuffled the papers into an orderly pile, studying what she'd written.

"Native to South America. Multiple cultures, including the Spanish and Portuguese, decorated everything with pineapple motifs," he read. "It was a sign of welcome. They liked to carve it into furniture, as well as the wood trim in their homes. It's still used as common ornamentation in modern hotels and inns, signifying hospitality."

Kali nodded. "The pillow covers in my room at the hotel on Lāna'i had pineapples in the design."

"Okay, but the hospitality angle doesn't seem like a con-nection to the body."

"Agreed," said Kali. "At least not on the surface. Lots of immigrants came to the islands, though, including the Por-tuguese. Big part of the current population. The Portuguese grow pineapples on São Miguel, one of their islands in the Azores. After the fruit was introduced to Europe in the mid-1600s, it eventually found its way to Hawai'i and became a major money-producing crop in the early 1920s."

"Right," he said. "That's about the time Lāna'i became one big pineapple farm."

"The research I found said roughly seventy-five percent of all the pineapples in the world were grown in Hawai'i during the height of production. When the last of the big pineapple companies pulled out, a lot of people lost their jobs. Then the Shandling Fruit Company swooped in and took over the empty fields on Lānaʻi in an attempt to revive the industry, but that only lasted a few years before they failed, too—despite all the big promises they'd made to the workers."

Walter was quiet for a moment, considering what Kali had said. "So there were a lot of pissed off, financially impacted people wandering around without a job to go to in the morning."

"Yeah," she answered. "By the time Shandling Fruit packed up and left Hawaiʻi in August of 1997 to reopen with a much smaller presence in Central America and Southeast Asia, it seems safe to assume there were more than a few unhappy people. So, not a stretch to think there could be some connection. It's more than possible that the guy who comes in to tell everyone to go home and stay there, becomes the target of some serious anger."

"And finds himself headless and stuffed into a refrigerator?"

"Yes, except . . ." Kali looked thoughtful. She eased the Jeep over and around a series of potholes, then turned back to Walter. "Except that he wasn't stuffed, was he?"

Walter frowned.

"His hands were folded, and it looked to me as if he had been placed inside the fridge pretty carefully." She hesitated. "Maybe even reverently."

Walter considered this. She waited, knowing that a thousand different scenarios were likely dancing around in his head. Outside the window, the rich green and turquoise shades of the island's interior gleamed in the sunlight. They'd passed though Keokea and Kula, and were approaching the turnoff for Highway 37 leading toward the airport and on to Wailuku. When they were less than ten minutes from their destination, she glanced back at Walter, surprised that he'd still made no comment. His head was turned toward the window, nodding gently with the movement of the car. Kali sighed. He was asleep.

She reached over with her right hand and poked him in his thigh.

"Hey there, sleeping beauty—wake up!"

His head jerked upright. "Damn," he said, stifling a yawn. "Sometimes I forget how mean you are."

"You used to tell me I was sweet."

"Yeah, when you were eight."

That was a long time ago, she thought. Long before she realized the world was filled with thieves and bullies and killers. Long before she knew about rainforests being destroyed and animal abuse and child molesters and garbage filling the seas. When she was eight, she reflected, she could afford to be sweet.

CHAPTER 4

Walter and Kali looked at the skeleton arrayed on the metal examination table. There wasn't much to see. Stitches had removed the clothing from the body. The hands were no longer carefully folded, nor was the body still bent at the waist and knees. Stretched out beneath the glare of lights, it seemed even smaller and more despondent than it had looked curled within the refrigerator.

Kali moved toward another table, where the clothing had been laid out. The deceased had been dressed in a short-sleeved shirt beneath his overalls, but the cloth had long ago begun to disintegrate. His shoes were leather, but thin and inexpensive, and the soles and heels revealed considerable wear.

"There's something about these clothes that suggests a different time period, don't you think?" she asked. "The shoes, too. They look a little old-fashioned."

Stitches nodded. "Indeed they do," she said, "that is, if you think the 1970s and '80s warrants the term 'old-fashioned.' And let's remember: Not everyone has the means to update their wardrobe on a regular basis. Many people hold on to clothing for a very long time, or wear hand-me-downs."

Kali frowned. "Granted. To me," she said slowly, walking around the table and viewing the items from different angles, "the coveralls suggest farm laborer, but the shoes say going-to-town day." She moved closer to where Stitches stood in front of the skeleton.

"Yeah," said Walter. "It seems like boots would be more appropriate for working in the fields."

"Again, you're projecting. Not everyone can afford boots. Or perhaps he'd decided to be ironic when he got dressed the day he died," said Stitches. Neither Kali nor Walter laughed, unable to separate her humor from her sarcasm even after years of working with her. "If the clothing was his," she continued, "it's unlikely he was wealthy, or, say, management. More likely to have been a worker, or maybe someone visiting. The fabric is of no substance, and there are no maker's labels." She stood back, allowing Kali enough space to view what was left of the man in front of them.

"That's all still assuming he was a farm laborer," said Walter. "And we don't even know if these were his clothes or if he was associated with the fruit fields. The empty land could have just been a convenient spot to stash a body."

"I don't know," said Kali, still frowning. "The pineapple and the fridge are a couple of steps too far, don't you think? The pineapple was unlikely to have been a casual afterthought, and as for the fridge, you would not only have to know there was one available, but have the means to move it. It seems unlikely a body would be brought here from somewhere else, hidden in the fridge, carried here in some kind of vehicle, and hoisted into a large hole. How many people would that take, anyway? Minimum of four, I'd guess."

"Yes, of course there are a multitude of details to consider, but for the moment, shall we stick to the clothing?"

asked Stitches. "If these clothes didn't belong to the deceased, then whomever they did belong to left something in the pants pocket."

Kali and Walter looked surprised.

Stitches smiled in satisfaction. "Front, right side," she said, watching them closely. "And he or she must not have wanted to lose it, because the bottom corner of the pocket where I found it was sewn closed to protect it."

They stared at the plastic evidence bag as she raised it. Inside was a small metal charm that suggested a stylized anchor. Kali took it and held it up to the light. She turned it over several times, then handed it to Walter.

"Sewn shut?" repeated Kali, intrigued.

"Yes," said Stitches. "Those that were left were small, neat stitches. Very even. I might even say they were made by someone who was handy with a needle."

Walter examined the charm closely. "Could you tell if there's any kind of marking on it?"

"There's nothing. No inscription, no initials, no manufacturing mark."

Kali's face took on a thoughtful expression. There was something vaguely familiar about the shape of the metal. Although the suggestion of an anchor was clear, the bottom piece was straight, whereas a typical anchor would generally be curved upward on its two points. "A lot of people, including fishermen, carry talismans," she said, unconsciously reaching up to slip one finger beneath the neckline of her shirt to finger the leather cord around her neck, from which dangled a collection of small talismans of her own. "Fishing charms. Some of them even keep the charms fastened to their nets to bring good luck."

Walter nodded. "Not uncommon, especially with the older generation. I've seen some beautiful jade and stone examples. But what's a fisherman doing in a pineapple field?"

"I don't know," said Kali. "He could have been a visitor or friend, or someone who had multiple jobs."

They considered the host of implications and possibilities in silence. Finally, Kali spoke. "Any clue on ethnicity?"

"Ah," said Stitches. "That may take some time to determine. The shape and capacity of the cranial cavity is usually one of the places we start with skeletal remains. What we do have right now is height. The femur, being mature and fully intact, indicates an adult with a height between five feet seven and five feet ten. There's also evidence that the right arm was broken at some point."

Walter sighed as he handed the anchor back to Kali. "That's something, I guess. I've got Officer Hara going through the records on missing persons. Do we at least have some idea how long this gentleman was left in the field? It would help if we had a ballpark date to narrow the search."

"Not yet," said Stitches. "Determining that will also be a challenge."

"I'd guess that someone would have to have known that that part of the field was no longer in use before burying someone there," said Kali. She passed the anchor back to Stitches, then walked over to a rolling metal cart where the wooden pineapple had been placed.

"The pineapple is a fascinating component," she said, gazing intently at the details of the design. She lifted it and turned it upside down. It had been created from a single piece of wood. There was a hole in the bottom, roughly square, with a cavity that was about six inches deep.

"I'm not sure 'fascinating' is an appropriate descriptor," responded Stitches, replacing the metal charm back into the small evidence bag. "Though the intricacy of the carving, in my inexpert opinion, appears to be of a high quality." She followed Kali with her eyes. "I see you've noted the hole. Fence post would be my best guess. While you're sorting out that bit, I'll be trying to collect enough DNA from the remaining hard tissues in the body for the forensics lab to work with. There's likely been substantial degradation, though perhaps not as much as would have occurred if the body hadn't been partially sealed."

"Partially?" asked Walter. "Looked to me like he was pretty well secured in there."

"Yes, but the rubber sealing material used to keep the refrigerator door closed had rotted away in large sections, so the interior was not airtight. External microbes had access to the body at that point, though there was likely a delay of some time before that occurred." Stitches glanced over at the pineapple. "At any rate, it's all yours. We didn't find anything on it, so you can add it to your evidence collection, such as it is. The charm, as well."

She waggled the small plastic bag in front of her, and nodded toward the pineapple. "I left a box in the hall beside my office door. The pineapple should fit." As Kali and Walter lingered, their gaze on the skeleton, Stitches cleared her throat impatiently. She crossed to the pineapple, lifting it. "I have work to do, and so do you. Let's get on with it, shall we?" She placed the ornate carving in Walter's hands and handed the anchor bag to Kali, then turned away from them without saying anything more.

Walter gripped the wooden fruit, raising a brow at Kali. They made their way through the door and into the hallway, pausing outside Stitches's office door where an empty cardboard box was sitting. Carefully, Walter slipped the pineapple inside, glancing at the writing on the box.

"*Bone saw*," he read, then hoisted the box up. "Yikes. When my wife leaves empty boxes around the house, they usually say something like *shoes*, or *wineglasses*."

Kali grinned. "I'd be willing to bet that Stitches gets as excited about a new bone saw as your wife does about a new pair of sandals."

"Yeah, bet you're right," he said. Together they left the building and made their way to the parking lot, where Walter finally shook his head. "And then there's you with dogs. I understand criminals. Even kids, to some degree. But I don't think I'll ever get a handle on the way you think."

"I wouldn't waste my time trying if I were you." She patted the box. "The fence post makes a lot of sense, though. I can see the pineapple sitting on top of it, maybe at the entrance to a road or property."

They climbed into the Jeep, the box holding the pineapple stored safely in the rear seat. Walter glanced at his phone as Kali started the car and pulled slowly out and onto the road.

"Couple of messages from Hara. We've got a good lead on that cock-fighting ring that's operating up-country, you know, the one we suspect is run by that brother-and-sister duo. The woman just checked in at the emergency clinic covered with gouges that look like they came from a pissed-off rooster. Not to mention, that couple who found the fridge have been running their mouths. We've got a ton of calls from everyone including the newspaper in Honolulu asking about it." He sighed. "Damage control time, I suppose. Other than that, Hara says he's come up with twenty-two names of still-unaccounted-for missing males since 1997, which is the date I gave him to start with. Seeing how it's the year the Shandling Fruit Company gave up and left."

Kali grimaced. "That doesn't seem like a lot, somehow."

"A lot of missing people eventually turn up, as you know. Different names, unexpected places, dead, hiding, whatever."

"Once we have more details, we should be able to narrow the list a bit."

"Agreed," said Walter. "I'll pick up my car from your house later on. Let's just head straight to the station."

CHAPTER 5

Officer David Hara, the rookie who was currently serving under Walter's supervision at the small Maui satellite police office near Hana, was sitting at his desk in front of his computer, his back very straight, his dark blue uniform shirt neatly pressed. He stood up respectfully as Walter and Kali entered.

"Captain. Detective."

Walter rolled his eyes.

"Sit down, Hara, for crying out loud. And spill something on your shirt, will you?"

Hara looked confused.

"Ignore him," Kali said to Hara. She watched as Walter tugged instinctively at the rumpled collar of his own shirt, which was spread to the limits of the available cloth across his wide girth. "He's just intimidated by anyone who doesn't look as though they spent the night being dragged through the underbrush by a loose house cat." What she didn't say was that she was aware of how Hara's extraordinary good looks made Walter vaguely uncomfortable, as though he were being personally judged by some unnamed force, and found wanting in comparison.

To help relieve Hara's obvious discomfort, Kali walked over to a long wooden table where a coffeemaker had been set up next to an electric kettle and a microwave. There was an apartment-sized refrigerator next to the table, and a small, newly erected shelf above the fridge. She took two clean mugs down from the shelf, and placed them on the table's surface.

"Coffee fresh?" she asked.

"Yes, ma'am. Just made it up," said Hara.

Kali smiled as she lifted the coffeepot and filled both mugs. "How do you take it, Hara?"

He smiled, looking slightly shy.

"You don't have to . . ."

"Nice shelf you built here, by the way. If memory serves, Captain Alaka'i said he was going to put one up, but that was what, five years ago? Six, maybe?" She replaced the coffeepot and opened the refrigerator door, reaching inside for a carton of cream. "I think I've noticed you like cream but no sugar, right?"

Hara's smile grew a little wider.

"Yes, that's right." He looked nervously at Walter. "The shelf—that was nothing."

Kali poured a splash of cream into one of the mugs, then lifted both, leaving the carton of cream open on the table. She walked to Hara's desk and placed one of the mugs next to his keyboard.

He looked up. "Thank you very much."

She smiled in acknowledgment, taking the other mug for herself. She walked to a desk in a corner of the room, sitting down with the hot drink held carefully in her right hand. This was officially her desk, though she rarely used it. There was a window behind it that was partially open, and she could feel the warm, outside air making its way into the room. It smelled clean, carrying the aroma of the nearby sea.

She took a sip of her coffee, releasing an audible sigh of pleasure.

Walter stood halfway between the door and his desk holding the box with the pineapple, watching the display of coffee distribution. He waited as Kali took another sip.

"I see," he said to her. "Get my own coffee, is that how it is?"

"Do I look like your secretary?"

"No, right now you look like *his* secretary." Walter's voice was dark. He glanced from Kali to Hara and back to Kali, his gaze slightly defiant.

"You didn't build a shelf," she said, shrugging. "Lazy bastard." She swung her chair around to face Hara, and raised her coffee in salute to him, then turned back to Walter, bearing a wide grin. "I believe I've heard you say more than once that enterprise should be rewarded."

Walter turned toward his own desk and placed the box with the pineapple on its surface. He pulled out the cushioned, wheeled office chair and made himself comfortable.

"Didn't want any coffee anyway," he grunted. Looking worried, Hara rose to his feet, moving swiftly toward the table and coffeemaker, but Walter waved his arm lazily in the air. "Don't bother, Officer, please. I'm going to let Detective Māhoe think she made a point, which will make her overconfident about her next move and thereby give me a slight advantage."

There was a look of bewilderment on Hara's face. He ran one hand through his short, dark hair, opened his mouth to say something, then turned back to his computer, his thought left unvoiced.

Kali snorted. She moved her mouse, opening her computer screen, and became suddenly businesslike. "Okay, Hara, the list you compiled—you sent a copy to me, yes?"

"Yes," he said. "And also to the captain."

"During our visit to the coroner's office this morning, Stitches suggested the pineapple may have once been a decoration on top of a fence post, which makes sense as there's a hole at its base, roughly square and a few inches deep." She nodded toward the box. "It's in there; you'll see as soon as you turn it over. And she found this in the pocket of the dead man's trousers." She reached into her bag and removed the anchor encased in protective plastic, tossing it to Hara. "It was sewn into the very bottom corner of one pocket, as though it was too important to risk losing. He may have carried it as a talisman."

Hara looked at it with a great deal of curiosity. "Okay to remove it?" he asked. As she nodded, he slipped it carefully into the palm of his hand. "It looks sort of like an anchor," he said.

"That's also what I thought," she said. "Let me know if anything occurs to you. Other than that, Stitches says our pineapple man stood between five feet seven and five feet ten."

"Right," said Hara. Handing the anchor back to Kali, he swung around to his desk. His keyboard clicked as he performed a search through the information he'd compiled on missing persons. "That means we can probably eliminate five names so far, based solely on height." He looked at Walter. "Should I do that, Captain?"

"Don't eliminate them, but flag them as unlikely," answered Walter.

Hara made the necessary notation, then sent his file to the printer. In a few seconds, the machine began to whir. Then came the sound of printing pages. Hara rose from his desk in time to intercept them as they were expelled by the machine. He stapled the pages together in three separate stacks, then handed a copy to Kali and one to Walter, keeping one for himself.

Each of them scanned the list, in which Hara had included all known information provided to the police about each of the unaccounted-for men at the time they had been reported missing.

"All right," said Walter, turning to Hara. "Go through our database again and see whose jurisdiction these fall under, then the national database one more time to see if any of these names can be eliminated as deaths occurring elsewhere. Then it's phone call time, I guess. Do some digging. Find out who was in a messy divorce, who owed someone else a lot of money—including IRS debt—and who had a criminal background. Pay attention to anyone who might have had a reason to disappear of their own accord. All the obvious stuff."

"Yes, sir." Hara hesitated, then added, "Shouldn't we already have that kind of information on file?"

"Not necessarily," Walter answered. "Depends on who reported someone missing, and how much follow-up there was. Lots of room for things to slip through the cracks."

"Or not be reported at all," Kali added. "Not everyone who goes missing is actually missed."

Walter nodded. "True dat. But find out what you can."

"I've just texted Tua over at the Hana Cultural Center," said Kali. "He's going to meet me over there so I can show him the anchor charm." She looked at Walter. "Care to join me?"

He grimaced. "Would love to, but I've got overdue paperwork that's got to be dealt with before the end of the day. Let me know if anything interesting turns up."

"Will do," she said, draining the last of the coffee from her cup and rising from her seat. She gathered her belongings and walked toward the door, her thoughts far away, imagining how important the charm must have been to the dead man, and wondering why.

*　*　*

The Hana Cultural Center and Museum was a modest building on the Uakea Road above Hana Bay. It was located on the same grounds as the former Hana Courthouse, which was listed on the National Register of Historic Places, and now used only occasionally for official business. Though the museum was only open to visitors for limited hours a couple of days a week, Kali knew Tua Kalani, the current director, who had been helpful to her on past cases.

Tua was waiting for her on the museum's steps, waving as she pulled the Jeep into a parking spot. She saw him stand up and dust off the back of his trousers as she made her way across the grass.

"Aloha, Tua," she called in greeting.

"*Aloha kakahiaka.*" He smiled as he said "good morning" and turned to open the door, standing aside so that she could enter. "Here to talk story today?"

"Maybe a little bit," she said. "Mostly I want to show you something and get your reaction."

He watched as she pulled out the plastic evidence bag and slipped the small anchor from inside. She offered it to him, and he took it, clearly intrigued.

"I guess this means you aren't worried about fingerprints," he said, grinning slightly.

"Already checked. There's nothing. So please give it a close look, and tell me if it suggests anything to you."

Tua walked across the front room to a door leading into a small office. There was a wooden desk in one corner. He moved a few items around until he'd uncovered an old, thick magnifying glass on a silver handle. He moved to the window, lifting the anchor with the fingers of one hand, holding the magnifying glass in the other. He studied the small metal trinket, turning it over carefully several times.

He went back to his desk and located a heavy magnet, then played for a moment longer with the anchor.

Kali waited.

"Well," he said finally, "it appears to be an anchor in design, as you've no doubt already determined; but it's not made of any precious metal such as silver or gold. Gold, of course, would be obvious. Silver or silverplate would likely show tarnishing if it was of any age. The magnetization is very strong, as expected with steel. Watch." He held the magnet above the anchor and it immediately became adhered to the magnet's surface. "So not valuable, if that's one of your questions." He looked at her intently. "Though value, of course is entirely relative. Something may have great sentimental or other meaning, but no measurable market value. It may have a significance entirely removed from what it's made of or sells for."

She nodded. "What about the symbol?"

"Yes," he said. Small wrinkles formed in his forehead as he frowned slightly. "Well, an anchor may mean many things. Security. A connection to water and the sea. It's also a common Christian symbol, used to represent the Christ figure as hope and conviction in an afterlife."

Kali tilted her head. "How about a fishing charm?"

"Those are very common, but usually we see fish symbols carved from stone. Jade is particularly popular with fishermen of Asian heritage." He looked again at the anchor. "Fishing charms almost always have some device for attaching them to a net, though I can see that this one has a small hole between the two sides of the anchor at the top, through which a thin line or string might be threaded to secure it. There's a belief among some fishermen that the power and beauty of the charm lures fish into the net. Blessings are sometimes performed to maintain or restore the charm's power."

"If you had to guess, is that what you'd assume this anchor to be? Some kind of fishing amulet?"

Tua shook his head. "Sorry, Kali. I'm not confident that it is." He handed the small anchor back to her. "And it could be both a religious symbol *and* a fishing charm, used by a fisherman who was also a believer. I wish I could be more helpful. Can you tell me anything more about it to put it into context? Some *kolohe* making trouble?"

"No troublemakers right now. It's part of a larger investigation, found in someone's trouser pocket."

He nodded. "Well, all I can say is that if someone was carrying it with them, it was likely to have been of personal significance." He laughed suddenly. "Unless they'd just seen it on the floor, caught in the sunlight, and decided to pick it up and take it home."

She sighed. "Yeah. Thanks for that."

Tua grinned. "Always happy to help."

They moved from the interior office toward the building's front door. She waited outside on the lanai as he locked the door behind them, then followed him down the steps onto the lawn.

"You know, I think I remember something not unlike this anchor somewhere else. Over on Lāna'i, one of the *ki'i pōhaku* carvings."

She nodded slowly. "The ancient petroglyphs on the rocks down in the south."

"Yes, they're on a group of huge boulders as you're driving toward the Palawai Basin. There are more up on the trail off Shipwreck Beach, but the one I'm thinking of is on a rock that also has carvings of a boat on it."

"I remember that scene. A sea battle, I think."

Tua shrugged. "Maybe. There's never been any agreement about what they mean. As far as I can tell, someone was merely documenting life in the islands. Probably only important events that warranted the effort the carvings would have taken to create."

"No doubt." She moved toward the Jeep, lost in thought, watching as Tua walked away.

"*Mahalo nui loa,* Tua!" she called in thanks.

He waved in response. "Anytime, Kali."

CHAPTER 6

Kali backed the Jeep carefully into the parking lot of George's Island Market. The lot was packed, which was not surprising given that it was off-season. The special room rates advertised by many of Hawai'i's hotels and resorts had attracted the usual crowds of tourists who'd despaired that spring would ever arrive in whatever snowy, icy town they called home.

The general store was typically the place where everyone restocked their coolers after the long, winding drive along the famed Hana Highway bordering the island's eastern shore, and today was no exception. College-age kids in surf shorts and bikinis mingled with couples and families in brightly colored vacation clothes.

Right now, the most pressing thing on Kali's mind was picking up a bag of dog food. It had been an extremely long day, and a hungry Hilo was more than Kali felt like dealing with this evening. She left Hilo sitting in the front passenger seat of the Jeep and told him to stay put. The sound of his moaning followed her as she walked toward the store's entrance.

Inside the cool, air-conditioned interior, she saw that

George Tsui, the store's longtime proprietor, was seated behind the counter next to the cash register in his worn, cushioned easy chair. Tourists were milling about, examining the products displayed on the shelves. George stood up and greeted Kali the way he almost always did, reporting on the day's headlines splashed across the front of his favorite tabloid newspaper.

"The government is putting mind control drugs into the drinking fountains in schools on the mainland," he said. "I wonder if it will do any good."

"I wouldn't count on it," Kali said. "For starters, when's the last time you saw a kid actually drinking water? I don't think they drink anything anymore unless it's at least fifty percent sugar."

"Good point. They should put those drugs into French fries, instead. Kids are always eating."

Kali walked down an aisle and chose the largest bag of dog food available. She slung it across one shoulder, then moved to the next aisle and selected a loaf of cinnamon raisin bread from a display of bakery goods, smiling as she reached in front of a middle-aged lady wearing a sun visor emblazoned with the logo of a nearby resort. The woman smiled back, her expression friendly and relaxed.

George looked critically at Kali's bread selection as she placed it on the counter in front of him.

"You should buy the whole grain kind," he said.

"I should, you're right. But if I did, it wouldn't get opened until it was too stale or moldy to eat, and then I'd just feed it to the birds and drive all the way back here to get a loaf of this."

"Seems like you've thought this through."

"Pretty much."

"Okay." He looked at the dog food as he rang up the purchases. "At least you buy the healthy, grain-free food for Hilo. He'll probably outlive you."

"True," she said as she handed him her credit card. "But not because of what either one of us is eating."

As she gathered up the dog food and bread, George glanced meaningfully toward the door. Hilo had abandoned the Jeep, and now stood looking inside the store's entrance, effectively blocking the exit of two women in shorts and bathing suit tops.

"Assistance needed near aisle three," said George quietly.

Kali sighed. The tourists stood at the door, frozen, regarding Hilo with a mix of wonder and alarm. Kali silently reminded herself to put the detachable doors back onto the soft canvas frame that covered the interior of the Jeep, which might actually serve the purpose of keeping Hilo contained.

"He's mostly harmless," said Kali, approaching the door, smiling again in what she hoped was reassurance, the bag of dog food under one arm and the raisin bread swinging from her hand.

The women looked at her incredulously.

"Mostly?" one of them repeated, her voice faint.

"Except when he's missed a few meals," acknowledged Kali, gesturing to the dog food. The women backed away, allowing Kali ample room to slip outside.

Hilo wagged his tail happily, sniffing at the bag. He followed Kali back to the parking lot, leaping onto the car seat unbidden. She climbed in behind the steering wheel and started the engine.

"People are afraid of you, you know," she said affectionately, reaching over briefly to scratch his ears. Hilo closed his eyes, leaning into Kali's hand, enjoying the attention.

She drove slowly out of the parking lot and back onto the main road. When she reached the driveway leading to her small clapboard house by the sea, Hilo leapt out and galloped toward the porch, where someone was waiting in one of the rattan deck chairs facing outward from the house. She could hear the sound of ukulele music, and as she pulled closer, she saw the police cruiser parked in the shade. She turned off the engine and slid to the ground, making her way leisurely toward the porch steps.

"Do you ever keep your phone ringer turned on?" asked Walter from the comfort of the chair. He was holding his old, burnished ukulele angled across his lap, and he ran his fingers across the strings, punctuating his words. "Or, even better, check your texts? I'm merely asking, of course, because technically you're on duty, and technically I shouldn't have to drive over here to hunt you down."

Kali eyed the ukulele. "I see you at least got in some time for a rehearsal. Don't think I don't know you've entered the contest at the festival that's coming up at the end of the month." She pulled up another aging rattan chair from the other side of the deck. "Nice to see you, too, by the way." She yawned as she sat down, hoping Walter would be brief so that she could go inside and take a nap without the extra guilt of having been seen collapsing onto the sofa.

"You'll change your mind about that in a minute," said Walter darkly. "Your presence is requested over on Lāna'i. You need to get over to the ferry dock at Lahaina first thing tomorrow. The police cruiser will be heading over, but you can take the ferry across if you miss it."

Kali leaned forward in her chair, instantly alert. She could feel the small hairs on the back of her neck prickle. She watched Walter's face carefully.

"They've located the head?"

"No." He waited. "But the search turned up another body. You'd know all this already, of course, if I'd been able to reach you."

Her sense of trepidation increased.

"And?"

"Scene-of-crime crew will fill you in on the details when you get there. There's another room booked for you at the

Hotel Lāna'i in town for tomorrow night, and the following one if staying over is necessary."

Nodding, Kali rose to her feet. "Okay."

Walter met her eyes.

"What are the chances it's only one more grave?" she asked, already knowing the answer.

He looked grim.

"Yeah," she said. "That's what I'm thinking, too."

She turned, looking out across the lawn to the lava-edged coast where land and water met. Beneath the softly undulating blue-green expanse of the ocean, and between the blades of tall green grass growing in front of her, other battles were in full play: deliberate deaths on vast scales, many plotted and premeditated, over everything from terrain and food to breeding grounds and shelter. Nor was the idea of people killing other people anything new. It was, she reflected, something humans had done since the first dispute over a hunting ground or a desirable woman had taken place.

She shook her head, trying to dispel the veil of darkness that was falling around her, fighting to keep it at bay. She looked at Walter and thought of his determination, his kindness, his belief that it was his duty and calling to strive for order and some semblance of decency, to mend the broken things that filled the world.

"Okay," she said. "I'll head over to the harbor first thing in the morning. I'll give you a call once I'm there."

With some difficulty, Walter began extracting himself from the deck chair. He stood and stretched, the ukulele in one hand.

"Oh, and Kali?" he called as he started down the steps. "Special request from the crime scene unit. They said to leave that dog at home, or they'd make you build your own raft to get back to Maui."

The steps creaked ominously as Walter made his way carefully down them.

Kali watched, half smiling. She whistled for Hilo, who appeared from beneath the lanai where he'd been dozing in the cool shade, and began a slow jog toward Elvar and Birta's home, her constant companion following; she was ready to make her request for more babysitting help. "Might be time to lay off the coconut pancakes, Walter," she called over her shoulder.

As he walked toward his car, Walter waved his free hand in the air without turning around, his middle finger pointing skyward.

CHAPTER 7

Kali stood in the roadway in the faint morning light, looking for oncoming traffic. There was none. She was on a small hill on Highway 31 close to where it became Highway 37 as it curved north, but her path was blocked by the carcass of an enormous pig. The feral pig population had spread throughout the island as droves of animals were forced to search for new sources of food in the wake of sugar plantation closures, and traffic encounters with them had increased in direct proportion. She guessed from bits of glass on the road near the carcass that it had likely been struck by a heavy truck.

By her estimation, the dead pig in the road weighed about three hundred pounds. It was positioned across the center-line, spilling into both narrow lanes. She could probably get around it by navigating the sloping, grassy road verge, but it had rained during the night, and the ground was soft. She sighed. The pig's body was on a blind spot, and someone coming along at a fast clip might wind up in a crash trying to avoid it.

Looking up and down the road in both directions, she willed another motorist—preferably one in a pickup truck with a winch—to show up. There was no one. From the hillside sloping down to the road, several chickens appeared, followed by a huge rooster. A few seconds later, more chickens spilled across the crest. She calculated that there were about forty altogether. She was aware of the wild chickens that were as much of a problem as the pigs, and even more cognizant that they were coming to feed on the remains of the carcass. Kali grimaced at the thought, knowing that the chicken problem had developed after 1992, when the destructive forces of Hurricane Iniki had smashed through the islands, destroying buildings that included enough chicken coops and holding pens to launch a feral population. Now they were everywhere, ubiquitous to the landscape, helping to feed the underground cock-fighting organizations that operated illegally throughout Maui.

She'd already activated her hazard lights, which blinked in a steady warning as she opened the back of the Jeep. There was a shovel there, but she knew the pig was too heavy to lift. Reluctantly, she hauled out the heavy towrope coiled in a corner in the back. Swearing under her breath, she dragged the rope out and wrapped one end around the smashed remains of the pig's hips above the splay of intestines and guts, hoping the whole animal wouldn't simply fall apart as she moved it.

After securing the rope to the rear of the Jeep she walked back to the newly re-installed driver's door, then hesitated. There were streaks of blood and inner pig workings on her hands and arms, and stains on the front of her jeans. She reached into the glove box and pulled out the rag she kept there to wipe Hilo, doing her best to clean her hands. It was useless. She climbed into her seat and released the parking brake, then slowly moved the vehicle forward until the slack in the towrope had been taken up. Carefully, she eased forward, dragging the pig until it was on the edge of the road, no longer blocking the passage of motorists.

She got out again, standing by the dead animal, surveying her handiwork. There were still pieces of pig and broken glass on the pavement. She removed the shovel from the Jeep's rear, scraping as much as she could onto the verge. It would have to do. She glanced at her watch, aggravated by the delay, doubly annoyed by the state of her clothing. The scent of the pig filled her nostrils.

The movement of the Jeep had caused the flock of chickens to temporarily disperse, but now they were returning, picking at the flecks of pig on the road surface as they closed in on the carcass. She climbed back into the front seat and radioed the station, telling the police cruiser to go ahead. She was a good forty-five minutes late already, and was going to have to clean herself up before she went anywhere.

By the time she'd reached the harbor parking lot in Lahaina, the first passenger boat of the morning was already pulling away from the dock. Her mood plummeted. She got out, taking her overnight duffel with her, and locked the Jeep. Shoving the car keys deep into her canvas messenger bag, she hung it cross-body style over her shoulder and chest, and shouldered the duffel. It had rained during the night. She navigated her way around the puddles that had formed in the parking lot's unevenly paved surface, and made her way toward the public restrooms.

She glanced down at the bloodstains on her jeans, rueful. Dealing with them would have to wait until she had access to a washing machine, but she took off her shirt and did her best to rinse the flecks of pig parts and blood streaks that marked it. She wrung it out and stuffed it into the bottom of her duffel, then scrubbed her hands and arms and put on one of the clean sleeveless shirts she had packed.

The next ferry was already boarding by the time she felt presentable. At the ramp, Kali spoke briefly with the crew member checking tickets, receiving a head nod as she showed her badge. She made her way through the hatch into the interior behind a group of three oddly dressed women in long, matching blue cotton skirts. One of them was old, with beautiful white hair, and Kali estimated the other two to be somewhere in their early twenties. Their hair was tied back in loose ponytails, their tanned skin giving the impression that they spent a lot of time outdoors.

The ferry crossing didn't actually take much longer to make the trip across the channel than the cruiser, and she consoled herself with the thought that the larger boat was far less bouncy and considerably more comfortable than the small speedboat. Other than the group of women, there were very few passengers on board. She chose a seat on the starboard side toward the bow as the boat's engines rumbled to life. As she wedged her duffel beneath the empty seat next to her, she looked around. Sitting against the bulkhead on the port side was a man with sunglasses and a black baseball cap with the brim pulled down, obscuring his face. He was holding an open magazine. Kali frowned. There was something familiar about him. Despite the attempt to camouflage his identity, a thick strand of bleached blond hair was visible beneath the bottom edge of his cap.

Kali felt herself bristle with annoyance. It was Chad Caesar, an actor from *Lights Out Maui*, a canceled television series that had been largely shot locally on Maui. He'd played the lead character, an investigative journalist from the imaginary *Honolulu Record* newspaper who managed to break a big story, uncover crime and injustice, catch a criminal, and wrap it all up neatly by the end of every episode.

The series had been hugely popular, having run for multiple seasons before being canceled abruptly, much to the dismay of legions of loyal viewers and fans. Kali had heard from several trusted sources that the show's cancelation had been the direct result of ridiculous salary demands from Chad. Instead of leaving Hawai'i with his tail between his legs, Chad had capitalized successfully on his status as a local celebrity to launch a blog and podcast focusing on local events, emphasizing crime, supernatural phenomena, UFO sightings, sea monsters, mermaid encounters, and occasional run-ins with a tropical, mountain-dwelling cousin of Bigfoot that he had dubbed the Palm Man.

Chad's public persona as Ruler of the News—a title he had chosen for himself to promote his podcast—was familiar to Kali. She also knew that his presence on the morning ferry was unlikely to be random. Instead of sitting down, she walked toward him, waiting in the passageway next to his row of seats. As the boat pulled into open water, she watched him tug the brim of his hat lower over his forehead, and turn his gaze to the back cover of his magazine, peering intently at the ad there. He was studiously ignoring her presence.

She crossed her arms over her chest and spoke clearly. "Good morning, Chad. What are you doing on this boat?"

He looked up at her, a brilliant, practiced grin on his face that gave full play to his unnaturally white teeth. He took off his sunglasses and pushed his cap back on his head, allowing a mass of artificially enhanced golden hair to spill onto his forehead and over the tops of his ears. His grin grew wider, crinkling the corners of his eyes.

Kali assessed him dispassionately. In her opinion, he was more pretty than handsome. His face was perfectly symmetrical, the features almost too well proportioned. It lacked what she privately termed "an element of interest." It wasn't, she believed, a face that she'd enjoy looking at for any length of time. Her thoughts flashed briefly to Mike: his crooked smile, the way the hair in his dark eyebrows had a tendency to spike in wild directions, the small scar on one cheek from crashing his bicycle into a fence when he was ten, how his ears were slightly uneven. It had been a face with character and grace, one that told stories.

Oblivious to her thoughts, Chad turned his charm dial to

its fullest setting. "Why, if it isn't my favorite lady detective! Fancy meeting you here. I mean, what are the odds?"

She snorted derisively. "What are the odds, indeed? Let's factor in your illegal police scanner and see what kind of numbers we come up with."

He made a pretense of surprise. His eyes widened as he regarded her solemnly. "I have absolutely zero idea what you're talking about."

She shook her head. "Sorry, Chad, you just aren't a good enough actor to be convincing."

Ignoring the slight, he looked at her more closely, then drew back with a wrinkled nose. "I have to say, Detective— your perfume choice is a little . . . *pungent* this morning, not that you asked." He was staring at her jeans. "Is that . . . *blood*?" His eyes grew even wider in mock fear. "Oh hell, are you trying to make a getaway? Did you kill someone this morning?"

Her eyes narrowed. She leaned toward him. "Not yet."

He smiled. "Then maybe you've just found another body abandoned somewhere?"

She straightened, staring directly into his eyes. "Just so there's no misunderstanding here, Chad, you will not be getting off the ferry when it docks. In fact, I encourage you to keep the same seat you're in now so you have a different view on your way back to Maui."

"But Detective," he said, pretending to be offended, "I have a whole day of hiking and snorkeling and cocktails already planned. My readers and viewers can't wait to hear about it."

She looked critically at the small knapsack on the seat beside him. "Got all your gear stashed in that?"

He smiled broadly. "Yes, ma'am." He lifted one foot into view. "Hiking boots, check." Reaching for his knapsack, he loosened the drawstring top and pulled out a water bottle. "Hydration, check." He held the pack open so she could see inside. "Plus an apple and a protein bar to stave off starvation, *and* my ID in case anyone needs to see it before accepting my martini order. So unless you plan to arrest me for wanting to take a day off, I have every intention of having a relaxing time on Lāna'i."

"Where's your snorkeling gear?"

"Ahhh. I'm trained to hold my breath for very long periods of time. I learned how to do that while free diving for pearls in the Maldives."

He winked at her, but she stared at him, unsmiling. "Free diving? I have half a mind to toss you overboard right now to see if you can dog paddle to shore."

He chuckled. "Let me prove it to you. Come spend the day with me. I don't mind if you forgot to pack your swimsuit. Or—maybe you already have plans? Something keeping you busy today?"

Taking a deep breath, Kali forced herself to turn away, silently cursing Brad and Jan and their big mouths. She moved a few steps back from him, into the space between the rows of seats. With an effort, she kept her voice calm as she looked over her shoulder. "Do *not* let me catch you anywhere within my sight today, Chad."

She grabbed her overnight duffel from where she'd left it, then made her way out onto the deck. Lāna'i was already in view, its towering cliffs clad in thick, emerald-hued vegetation. The waters of this channel were warm and relatively shallow, compared to the deeper seas beyond the islands. The channel was a primary migration route for humpback whales that returned each year to give birth and nurture their young. On many past occasions, she'd watched the huge animals frolic and breach in the channel during the crossing between the islands. Today, the sea appeared to be empty. She stood at the rail, enjoying the sensation of the moving air as it cooled her face and lifted her hair, trying to release the irritation Chad's presence had awakened in her.

She stayed on deck until the boat eventually slowed, and the ferry pilot maneuvered skillfully into a slip and cut the engines. The few onboard passengers made their way to the area on the deck across from the dock as the gangplank was locked into place. Kali was the first person off. She waited briefly on the dock, watching as Chad made his way behind the other passengers and across the gangplank. The three women in the long, blue skirts were just ahead of him, and passed her on the pier. The woman closest to her was the elder of the three. She slowed, staring openly at the tattoo on Kali's upper arm, shaking her head. She muttered something, but Kali couldn't make out the words.

"Excuse me?" she said. "Were you speaking to me?"

"That mark on your arm," the woman said with disdain. *"You shall not make any cuts in your body for the dead nor make any tattoo marks on yourselves: I am the Lord.* Leviticus 19:28."

Kali watched in bewilderment as the woman walked away, and turned just as Chad stepped past her. She was about to warn him again, but he spoke before she had the chance.

"Five o'clock, Detective? Shall we say the lobby bar at the Four Seasons? The property by the water, not the up-country hotel. Drinks are on me, natch."

She raised her brow at him, determined not to let him get a reaction out of her in public. "I can't imagine ever being thirsty enough to say yes, Chad. But best of luck to you chatting up someone less discerning and far more desperate. And," she added, "remember that it'll be tough to hold a glass if your hands are handcuffed behind your back for interfering in a police investigation."

His face lit up. "So you are here on official business. Good to know. And as far as the handcuffs go, you have my permission to slap a pair on me any time you like." He blew a kiss in her direction before making his way rapidly along the waterfront, away from the small harbor.

Tomas was there, leaning against the hood of his police car, waiting for her. He watched Chad's retreating figure.

"What was that all about?" he asked as she drew closer. "One of those fleeting cruise ship romances? He looks vaguely familiar."

Kali groaned. She opened the rear door of the car and placed her duffel on the seat. She watched as Chad disappeared from view around a bend in the road. "Yep. That's the one and only Chad Caesar."

"Oh. The actor, right?"

"Pain in the ass. I think of him as a tall, blond hemorrhoid."

Tomas threw back his head and laughed. "Anything I can do to help?"

"Just keep an eye out for him near or at the crime scene. He has a podcast blasting made-up news all over the islands. We're pretty sure he's using a police scanner, though we haven't found one yet. He probably heard about the body being discovered on local news, thanks to that couple blabbering. But he's definitely got some kind of inside scoop on what we're doing before information is released to the public."

They climbed into the car. Tomas started the engine and turned the conversation to the investigation.

"You'll see the search efforts have stepped up considerably since we don't know what else—or who else, rather—is out there, and there's a lot of field to dig. We've had an aerial map created, but nothing clear has shown up, so Honolulu sent over a couple of people with additional ground-penetrating radar equipment to assist in the field."

She nodded as he continued speaking.

"Here's what we've got so far on the second body: male,

buried about one hundred yards from the first, but not in a kitchen appliance. This one was wrapped in some kind of material, mostly rotted away. Nothing but a skeleton and what's left of the clothing. It appears to be fully intact. Stitches is waiting till you've had a chance to see it before we move him."

Kali was silent as she turned these facts over in her mind. As she mulled over the few similarities, which seemed to be limited to another male body in a pineapple field, Tomas pulled off the paved main road and onto a bumpy secondary one leading into the island's interior. A sudden gust of wind threw sand and debris against the side of the car, and she watched apprehensively as the field came fully into view.

CHAPTER 8

The pineapple field was buzzing with activity. Kali wondered briefly if there had been this many people weighing down its surface since the fruit production had ceased years before. A slender, dark-haired man standing next to a tent at the command center looked up as Kali and Tomas pulled to a stop next to a collection of other vehicles. She recognized him as the scene-of-crime officer heading up the team on Lānaʻi. He was dressed, as were a number of other people, in the white plastic coveralls so omnipresent at a crime scene. As Kali and Tomas climbed out of the car, the man gave a brief wave, then pointed to a couple of packets stacked on top of a folding table in front of the tent.

Kali and Tomas approached the table. Tomas reached for one of the packets, tossing it to Kali. She caught it and shook out the thin plastic garments contained inside: a spare set of coveralls, an elastic-edged cap, and a pair of booties to pull over her shoes.

"Let's get you dressed so you can see what we found," Tomas said, glancing toward a spot behind him where several people were grouped around an opening in the ground.

"Coroner's waiting for you, Burial Council has come and gone—and just a heads-up that Chief Pait's here, too."

Kali tried to keep her face neutral, but knew she had failed by the twinkle in Tomas's eyes. The presence of Maui Chief of Police Leo Pait meant that there was likely a public relations aspect to the investigation that would have to be taken into consideration—a situation that had often caused Kali a great deal of aggravation.

"I'll leave you to it, then," said Tomas. "My team is going to start on the next section of field. Just in case."

He walked away, and Kali pulled the plastic suit on. It was baggy and almost immediately hot. She pulled the cap over her hair and slipped the booties over her shoes, then made her way along a newly defined path to the grave site. She could see Stitches engaged in conversation with Chief Pait. She listened as she approached.

". . . two males," Pait was saying, shaking his head as he leaned over slightly to look into the open ground near his feet. "I need to know this is the full extent of it, Doctor." Both he and Stitches turned to Kali as she stopped in front of them. Pait straightened himself to his full height, gazing down on her. Kali was struck, as always, by how thin and narrow and pale he was; his frame was topped by a head full of glistening, snowy hair. Standing on the edge of an open grave, even framed by brilliant sunlight, he looked as if he could be a spirit who'd just stepped out of the deep, sleeping night of the earth to briefly visit the bright, living day.

"Detective Māhoe. Just the person I need to see," he said. "Let's take care of this quickly, shall we? The tribal officials have already been, by the way. You can pack him up."

"Good morning, Chief," she said, choosing not to comment on the untenable directive he'd just issued. She nodded at Stitches. "Anything interesting so far?"

"Dr. Stitchard was just noting that both bodies are male,"

said Pait, his voice exuding conviction, as though this small fact was of huge significance.

"Yes, well, statistically speaking—" began Stitches, but Pait interrupted.

"Not my concern, statistics. Bodies in pineapple fields, yes. Statistics—well, far less interesting."

Kali and Stitches exchanged glances. Seeing how Stitches had her lips pressed together, Kali understood the supreme effort it took for the doctor to refrain from commenting.

Pait turned to Kali. He gestured toward the command center. "I've got to make a public statement about all of this later today," he said. "What's your theory so far, Detective?"

She took a deep breath. "I don't have one. I just got here, as you see."

Pait frowned. "Well, off the top of your head?"

Kali held up both hands, palms facing the sky. "Turf battle? Pineapple wars? The bodies of the defeated left behind to fertilize the fruit? Really, Chief, at this point it's impossible to formulate a likely theory."

"Later today, then. Be in touch." Pait nodded to the women and turned away, walking back in the direction of the tent.

"Well then," said Stitches. "Since you seem to have been given a time line for solving who-only-knows what kind of crime, I suppose I should brief you." She pointed to the exposed skeleton in the hole, and Kali noted that there was still hair visible on the skull. "Not counting the foot shorn off at the ankle—thanks to the somewhat eager volunteer digger who stumbled upon this gentleman with his shovel—there are no obvious injuries like bullet holes or a missing head, but the neck is broken, though that may have happened long after death. What else can be determined remains to be seen. There is, as you can see, a hibiscus root growing through the rib cage, which isn't surprising given the relatively shallow nature of the grave." She looked the body over. "What I can tell you definitively at this point is that this is an adult male who had brown hair and stood about six feet three inches when alive. Of course, ethnicity has yet to be determined."

Kali listened, walking slowly around the grave while Stitches spoke. She stopped at the foot of the hole, where she could take in the full length of the dead man. The hands, like those of the first body, were crossed over the chest. Above the pelvis hung what remained of a wide, drooping leather belt with a rusted metal clasp. The clasp was shaped like a sunburst, more decorative than the typical buckle found on a man's belt. Any clothing had long since rotted away. Kali pulled out her phone and took a photo of the belt buckle.

"The hands," said Kali.

Stitches nodded. "Yes."

There was the rustle of ground birds from somewhere nearby, and the muted chatter of people going about their business at the crime scene. Kali closed her eyes and listened to what might be discernible beneath the surface noise. She imagined the snaking root and the toothed leaves of the yellow hibiscus, the lovely *ma'o hau hele*, making its way through the earth, reaching into the dead man's ribs and wrapping around the space that had once held his heart. *Who left you here?* she wondered to herself, but there was no answer to be heard.

"Let's get him back to Maui and see what he has to tell us," said Stitches, breaking into her reverie.

Kali stood back, watching as the body was removed with care from the ground for transport back to the county morgue. Once the bones had been gathered, Tomas returned, stepping carefully into the empty space that had been left behind. He carried a sifting screen, a bucket, and a box of plastic evidence bags. There wasn't enough space for two people to work next to one another, so Kali crouched on the edge and worked her way through the mound of earth that had been removed as the body had been revealed. She thought of the man's damaged skeleton, and of the bone breakers who had once roamed the islands, working as free-lance thugs for the many minor chieftains who had warred regularly with one another along the coastlines.

She'd been told these stories and others by her grand-mother, the celebrated Hawaiian author and historian Pualani Pali. Pualani had been the *kahu* who served as the spiritual leader and wisdom keeper of Kali's family, a posi-tion of great status. Because of this family connection and her close relationship to her grandmother, Kali's upbringing had included an immersion in not only the spiritual beliefs and legends of Hawai'i, but also in the culture, geography, and botanical features that made this remote Pacific island chain so unique.

She'd studied the vast collection of tales handed down orally through generations of Hawaiian people, later gath-ered and assembled by anthropologists and historians, each story having a multitude of variations depending upon the teller of the tale. This knowledge had proven invaluable in her position with the Maui Police Department, and in her role as a consulting expert throughout the entire chain of is-lands, particularly in cases that suggested a connection be-tween a crime and Hawai'i's rich mythology. Her position was unique: Not only was she a native Hawaiian with a de-gree in cultural anthropology, she had been identified by her grandmother as the *kahu* of her own generation, a position always handed down from grandparent to grandchild.

Pualani had tailored Kali's education to help her fulfill this role, and learning even the darkest tales became part of her lessons. Her mind wandered from the burial site across the distant hills and slopes, through the long, deep valley to the past where so much blood had seeped into the ground beneath the trees, feeding their roots.

Tomas's voice interrupted her thoughts, bringing her suddenly and firmly back to the field.

"Here we go," Tomas crooned with satisfaction, climbing from the hole and passing a small metal object to Kali.

Kali lifted it with her fingertips, peering at it closely, and then placed it in the palm of her left hand. A wave of familiarity washed over her. It was a tiny anchor, the arm at the bottom of the shank flattened out into a straight bar, and a small round hole where the top bars met. To all appearances, it was identical to the one that had been found in the pocket of the headless man.

"Here we go indeed," repeated Kali softly. The possibility of mere coincidence, or that two random burials had taken place in the same location, vanished. She surveyed the huge sweep of pineapple field. The majority of it had been turned over, but there were areas that still needed to be searched. Her eyes followed the line between the first grave and the second. Though there was considerable distance between them, they appeared to be roughly aligned with the edge of the service road that bordered the field. She turned to Tomas, who stood waiting for direction. "Ask the crew to concentrate on the field's perimeter where it's accessible by the service road," she said.

He nodded his assent, and headed off to speak to the backhoe operator. She texted Walter, receiving an almost immediate reply that he'd take a launch over to meet her early the next morning.

Kali sat back on her feet, wondering how many other lonely things the *ma'o hau hele* roots might have brushed against as they reached downward in their search for water and nutrients. She looked at the shrubs scattered across the landscape, imagining their flowers filled with the souls of the nameless dead.

CHAPTER 9

Kali spent the night at the Hotel Lānaʻi, rising early to meet with Tomas for a quick breakfast in the small dining room. Walter had already texted that he'd arrived at the command center and was waiting for them to make their way there.

Their coffee cups had just been filled by a quiet, shy waitress when there was a crackle from the radio that was secured within a pouch in Tomas's duty belt. At almost the same moment, Kali's cell phone began to vibrate, jiggling slightly on the table where she'd placed it. They exchanged glances as each answered, and Tomas signaled to the waitress that they needed to leave. She hurried over with two paper to-go cups, transferring their coffee from the mugs on the table. As they made their way to the door, the same waitress met them, thrusting a large paper bakery bag into Tomas's hand.

"Coconut donuts." She smiled. "For the road. I put in extra."

Tomas nodded, accepting the bag with gratitude. "Mahalo, Claire."

Kali looked at him as they crossed over onto the lanai. "Let me guess," she said. "You let her off a speeding ticket."

"Not even close," he said. "Her kids are on the softball team I coach. One of her daughters is having a hard time, so we're working on her batting technique."

They stopped on the bottom step, out of earshot of the staff and guests. Kali turned to Tomas.

"I'm guessing that we got the same message," she said.

"Another body. They're still uncovering it."

"That's three. What do you make of this?"

He shook his head. "Who knows? Creepy as hell, though."

"Makes you think. All those stories about the monsters on this island. Man-eating fiends that hunted the living."

"They were conquered, remember? Banished a long time ago."

She looked at him quizzically. "You've been in this business a long time now. There are always plenty of monsters to spare. And not all of them are found in the shadows of old stories."

He made no response as they walked to the street where the patrol car was parked. They climbed inside, and Tomas pulled away from the curb. The sky was clear and bright, and Kali watched the morning shadows slip by along the road's verge as Tomas drove toward the pineapple field. The old legend that he'd referred to painted Lānaʻi as an island haunted by malevolent spirits. In the traditional tale, it was the wayward son of a powerful Maui chief who finally vanquished and expelled the evil forces that had taken up residence among the sloping valleys.

As though he'd been thinking about the same details, Tomas turned to her.

"It was Kauluāʻau, right? The chief's son who did the housecleaning here? I forget why he was in trouble."

"For pulling up all the breadfruit trees on Maui," she said. "Kauluāʻau's father sent him here as punishment, but he eventually redeemed himself by casting out the evil and making the island safe again."

"I wonder . . ." said Tomas, his voice trailing off.

"Yeah," said Kali. "Seems like he might not have checked under *all* the rocks."

They'd reached the turnoff that led down a gentle slope to the investigation assemblage area. By the time Tomas had set the parking brake, Kali already had one foot out of the door. Tomas followed her as she hurried to the edge of the field, past the site where the refrigerator had been discovered and the second body had been found, and onward another two hundred feet to where Stitches, Walter, and a few of the SOC crew were waiting. The volunteer diggers stood silently behind them.

Kali stopped next to Walter.

"Good timing getting here," she said.

"Yeah. Most of another skeleton has been uncovered, but digging's on hold." He looked at the white bakery bag in Tomas's hand. "What's in that bag?"

Tomas passed over the pastries. Walter reached inside, removing a large donut covered in toasted coconut.

Stitches looked up at Kali. "Glad you're still on-island," she said. "We can't get a Burial Council official here until about noon, but they said if you're willing to act on their behalf, they have no problem with that. Everyone's pretty sure these aren't ancient remains."

Kali nodded. "Of course. What have you found so far?"

Walter and Stitches exchanged looks. Walter swallowed the piece of donut he'd been chewing and cleared his throat.

"Another male. Except . . ."

Kali waited.

"Except he doesn't appear to be alone," said Stitches. "As we widened this latest grave, we could see the elbow bone of a second figure protruding into the first skeleton's humerus, and also a tarsal from another foot, so it looks like there's another full skeleton buried very close. Side by side."

"Hands folded?" asked Kali.

"The first one, yes," Walter answered. "They've just started uncovering the second person."

Kali moved closer to the hole. "Any sign of another anchor charm?"

"Not so far," said Stitches, "but there's a lot of earth to sift through."

Walter turned back to the waiting team. "Okay, everybody," he called. "You know the drill. Careful."

After a few moments of reorganization, the digging continued. As the mound of red-hued soil grew larger, Walter rejoined Kali, Stitches, and Tomas where they stood a little way back from the hole in the ground.

"Do the two new bodies have skulls attached?" Kali asked.

"The first one, yes," answered Stitches. "But we've not gotten that far with the one buried beside it."

They each considered the ramifications in silence.

"Four people popping up in the same field without anyone noticing that any of them had gone missing is statistically unlikely in a population as small as the number of people on Lānaʻi," Walter finally said. "This whole thing is giving me a big case of the heebie-jeebies."

"Yeah. Same." Kali looked back to the small crowd that had gathered around the pair of bodies, feeling uneasy. On the other side of the service road that ran the length of the field, thick shrubs and small trees formed a natural barrier between the plantation and the countryside beyond it. A long length of police tape had been erected along the edge. She suddenly became aware of movement; several figures became apparent, moving slowly through the vegetation.

"We've got interlopers," she said, indicating with her eyes the line of shrubs where she'd seen people moving about.

"Damn it," said Walter. "Guess it was just a matter of time. I knew that tourist couple was never going to stay quiet about what they found. The body in the fridge has been all over the news, and when the police launch left port this morning, I noticed that the next ferryboat was packed. Word's out, I think. At least about the first body."

"Yeah, it's all over the news *and* the fake news," she said darkly. "We're going to need to set up a dedicated phone line for incoming calls." She moved closer to Tomas.

"Company," she said, indicating the far side of the service road.

He followed her line of sight. "Okay," he said, resigned. "I'll go run them off."

"I'll help," she said. "Just give me a minute." She turned back to Walter. "Are you staying over here tonight?"

"Can't," he said. "I've got to make an appearance in traffic court first thing in the morning. You'll have to fill me in as this unfolds, especially if this isn't the last of it—but I'm going to need you around, so don't stay longer than you have to. We got a heads-up from another arrest we made in the cock-fighting ring that there's a big meet-up planned in the next few days. Vice says they can use our help."

Kali sighed. "Okay. I'll plan on heading back tomorrow, but I guess that depends on what else the day turns up. I should probably bring over my tent and camping gear and just set up house until the whole field has been turned over."

As Walter turned to rejoin Stitches, Kali caught up with Tomas. Together they walked from the field to the service road and ducked beneath the plastic police tape, moving steadily across the rough earth toward the shrubs. As they drew closer, they could see a crowd of people, standing in groups except for a few who had separated and moved to the back. Two of the women dressed in long skirts from the group Kali had seen on the ferry carried signs with sentiments that opposed the digging: LET THE DEAD REST; STIR

NOT THE SOULS OF THE DEPARTED; while a few other signs challenged the police. CATCH THE KILLER, read one, while another had the words MURDERER IN OUR MIDST scrawled in red paint. Kali expected them to disperse when they caught sight of Tomas's uniform, but instead they just waited. Kali felt her jaw clench when she spotted Chad standing near the front.

"What did I tell you?" she said when she was close enough for him to hear.

"A funny thing happened on the way to the beach," answered Chad, his smile flashing in the sunlight.

Kali's eyes swept the crowd, estimating that there were approximately twenty-five people there. "Did you hire these people?"

"Hire them?" said Chad, feigning surprise. "These are some of my loyal local fans."

"And this is a police investigation," she said.

"Ah, I believe what you mean is that this is a crime scene," countered Chad. "And I'm here in my capacity as a journalist to get an official statement about why this pineapple field is filled with dead bodies. That, and why the police are trying to hide it from the public."

There were murmurs of assent from those standing around Chad.

"That's right," said a short, stocky man standing beside him. "There's a serial killer loose. What are the police doing to find him—or her—and protect the public? Most of us have kids. We're too afraid to let them out into our yards."

The other voices became louder and more adamant. The two women holding the religious signs began to sing a hymn. Kali wondered where their older, tattoo-opposed companion was. To the rear of the crowd, one person stood slightly apart from the others, saying nothing. He was tall, his face concealed by a straw hat with a wide brim.

Tomas looked at Kali, one eyebrow raised, then turned back to the assembly of people.

"All right, that's enough," he said. "An official statement is forthcoming. Meanwhile, I need you to disperse. Your presence here may very well contaminate the area where we're working."

"We're on this side of the police tape," Chad pointed out. "Well within our rights as observers. And as a journalist—"

Kali laughed. "For crying out loud, Chad, how many times does someone need to explain to you that having a blog or a podcast or whatever the hell—"

"Blogcast," said Chad, his voice smug.

"—does *not* make you a journalist," she finished. "Let's see some credentials. I'll let you slide if you show me a diploma with a journalism degree, or a press pass from an accredited news association—*not* something you generated online and printed out in a fancy font."

"I have an Emmy nomination for my role as an investigative journalist."

"*From a television show!*" Kali nearly shouted. She took a deep breath, trying to control her mounting annoyance. "And I don't believe you actually won the award, did you?"

"Oversight and politics," he said, completely unruffled.

Tomas intervened. "Okay, that's enough. All of you, stay on that side of the tape. That includes you, Mr. Caesar. No pictures. No recording. As I've already said, an official police statement will be issued later today. Understood?"

"Freedom of information, Officer!" yelled the man standing next to Chad. "You can't stop the people from learning the truth! It's your job to protect us!"

There was more agreement from the others, this time louder. The women in the blue skirts laid their signs on the ground and joined hands with one another, raising them above their heads. One of them bowed her head and began to pray aloud.

"You will be safest when you follow police directions, which, this morning, are to stay on that side of the barrier and follow all police orders," said Tomas, his firm voice rising above the din. "Otherwise, you will be removed from the area. In handcuffs, if necessary." He spoke into his radio. A uniformed officer on loan from Maui waved to them from the area where vehicles had been parked in a line, facing the field next to the command center. Tomas and Kali stepped away from the crowd and watched as the officer got into a truck and backed out of the line, driving slowly toward them along the dirt service road.

"We've called in extra volunteers to help today," said Tomas, his voice quiet, "but we're about tapped out. This is slow going."

"Relatively shallow graves, though, which helps a little. Hopefully we can get out of here soon. So far, the body in the refrigerator was buried the most deeply. Maybe that was to help make sure a heavy rain didn't wash off the soil and expose it. I wonder if the pineapple man was more important to the killer than these other people."

"Or maybe," said Tomas, considering, "the killer just ran out of refrigerators."

When the approaching truck came to a halt, Tomas moved away, speaking briefly to the officer who was driving, then rejoined Kali, who was busily scanning the faces in the small crowd around Chad. The tall, hatted man in the rear had distanced himself even more from the others. There was something familiar about him. Kali slipped beneath the tape, walking around the other people. The tall man was aware of her approach, and turned to walk away.

"One moment, sir," she called.

The man hesitated, but took a few more steps away, walking parallel to the service road.

"Sir!" she called again, her voice firm. "Wait where you are, please."

The man stopped, standing still as Kali caught up to him. She could tell, now that she was close enough, that he was elderly.

"Are you with the others?" she asked, indicating Chad's fan group.

The man smiled in response. "Well, yes and no. We all arrived at about the same time, you see. I more or less tagged along as they seemed to know where they were going. I assure you I am not here to cause any trouble."

His voice was familiar. Kali studied his face. "Could you please remove your hat, sir?"

Again he smiled slightly, then took off his hat, standing quietly with it in one hand, pressed lightly against his thigh.

"You're the gentleman from the hotel. You were a guest there a few nights ago when I was staying there."

He shook his head.

"Not a guest. I'd enjoyed dinner there, and was merely pausing briefly on the lanai."

"To greet the moon."

He bowed, the motion brief. "Yes. To greet the moon."

She was confused. "Do you live near the hotel?"

He nodded. "Quite near. I've lived on this gracious island since I was a much younger man."

"Were you with the pineapple company?"

His eyes clouded over. "I was not, though a member of my family was."

"And who was that?"

"Ah. My son-in-law."

Kali waited, but the man said nothing more.

"And why are you so interested in what's going on out here?"

The man smiled, but the gesture seemed half-hearted. "Even at my age, curiosity is alive and well. I heard that there was an unfortunate discovery here in the field, and naturally wondered what that might be. When I spoke to you that night at the hotel, I didn't realize you were a police officer." He looked back in the direction of the crowd. "Nor did I know that these people would be troublesome. I should have come on my own."

She watched him closely.

"Did you hear about all of this through Chad Caesar?"

He looked at her blankly. "Chad who?"

"The blond actor who led everyone here?"

His brow furrowed. "I'm afraid I don't know him, or even that he's an actor. But yes, he did take charge of the group, steering the others to this location."

She nodded. He didn't seem to be the type of gushing follower that Chad naturally attracted. "I'm a detective, by the way. Kali Māhoe. And you are?"

There was no change of expression on his face.

"My name is Bill Bragden."

"Well, Mr. Bragden. I'm very interested in learning more about the plantation and the people who worked here. Is there a chance you could put me in touch with your son-in-law?"

He tilted his head slightly, his gaze sweeping the field behind them. "I'm afraid that won't be possible. He disappeared, you see. Spent a good number of years making my daughter's life miserable, then he went to work one day and never came home."

Before she could comment, she caught sight of Tomas, waving wildly, signaling to her that he needed to see her. There was an urgency to his gesture. Kali turned back to Bill, distracted.

"Where can I find you later today, Mr. Bragden? I'd like to speak with you about your son-in-law, but this isn't the best time."

He nodded. "I can see that. I'm quite easy to find. White house with bright red shutters on Boat Street. Drop by whenever it's convenient. I have nowhere to go."

She turned toward Tomas, jogging back along the road to meet him.

"What's up?" she asked. Behind him in the distance, she could see that the old man had turned away. He was standing very still, gazing out over the field.

"I don't know," said Tomas, "but they need us at the new grave site immediately."

She looked in the opposite direction, toward the area currently being excavated. Stitches was standing in the hole, and Kali could see Walter and the others squatting around the perimeter. She walked quickly toward them, hearing the thud of her shoes fall into rhythm with Tomas's footsteps. As they reached the grave, the others turned toward her, their faces serious.

"What's going on?" she asked.

Walter rose and stepped aside, pointing to the cavity in the dirt at their feet.

"See for yourself," he said.

Kali looked into the grave in astonishment, then met Stitches's eyes.

"Is that . . . ?" she asked.

"Oh yes," said Stitches. "I can confirm that this grave holds the bodies of one adult male, one adult female, and one female infant. An 'ohana, yes?"

Hearing the Hawaiian word for family, Kalie fixed her gaze on the row of skeletons, lingering on the tiny form nestled beside the female body.

"I would suggest," said Stitches, "even at this stage of examination, that the child is quite, quite young. Also, we found another anchor charm beneath it."

"Under the tiny keiki?"

"Yes. It may have been wrapped in something that's since rotted away, but that's where it was."

"All of them, left out here in this damned, dried-out field," said Kali, her voice barely a whisper. A wave of anger swept through her, followed by a surge of responsibility. The bodies of the victims had been found and could be laid properly to rest, but that wasn't enough. She had to find who had been responsible—who had placed the little charms, filled the holes with dirt, and then walked away from the dead.

CHAPTER 10

Over the course of the morning, the three bodies from the mass grave were removed from their resting places and prepared for transport. The search in the remainder of the field had taken on a new urgency, and Kali watched as the patched, grassy areas abutting the service road were explored by several people pushing wheeled radar units across the ground. Along with some of the volunteers, she walked slowly through the nearby rows of mixed red earth, pushing a long metal probe into the ground in the hunt for more bones. There was nothing more to be found in the path line where the other bodies had been discovered, so the search teams moved to the interior of the field.

As the sun grew higher, Kali's energy began to diminish. The heat was becoming oppressive, and though she'd been loaned a pair of gloves, the constant thrusting required to use the probe had left blisters on her hands. She looked around for Tomas. He had stopped beside one of the volunteers, who had struck something in the earth. Instinctively, her whole body tensed.

"Just a rock," he said as she approached.

Her momentum waning, she held the long probe balanced on her shoulder. "Feel like loaning me your car?"

"Sure," he said. "Keys are in the ignition. If you tell me you're running away, I won't blame you. It's hot as hell out here."

She grinned. "What are you talking about? This is paradise, brah. All the brochures and television ads say so."

He wiped the perspiration from his chin with the back of his hand. The gesture left a streak of dirt across his skin. "Right. Easy to forget that sometimes."

"There was a guy in the crowd earlier. Tall older man who told me his name is Bill Bragden and that he's a local. Ever hear of him?"

"Bill? Sure," said Tomas. "Quiet guy, been here for as long as I can remember."

"You know anything else about him?"

Tomas frowned. "Yeah, I think there was something. I can't remember the details. Something that happened a long time ago. I think one of his kids died. It was before my time on the police force, but I think it got mentioned at a gathering. Maybe some cookout or a festival a while ago. Why?"

"I don't know. He was curious about what we're doing here."

"By now, everyone on this island is curious. You might have noticed there's not a whole lot of anything else going on. Or maybe he's just following that actor around."

"I don't think so. Yes, he was with Chad's entourage, but he's not really one of them. He didn't seem to know who Chad is. Regardless, I'd like to talk to him. He gave me his address."

"Sure. I'll let you know if there's any more excitement."

"Yeah, do that," she said, stifling a yawn. "I'm going to find Walter and take him with me."

She trudged down the service road to the parking area.

Walter was there, talking on the police radio to the station on Maui. He ended the call as she approached.

"I'm sick of talking to people about roosters," he said, following her to Tomas's police cruiser. "Where are you going?"

"To talk to a Mr. Bill Bragden, someone who was in that crowd following Chad around earlier. Feel like coming with me?"

He didn't hesitate. "Yes. And for once, I hope wherever we're going includes an air conditioner."

They climbed inside the car. The windows had been left down, but the interior upholstery was still hot. As she and Walter clipped their seat belts, her phone buzzed. The screen showed a text from Tomas, along with a photograph. The message said: This is the one found under the infant's body in case you need it. The attached image was a close-up of a small, silver anchor charm.

Got it, she texted in reply, feeling a wave of frustration wash over her. She turned to Walter. "Picture of the anchor," she said.

He nodded. "It's going out on the news later today, too. I'm not in favor of it, but Pait insists. There won't be any mention that it was found with the bodies, just an appeal to anyone who might recognize it to get in touch with us right away."

"I don't like it either," she said. "But maybe it will stir something up."

"What's the story on this little field trip we're taking?"

"I met this guy at the hotel the first time I stayed over after our pineapple man turned up. He seemed polite. And old. But he was at the field again today, watching with the rest of Chad's groupies."

"That doesn't mean anything. Why the interest?"

"Tomas says he's been around for a long time. And Bragden told me today that his own son-in-law, who worked for the pineapple company, disappeared."

"Got it. You talk and I'll listen, okay?"

She cleaned the lenses of her sunglasses and adjusted the seat, then eased out of the parking space and followed the service road back out to the main road. She could see Chad and his followers still keeping vigil on the far side of the police barrier. He was watching her as she drove away, and she held her hand out of the window, pointing her index finger directly at him. She could see him grinning.

"You've got to stop letting that guy get under your skin," said Walter, watching the interaction.

"Yeah. While I'm at it, I'll stop the tides from washing in and out, too."

The road wound inland, back into town. Bill's address was easily located, and Kali parked along the curb outside of the house. They climbed out of the car and stood facing the modest structure. It had a tin roof and a small, fenced front garden that looked as though someone spent a lot of time tending it, with several large bird-of-paradise plants and red-and-blue ginger bushes blooming near the gate. A short walkway led through the garden to the front door, which was open. Kali walked ahead and knocked on the exterior screen door, then stood waiting patiently. From within, there was the faint sound of classical music, and feet approaching across a tiled floor.

Bill's figure filled the doorway. "Come in!" he said, stepping aside. She pushed open the screen door and entered the cool interior, followed closely by Walter. They paused just inside the entrance. There was no formal foyer, and the cool, tiled interior was immediately on view.

"This is Police Captain Walter Alaka'i," she said, introducing Walter. Her eyes swept the room. She was immediately fascinated by her surroundings, and struck by the dated nature of the furnishings and décor. Everything seemed to be upholstered in a faded, flowery pattern of pink roses and winding green vines against a cream background. The room's multiple shelves were heavy with small figurines and vases, and there was a glass-fronted cabinet on spindly legs that was filled with a set of matching china. Standing in front of the overstuffed sofa was an ornate wood-and-glass coffee table covered with decorative bowls and glossy magazines.

She looked closely at the cover of the top magazine in the stack, noticing that the publication date was several years old. Visible through a wide doorway into the back of the house was a kitchen, and a second arched opening that revealed a room where the end of a piano could be seen.

"Please, make yourselves comfortable." Bill gestured to the sofa, noticing Kali's gaze. He smiled, but there was reservation in the expression. He sat down in one of the two matching easy chairs that faced the sofa from an identical angle, separated by a small table. The chair and sofa arrangement was clearly positioned to maximize ease in conversation between those who might be seated there. Kali wondered if Bill had a lot of guests who stopped by to pass the time with him.

Walter sank down into the thick cushions of the sofa. Kali sat next to him, facing Bill, her attention caught by a large glass figurine of a rearing horse rising from what appeared to be a bouquet of pink glass roses. Bill sat back in his chair, following her eyes.

"Bit of a time capsule, isn't it?" She felt her face flush, suddenly aware that she'd been staring and that Bill likely thought her rude. "I'm sorry, it just . . ."

"Doesn't seem like the home of an old bachelor?" He laughed softly. "I'm afraid I don't have much of an imagination—or strong opinion, for that matter—when it comes to these things. Everything is exactly as it was when I lost my wife some years ago. I dust and sweep and polish when I remember to, but otherwise things stay the same." He hesitated, then reached out with one hand to finger the edge of a candy bowl on the table between the chairs. "I find it oddly comforting. There are no surprises."

Kali nodded, thinking of the glass coffee press on her kitchen counter. It was still in exactly the same spot where Mike had kept it, and she liked knowing that it was there; an imperfect yet unbroken thread to past mornings that had been filled with banter and companionship.

"I understand," she said quietly. She looked at him closely, trying to guess his past occupation. She noticed the long fingers of his hands, and thought of the piano she'd glimpsed, and of the music playing in the background. "Are you a music teacher?" she asked.

He tilted his head slightly, smiling. "Yes. Was, at least." He lifted his hands from where they rested in his lap. "I escaped arthritis in my fingers, but I'm afraid my wrists weren't so lucky."

"I'm sorry to hear that. Did you teach here in the local school?"

"No, privately. Before I moved here with my wife, I played in a community orchestra in Northern California and taught at the high school in our town. Once we were here, it was easier to have students come to me, at the house. There were some young people, but a surprising number of adults as well." He paused. "Am I in some kind of trouble for joining those other people at the old pineapple farm?"

Walter shook his head. "We're just gathering information."

Kali remembered Tomas's mention of the loss of a child. "You moved here with your wife from California. Was it just the two of you?"

He hesitated. "Yes, it was only the two of us—my wife, Linda, and I. But we had an adult daughter who already lived here with her husband. Lily. Our only child. She was what brought us to Lāna'i, you see."

He looked away. Kali followed his gaze to a trio of photos in matching silver frames set among a display of silver spoons. The center photo showed a much younger version of Bill beside an attractive woman, with a third person standing between them. The youngish woman in the center bore a strong familial resemblance to Bill and the older woman. All three faces looked happy and at ease.

"Our daughter's husband, Matthew Greene, was a scientist who worked for one of the big chemical companies. They were both thrilled when he found out he was being sent to Hawai'i to test and monitor some new soil fungicides and plant herbicides his company had created. They were supposed to make the pineapple plants stronger, and increase the crop yield."

Kali listened, remembering reports that had surfaced about the plantation workers falling ill, and a growing number of sicknesses and cancer cases among them. Rumors had circulated that the illnesses were the direct result of exposure to the sprays used on the crops, despite denials from the chemical company. She glanced at Walter, and their eyes met. She knew that he also was thinking of the chemical controversy.

The sunlight fell in a shaft across Bill's cheek, creating a thin river of brightness that spilled downward across his chest and one leg, and onto the floor by his feet. He was smiling.

"We came over to visit as soon as Lily and Matthew found out he'd be here for a while, and we had such a wonderful time. Matthew's company had said he'd likely be here for about three years. We made one more trip during that time, and he gave us a tour of the operations and we got to explore the island. My wife, Linda, and I stayed on for another week to visit Maui and O'ahu, and we fell in love with all of it—the people, the places. The extraordinary beauty of it all."

He looked down at his hands and lowered his voice. "But things changed. Lily grew ill, you see. And, unfortunately, we began to suspect that Matthew was abusing her. She refused to talk about it. She was finally hospitalized for depression, following what seemed to be an attempt to take her own life with an overdose of pills. We came back to help at once. When the weeks dragged into months and she didn't get better, we rented a small house to be close by."

"Was she able to leave the hospital?" Walter asked.

"Yes," he said, his voice strained. "Once she'd been discharged, we tried to get her to leave Matthew and come back to California with us, but she refused." He took a deep breath. "So we sold our home on the mainland and bought this place." His eyes wandered around the crowded room. He laughed, but it lacked joy. "Linda insisted on shipping everything over. She wanted it to be just like home, I suppose. A sense of the familiar, what she saw as a continuation of normal. But then Lily died. A fall down a stairway was the official cause of death, but I've never believed it. I think Matthew was responsible."

Walter frowned. "Did you express this to the police?"

"Oh, yes. But they didn't seem to take it seriously."

Kali watched Bill's face closely. "You must have been devastated."

"Destroyed," he said.

"Did you ever confront your son-in-law with your suspicions?

"I was going to," he said.

"But?"

The silence lengthened. Kali gave him time to gather his thoughts, knowing that it was better not to interrupt the flow of memories. Finally, he raised his head and turned to her.

"He disappeared before I had the opportunity."

The words fell like darkness. Bill sat back, the shaft of

light no longer illuminating his face. There were other shadows there as well. Kali and Walter waited.

"It was I who reported him missing. My wife and I had been away for a few days. When we returned, I went to talk to him, but he wasn't home. His house looked as though he'd simply gone out one day and had forgotten to come back."

Now Kali spoke, trying to recall if she had seen the surname Greene on Hara's missing-persons list. "What year was this?"

"December of 1997. The announcement had come in late summer that the fruit company was shutting down operations. They were too small to compete with the big companies, though they also tried moving their operations to places where labor was cheaper. Eventually, they simply went out of business. All of this meant that the chemical company Matthew worked for would likely be recalling him to the mainland."

"Was he bothered by that?"

"No, I don't think he minded. After he went missing, there was an investigation, but nothing ever turned up. There was no sign that he had ever left the island. Then, when I heard about the bodies . . ."

Again he fell silent, as though not wanting to put his thought into words.

Walter spoke quietly. "When did you lose your wife?"

"Ten years ago. An accumulation of grief, I imagine. Some people would find that improbable, but I believe it's true. One day, she reached her limit of dealing with the sorrow she'd held on to for so long. Then she was gone."

Inside, Kali's own grief stirred in response. She acknowledged it, then pushed it away. The acute sense of loss that she held constantly at bay subsided, its sharp edges buried, for now, by the loss experienced by a stranger. She watched his face, focusing on his reactions.

"I'm very sorry," she said. "I don't have children of my own, so I can only imagine the toll such a loss would take. Have you thought of anything over the years—anything, however small, that you haven't already shared with the police—that you'd like to tell us now? Any reason that someone may have wished to cause your son-in-law harm?"

Bill shook his head. "No, nothing I haven't already shared with the authorities. The police initially thought it might have been a case of misadventure—that he'd drowned and the currents had pulled him out to sea, or that he'd fallen off a cliff into some deep ravine while out hiking. He used to go to that beach up at Polihua, where the undercurrent is so notoriously powerful. Be he was never found."

She looked over at Walter, who nodded imperceptibly. She pulled her phone out of her bag and opened the image of the anchor sent to her by Tomas, then passed the phone to Bill.

"Can you tell me if you've ever seen anything like this before?"

He took the phone, squinting slightly as he studied the photo. Kali watched his face as he turned the phone slightly, looking at it from another angle. There seemed to be surprise in his expression, but he quickly recovered his composure. Kali felt the energy in the room shift.

"There was a church here for a while," he said, his voice guarded. "They came around to people's houses. Witnessing, I think they call it." He looked up, but he didn't meet her eyes. "They all lived together."

"Do you mean it was a commune?" Kali asked.

He hesitated. "If you like. Commune, cult. Difficult to say. They talked a lot about the Bible, and they passed out brochures. I think they may have used this symbol in their outreach."

She watched him. He seemed suddenly restless. He turned

his head slightly, and his gaze suggested that he was looking far away into some other place or memory.

"Do you recall their name?"

Bill said nothing. After a moment, he looked up, as though startled from his reverie to find other people in the same room.

"No. I don't think so."

Kali rose to her feet. As Walter stood up beside her, Bill also stood and led the way to the front door. He turned to Kali, his voice hesitant. "Can you perhaps share anything with me about what you've found out there on the old farm?"

"Not at this time, no." She watched as his eyes clouded over. "But I promise you we're doing everything we can."

"If you're willing," said Walter, "it would be very helpful if you could help us locate someone from your son-in-law's family who could provide a DNA sample, or any existing dental or medical records."

Bill nodded. "Of course. I would be happy to do that." He faltered, looking at Kali. "It would be good to know, one way or the other. You understand?"

"I do," she said. She reached into her bag, removing her wallet and offering him a card. "Officer Alva will be in touch with you later today or tomorrow morning about locating a DNA sample, so please gather any contact information you have on family members of your son-in-law. And please feel free to call me directly at any time. We'll speak again, as soon as I have something definitive to share with you."

He stood next to the door, opening it and stepping aside so that she and Walter could walk out. Kali took a few steps down the paved pathway, then stopped and turned back to him.

"I'm very sorry about your wife," she said. "And your daughter. Whatever happened, I know it must have caused your family great pain."

He nodded. "Thank you."

She reached the car and climbed inside, feeling the heat that had accumulated in the seat penetrate her shoulders and the backs of her legs in a molten burst, as familiar and comforting to her as Linda Bragden's embroidered pillows and knickknacks were to Bill. She understood that the material things crowding every surface of his home provided an association for Bill to the family he had loved and lost. And, she considered, his home also bound him to a man who was likely not missed at all. She looked back at the closed front door.

Walter climbed in beside her and slammed the door.

"Loss or not, he's hiding something," she said.

"Yep," said Walter. "No doubt about that."

CHAPTER 11

Instead of heading immediately back to the pineapple field, Kali kept south on Highway 440, known locally as Manele Road. The presence of Lānaʻihale volcano was strong here, its long spine towering through cloud forest in a roughly north-south direction to her left, its slopes covered with densely growing ferns and thick groves of trees that were punctuated by majestic Cook pines. She knew that though the volcano's last eruption was more than a million years ago and that it was usually referred to as extinct, it was, in actuality, merely dormant, and wondered if it would ever stir again during her lifetime.

"Now what?" asked Walter, as they passed the turnoff to the plantation and kept driving.

"Maybe nothing," she said. "But let's at least go and see."

The petroglyphs that Tua had referenced were located on a slope on the volcano's side. She drove for about ten minutes before pulling the car over onto a clear patch of rough ground that had plainly been used as a parking area by others. They got out, making their way toward a hill rising above the plains of Palawai Basin, following a rugged track leading upward. The footing was slippery, and their feet skidded on the loose scree that covered the path's surface. Walter grumbled in protest as he kept up with her.

It didn't take long to find what Kali was looking for. On the face of a giant rocky monolith rising from the ground at the foot of the volcano was a collection of ancient petroglyphs. The original carvings had been desecrated in areas, and other, newer graffiti carvings had been added, but she had no difficulty identifying the original art. Her grandmother had written about these petroglyphs, commonly known as the Luahiwa carvings, and had interviewed other historians and archaeologists in the preparation of her highly respected work on Hawaiian culture. She'd read to a younger Kali from the book's pages, and Kali had studied the photographs closely. Eventually, her grandmother had taken her across the channel to see them for herself, and to offer a child's point of view on what the carvings represented.

Even among learned academics, there was no consensus on their meanings. Kali had been taught that they were likely a record of life on the island—a time capsule of events that were significant to the island's inhabitants, ranging from a collection of warrior figures, various animals, and boats. She searched among them, finally pinpointing the anchor carving that Tua had referenced. It was located not far from the carving he'd mentioned of what appeared to be a vessel of some kind, set into the stone face about eight feet from the ground and measuring nearly six inches across its base. Like a few of the other petroglyphs, its outline had been darkened by someone who'd dragged a burnt matchstick along the edge to define the shape and features—a practice frowned upon by historians attempting to protect the area from alteration and damage.

Kali and Walter studied the anchor image, comparing it to the photo of the anchor charm stored on her phone. Other than the slightly uneven lines of the stone carving and the small hole in the metal anchor, they were very much the same. She punched in Tomas's number, waiting for his answer as she and Walter followed the stony path back to the car.

Tomas's voice sounded even more tired than it had the last time they'd spoken.

"Don't tell me you're lost," he said. "I won't believe you, though I would understand completely if you were at least trying. It's hotter than hell here in the fields."

"Funny you should mention hell," she said. "Do you remember a local church group here that used to go around knocking on people's doors?"

He laughed. "That description's not specific enough, I'm afraid."

"This particular church isn't active anymore, but they were while the pineapple production was still strong. Also, Bill Bragden's son-in-law went missing after Bragden's daughter died. Bill made some allegations about domestic abuse. Do you remember hearing anything about that?"

There was silence as Tomas mulled over her questions.

"That was too long ago for me," he finally said. "I think you should talk to Bobby Keawe. He's retired now, and is in pretty poor health, but he was Lānaʻi's Maui County cop back then. He's in a nursing home over on Oʻahu near his kids and their families, but he'd be happy to talk to you, I'm sure. I'll bet he's been following the news here pretty closely."

"What's wrong with him?"

"Had a stroke. Can't live alone anymore because of partial paralysis, but there's nothing wrong with his memory."

"Do you know if Keawe worked the missing persons case?"

"He was the only cop here at the time, so he was bound to have been involved."

"Okay. Text me his contact details?"

"Will do. Where are you, anyway?"

"Up at the Luahiwa petroglyphs. Something very like our anchor is carved into the big rock up here."

There was a low whistle from the other end of the phone. "Damn. Why didn't I think of that connection?"

"There may not be any."

"Still. Keeps popping up, doesn't it? Be careful driving back. Lots of deer roaming around up there."

The image of the pig smeared across the road back on Maui flashed through her mind. "Yeah, I will be," she said. "See you in a bit."

They headed back toward the pineapple field, with Kali driving.

"Do you remember Bobby Keawe at all?" she asked. "Tomas said he was here on Lāna'i, but going back a while."

"Yeah, but only vaguely. He was getting close to retirement when I knew him, though he was still running things over here."

"He's not in the best of health, and is in a care facility over on O'ahu somewhere. Tomas is sending his contact info. We should find out about that old missing person's case involving Matthew Greene, and see if Keawe knows anything about churches that were in business over here while the plantations were still active. I feel like the anchor may be connected to them."

"You want me to call him?"

"Do you mind? Maybe he'll remember you."

"Sure. As soon as you have his number, send it along. Meanwhile, you can drop me off at the harbor. I'm taking the launch back to Maui."

"Okay. I'll be back at the hotel for the evening, so let me know after you've talked to him."

"Do we have a name for the church?"

"No, but I'm hopeful that maybe Bobby does."

*   *   *

Kali left Walter at the dock and returned Tomas's car to the makeshift parking area at the command center along the pineapple field's edge. She found him and made her request that he send Bobby Keawe's contact information directly to Walter, then tracked down a volunteer to give her a ride back to the hotel. After showering and changing her clothes, she went into the dining area to get a grilled fish sandwich to take back to her room. She sat at a small table next to the room's window where her computer was set up. Her notes were spread out on the floor at her feet, and she leaned forward occasionally to lift a page and study it as she ate her sandwich.

She sorted the notes, then resorted them into different stacks, trying to find a pattern or order to what had so far been discovered. She had just given up, and was stretched out across the bed staring at the ceiling when the phone buzzed and Walter's name popped onto the screen.

"Kali? I spoke at length with Bobby. He remembers the Matthew Greene case pretty clearly. Said he was pretty sure the guy was slapping his wife around, and he took a special interest because he'd heard the wife was dying and the idea of her being mistreated on top of that really got under his skin. After a neighbor called the police, Greene was brought in for questioning, but the wife was unwilling to make a complaint of any kind. Bobby says he used to park his police unit in front of Greene's house at night, partly to reassure the wife that he knew what was going on, and partly to shake Greene up."

Kali frowned. Abuse was one thing, but abuse of a dying woman struck her as particularly appalling. "And?"

"Then the daughter died. It was ruled an accident after she was found at the bottom of her front steps by a neighbor. She had grown pretty weak and wasn't supposed to be out of bed, but the neighbor who found her said he saw her outside every few days, sitting in her garden in the sun."

"How long afterwards was it before Greene disappeared?"

"Two weeks. There was an investigation into his whereabouts, but nothing ever came of it."

"Were the wife's parents suspects?"

"Both were questioned, but apparently they were off-island when Greene went missing."

She reached for a pen and pulled a page from her notes. She jotted down a few of the details that Walter had gathered, frowning.

"How could the time of his disappearance be narrowed down specifically?"

"Well, that's where things get a little cloudy. The parents went over to Kaua'i to have a private memorial ceremony for their daughter at an undisclosed location up in the cliffs on some path that she loved to hike. Bobby thinks they took her ashes there to scatter, but they never told him that for certain. That was on a Friday morning. Greene wasn't with them. He went in to work that day, though the field was mostly closed. He was clearing up his end of things, but then he didn't show up on Monday, and no one saw him anywhere around over the weekend—but no one was looking for him either. Production had completely stopped, and the plantation was in the final stages of shutting down, so no one was really keeping any kind of schedule. The parents got back to Lāna'i from Kaua'i the next day, on Tuesday. Bragden had their ferry tickets for the crossings back and forth, and crew members on the ferry at the time positively identified them as having been on board going over and going back."

"That's all very convenient. Who keeps their ferry ticket once they get home? I can't remember ever doing that."

"Yeah, Bobby said as much. He felt like Bragden may

have had something to do with Greene suddenly vanishing, but I don't get the feeling he was very motivated to pursue it after an alibi had been established."

"Okay, so what about the church?"

"Ah, the Eden's River people."

"Catchy."

"Bobby said they were basically a bunch of pains in the ass, banging on people's doors to try to share their view that native Hawaiians are all godless savages who need to be saved from practicing native witchcraft. Seems they just wanted to help everyone get into heaven."

"Wow. That's quite a mission statement."

"Mission is exactly the right word. It was founded by a family, led by a patriarch by the name of Abraham Waters, who was apparently a true zealot. I just texted you his photo. Turns out his 'church' was actually both a cult and a commune based in Christian beliefs. But they used the anchor as one of several symbols in their ministry, along with a cross and that little fish you see on the backs of people's cars that signals to everyone they're better than you are. The group name was tied to Biblical imagery connected to water: water into wine, walking on water, all that kind of thing."

"Was he a con man or just delusional?"

Walter took the question seriously. "Delusional, I think. I did a background check on him, and some interesting things came up."

"Such as?"

"First, his name was originally Greg Waterson. He was a high-profile sports doctor—a surgeon—in the Chicago area, who'd gotten a lot of publicity for his so-called miracle touch in the operating room, successfully treating people for injuries that other doctors had given up on. Then Dr. Waterson became the focus of a big lawsuit following a botched knee operation that left a rising high school soccer star permanently sidelined. The Watersons had a second home in

Napa Valley in the wife's name, and they sold that house and used the considerable proceeds to fund their move to Hawai'i in 1993. They also got huge donations from other like-minded people who still believed in him, and who were encouraging him to develop his vision of a healing retreat center out here in the islands."

Walter filled in more details, explaining that the Watersons had one child: a daughter whose name was Abigail. During the lawsuit, Waterson made several statements that alluded to a deep conviction that his skills as a surgeon had been divinely bestowed upon him, and that the botched knee surgery wasn't botched at all—rather, it was proof that God didn't want the young soccer player to play college-level sports, and had prevented the surgery from being successful in order to prevent a future that he wasn't meant to have.

"I've heard that a lot of successful surgeons come with— or develop—a kind of God complex." She thought for a moment. "I think if I had to have major surgery, I'd want the doctor with the scalpel to be as confident as humanly possible."

"Yes, but maybe not crazy with power," said Walter.

"I guess a name change helped create distance from his sports surgeon identity and any negative publicity surrounding what happened."

"That," agreed Walter, "plus the Biblical name fed into his project here. In fact, all members of the commune adopted the last name 'Waters,' and many of them, like Waterson, made it a legally recognized change."

Kali pondered the information Walter had gathered. "So, tell me how a successful surgeon parlays his skills into running a commune?"

"Easy. As we know now, Waterson was pretty religious already. His daughter's named for someone from the Old Testament, and he was very active in a number of Christian groups connected to his church. He had plenty of well-heeled friends who lined up to donate money after he pitched the idea of establishing a Christian wellness retreat on Lāna'i. Bobby says that for a while it even became a haven for wealthy creative types—musicians, actors, artists— flying under the public radar for a little rest and rejuvenation. For a while, Waters kept the religious aspects very subtle, and offered things like meditation and healthy cooking courses for guests, along with evening seminars on how to achieve goals. Life coach stuff. Hard to say when the shift occurred into cult and commune, but gradually that's what it morphed into. He kept it small, and maybe that was a deliberate ploy to keep from attracting national attention."

"Where's this guy now?" she asked.

"No one's quite sure. Bobby says he and his followers annoyed and/or offended too many people on Lāna'i and got run out of town."

"Before or after Greene went missing?"

"Not until a few years later."

Kali was silent, considering all that Walter had just shared.

"I still don't see a strong connection between all of these things," she finally said. "Did Waters have some connection to the Shandling pineapple operations?"

"No record of that, but his daughter had an after-school job there for a while, before the commune was good-sized. She was pretty young. She was thirteen when the Shandling company closed up shop. Bobby says he thinks Waters planted her there to entice people to check out the retreat— so it's likely that at least a few people who lived at Eden's River over the years had jobs connected to pineapple production."

She sat on the edge of the bed, swinging her legs. She felt agitated, and wasn't exactly sure why.

"By establishing it as a church, Waterson was able to stay tax-exempt, and all those donations from visitors and residents added up. There's no official estimate about other valuables that may have been given to the organization, like jewelry or art. He also ran a Bible-based school attended by his kid and a few of the children of commune members."

"Was the proselytization just about lending credence to the church claims?"

Walter laughed. "Probably didn't hurt the image, but Bobby told me the funny thing is, the members really bought into the agenda. He said they could be annoying as hell spreading their message, and that the locals didn't like the whispers about Abraham's policy of sexual freedom, but that they also did a fair amount of good. Donated tons of food to the local food bank, helped some of the older local citizens run errands and do yard work."

"What went wrong?"

She could hear the grimace in his voice as he answered.

"Seems like too much free love comes with a price. There were a lot of younger women that became followers. The doctor was quite a looker. Movie-star handsome. Some of them joined up after leaving behind concerned parents or pissed-off husbands. Several of those people made the trek to Lāna'i to entice their loved ones home, and things got ugly. Police had to be called to break up fights and shouting matches."

She looked at her phone, pulling up the photo that Walter had sent of Abraham Waters. She estimated that it had been taken when he was in his late forties. He was classically handsome, and she wasn't surprised that he found it easy to influence women. "Okay. So it all goes belly-up on Lāna'i, and Waters moves his operation elsewhere, but keeps it on the down-low."

"No proof of that, but that's what I'm betting on." He sighed. "I guess you could say not enough went wrong to keep him from carrying on. Nothing, at least, that smacked of a potential Heaven's Gate or Jonestown."

"Can you find him?"

"Looking for him right now. Hara's got a short list of past members; it shouldn't take long to find a trail." He yawned. "You coming back tomorrow?"

"Yeah. I'm going to check in with the search crew in the morning just in case there's anything else to see, then head for the harbor."

"Roger that. Get some sleep. We'll talk tomorrow."

CHAPTER 12

It was late afternoon the next day by the time Kali arrived back at the harbor on Maui. She was completely drained. There had been an exhaustive search of the remaining fields. The discovery of the trio of skeletons had galvanized the crews, and extra help had been brought over from Oʻahu and Maui, including Hara, who had been given the task of keeping the public at a distance from the field. Tomas had gathered additional trusted volunteers from the community, and an intensive search had commenced. Nothing more had been found.

Her last night at the hotel had been marred by disturbing dreams: a pineapple field filled with upright corpses instead of pineapple plants, each one faceless, each one wearing a pineapple mounted on its shoulders in place of a head. They'd stood in rows, silent and patient, waiting to be named. She'd finally given up on sleep, and had lain on the bed, staring at the ceiling until dawn began to wash across the sky. In the morning, she returned to Maui with Hara and Stitches. There was little conversation; each of them was as tired as the next.

She drove home slowly, stopping first at Elvar and Birta's house to collect Hilo. She could hear the clank of Elvar's hammer hitting steel as she made her way along the driveway. She parked and followed a path to the back of the house. Both Birta and Elvar were on the terrace. Birta had apparently been reading a book in one of the long lounge chairs set beneath the shade of the roof overhang, but was now holding it aloft in one hand while struggling to hold Hilo's collar with the other. She looked up in relief when she saw Kali, and released the dog. Hilo bounded toward Kali, then ran a circle around her, delighted. Elvar stood next to his forge, watching and smiling.

"Thank goodness," said Birta, sounding slightly ecstatic. "Take this animal home, please. And expect him to be sick. He ate what I think was a mongoose earlier today. It was difficult to tell, as it was mostly rotted."

"Great," said Kali, anticipating the likely drama of a moaning Hilo leaving bits of mongoose throughout the house.

Elvar laughed. "She's exaggerating, Kali. I got to him before he ate any of it. So he's mad at me, I think. But happy to see you."

"Well, thank you both. Again." She sighed. "And dinner's on me, of course, whenever it suits you."

"Thank you," said Elvar, bowing slightly. "It's not necessary, of course, but we would be happy for your company."

"Yes," said Birta darkly, "provided it's somewhere that won't allow dogs. It would be nice to enjoy a meal without being stared at the whole time by someone with slobber dripping from their oversized jaw."

Kali looked down at Hilo, who was gazing at her in absolute adoration. "Where are your manners, Hilo?"

Elvar placed his hammer on the flat surface of his anvil. "He has excellent manners. Birta is just overly sensitive."

"Yes," agreed Birta. "Overly sensitive to the possibility that your enormous dog views us as the dessert course."

Kali turned away, laughing. Hilo pressed his body against her leg. "Well, I appreciate your patience and generosity. Truly." Her eyes twinkled. "Birta, maybe I should get you a puppy as thanks."

Birta took a sharp intake of breath.

Elvar watched, hardly containing his grin. "Great idea, Kali! I'll help you find one, and as soon as Birta's forgotten, we'll bring it home as a surprise to her."

"Oh no you won't," snapped Birta. "Absolutely not. I won't have it. Animals and I . . ." Hilo trotted over to her, nuzzling her arm affectionately, then walked back to stand beside Kali. "Animals and I don't really get along."

"Hmmm," said Kali. "Hilo doesn't agree. He loves you, Birta. He loves you both. But we'll get out of your way now. Lots to do." She made her way back to the driveway, turning to wave, Hilo in tow.

"See you soon," said Elvar.

By the time she reached the driver's side of the Jeep, Hilo was already waiting. She opened the door, and he leapt into the passenger seat. She pulled out onto the road, making the next turn into her own driveway, flooded with pleasure to be home. She brought her duffel bag inside, dropping it on the floor next to the sofa. She lay down on the soft cushions and fell asleep almost immediately, wondering how thorough the investigation into Matthew Greene's disappearance had been, and if Bill Bragden or his wife had really been considered a serious suspect. Certainly there was motive if their only daughter, already ill, was being abused.

After a half hour, she got up and changed into an old tank top and a pair of cutoff leggings, then made her way down to the beach, Hilo racing ahead of her. Gradually, she went from a slow jog to a full run, allowing her mind to wander while her body strained and sweated. She had tasked Hara with searching for anything he could find on Eden's River, and had left Tomas gathering what information he could from his local contacts while they waited for medical records to be sent from Matthew Greene's family on the mainland. She felt frustrated, running harder, her shoes digging into the damp sand along the water's edge. She could feel the muscles in her legs burn, running harder still, until sweat had soaked her clothing and her breathing came in gasps.

She climbed the short coastal path upward, walking slowly toward her house, allowing herself to cool down while her heartbeat returned to normal. The sight that greeted her as she left the trailhead and made her way into her own yard was an unwelcome one. The sun was already moving low toward the horizon, but she could see that the hammock on her front porch was occupied: it hung low with the weight of a visitor, swaying back and forth in a slow, deliberate swing, set in motion by the thin, brown leg stretching from the faded blue fabric of the hammock to the porch floor.

Kali came to a stop, taking a deep breath, willing herself to remain calm. She recognized the leg and the bare foot attached to it. His tail wagging happily, Hilo left her side and made a beeline for the porch. Kali could hear a woman's voice greeting him. It was Makena Shirai, Mike's only child.

Kali made her way unenthusiastically across the lawn and up the steps. Makena was scratching Hilo's back at the base of his spine where his tail began, and he was moaning in pleasure. Kali looked at her visitor, and made an effort to keep her voice level as she spoke.

"Hello, Makena." The greeting held neither enthusiasm nor warmth. "If you stopped by for tea, I haven't made any. Afraid I'm fresh out of crumpets, too."

The young woman in the hammock sat up and swung her

other leg to the floor. Kali could see dirt embedded between her toes and beneath her nails. The dress she wore was at least two sizes too large. The straps across the shoulders that held it up revealed a concave chest and deep, sunken spaces beneath the collarbone; her bare arms were riddled with old needle marks. Kali was surprised to see that despite the overall appearance of undernourishment and general dishevelment, the girl's eyes were uncharacteristically clear. She felt a sweep of apprehension.

Makena frowned. "Why do you always have to be such a bitch?" she asked, her tone petulant. She stretched her hand beneath Hilo's chin, scratching vigorously. "It's like it's your default setting or something. At least Hilo's glad to see me."

"Hilo's glad to see anybody who'll scratch him or throw something for him, or share a sandwich. That's the thing about dogs, Makena. They're completely without expectations."

"Unlike you, you mean." Makena's brow wrinkled.

Kali ignored the comment. She knew it would be useless to express any of the hopes she'd once held for this girl, remembering with sadness and barely concealed regret the bright young child who'd almost become her stepdaughter.

"Where have you been, anyway?" she asked. "I suppose by now you've used up the tray full of needles and painkillers you stole from the hospital."

Makena stopped scratching the dog and leveled her gaze fully on Kali. "Oh, you mean that night when I saved your life? And I was there for the inquest, like a good girl. Everyone said I was a hero."

"You were. And then you did your disappearing act. If you'd stuck around, I would have said thank you."

"That's okay." Makena pushed herself out of the hammock and into a standing position. For just a moment, she swayed slightly. She looked at Kali, but her eyes, clear moments before, now had a slight glaze to them. "I came here because I wanted to tell you . . ." Before she could finish, she lurched forward and fell, turning slightly so that she landed faceup on the floor. Kali leapt toward her, but was too late to catch her. Makena's thin body landed with a thud, her head making solid contact with the floorboards, her eyes rolling backwards into her skull.

"Great," muttered Kali. "Just what I need tonight. An unconscious junkie on my deck."

She checked the girl's pulse and breathing, then pulled a cushion from the nearest chair and lifted Makena's head just high enough to slip it beneath the matted tangle of dark hair. Makena stirred, then reached for Kali.

"Hush. Don't try to sit up or say anything. I'm calling 911."

Makena's eyes flew open. "No," she said. "I don't need anyone except for you right now." Her voice sounded weak, but coherent.

Kali knelt beside the thin, dirty figure as she pulled her phone from the side pocket of her leggings. Hilo whined, pushing himself between the two women, licking Makena's bare arm.

"Yeah, you need me *and* a detox team." Kali scanned the girl's face. "Whatever you're up to, Makena, I don't have time for it. What did you take? And how much, and when?"

"I know what you think, but I'm not high. I swear it."

Kali lifted Makena's arm, surveying the needle scars that ran its length, looking for fresh marks. "You're always high," she said. "It makes you boring."

Makena tried to roll over onto her side, using her other arm to push herself into a sitting position. Kali pressed her hand against the girl's chest, preventing her from rising.

"Lie still."

"I mean it, Kali. I'm not using. I'm clean, and I'm going to stay that way."

Kali shook her head. She'd heard these proclamations before, and knew better than to be sucked into whatever fantasy Makena had concocted for herself.

"Let me guess. Spiritual conversion? Psychological breakthrough?"

"No, sorry."

"Then what? You've got two seconds, then I'm calling for help."

"I'm pregnant."

The words fell onto the porch, across the sloping yard, spreading into the air where they mingled with the cries of birds above the beach. Kali felt them envelop her. She knew they were true. Not good. But true. She sat back on her heels and looked down at the girl stretched out in front of her.

"Are you absolutely positive?" She regretted the words, and their tone, the moment they left her lips. Makena searched her face, her expression unfathomable. Kali bit her lip and tried again. "I mean, did you do one of those drugstore tests, or did they tell you at the clinic?"

"Stick test. Three of them." Makena looked away.

There was silence as each woman considered the significance. Kali knew better than to give voice to all of her own concerns: Makena's ongoing drug use, her poor health, her deplorable personal hygiene. Certainly there had been plenty of other young mothers like her who had given birth to normal, healthy infants—babies without an immediate dependency on drugs, and who were strong enough to survive. But the odds were not good.

Her mind jumped to a variety of sad and distressing future scenarios as she helped Makena to her feet and guided her inside to the sofa. She pushed the thoughts away, wanting to be optimistic, charitable even.

"Sit down. I'll make up the spare room. You can stay here for a few nights until we figure out a plan."

Makena nodded.

Kali considered the girl's uncharacteristic silence as she brought a set of fresh sheets and pillowcases from the hall closet to the small spare room that she used as storage space, placing them on a stack of books. A camping cot that served as guest accommodations for her rare visitors was folded up against the wall. She brushed a thin, fine layer of sand off the exposed top edge and unfolded it. On the floor behind the cot was a thick foam rubber pad, rolled into a column, which she pulled out and spread across the surface of the cot.

Instead of making up the bed, she gathered the sheets and pillowcases and sat down on the edge of the cot, clutching the stack of linen in her arms. She looked through the door to the living room. The back of the sofa was visible, and she could hear Makena's voice, talking softly to the dog. She remembered, suddenly, a long-ago morning on Oʻahu, when she had volunteered to teach Makena to surf while Mike was busy. It was an attempt at bonding, but it had felt like something more—a sharing of knowledge and tradition, two women from different generations communing with the vast, restless sea. That day, Kali had been filled with hope for the future and all that it might hold: a family, even ready-made, and the welcome responsibility of teaching the child by her side how to become a woman.

She caught her breath in sudden grief. This girl was ill-equipped to care for a baby, and had already proven beyond the shadow of a doubt, unable to care for herself. She wished for a moment that Mike was here to help sort this out. The fleeting thought was replaced instantly with a feeling of gratitude that he had been spared. His life had ended tragically in an act of violence, but at least it had been swift and he'd been spared the anguish of watching his only child deteriorate over the years.

She rose to her feet to finish making up the bed, choosing two thick pillows and a light, soft quilt in case the night became cool. She would make something to eat and see that Makena went to bed with enough nourishment inside of her to pass along to her baby. At least for tonight, there was nothing else that could be done.

CHAPTER 13

Kali sat beside Walter in the patrol car. It was morning, and she'd left Makena at her house, still asleep. Walter started the engine and they waited for the air-conditioning to get up to speed before they pulled out onto the road. The windows were still rolled all the way down, and the hot air that had already settled across the dashboard and the seats had yet to cool.

The weather had been unusually scorching. Kali longed for a strong trade wind to lift the heat and carry it away— and there would be no argument from her if the wind chose to take the burden of Makena along at the same time.

Walter had asked her to ride along to follow up on a lead to the illegal rooster fighting he was investigating, as she had history with Angelo Mendoza, who was a suspect. A bust of a staged fight had been attempted the night before, but someone had gotten word that the police had found out about the cock fight, and there had been nothing to be found at the address where the event was supposed to have taken place.

Kali moved the conversation to Makena. She'd just finished filling Walter in on the details of the pregnancy, but he had yet to respond. She glanced at him, waiting until he'd adequately processed the story before she said anything more.

He sat quietly, staring ahead, then grunted. "She say anything useful, like who the father might be?"

"I haven't pushed the conversation that far yet."

"Odds aren't great that this will end well," he offered. "Lots of babies born to heavy drug users . . ."

". . . are stillbirths, or arrive with their own drug dependency already in place. Yeah. I know."

"How far along do you think she is?"

"About five months, from what I was able to gather, though she doesn't look it. Skin and bones. I'm not sure how much attention she's been paying."

Walter turned, looking intently at Kali. "Hey, you know what? This kind of makes you a grandma." He threw his head back and laughed, the deep sound reverberating throughout the car.

Kali took on a murderous expression. "You're hilarious, as usual. She's no relation of mine."

"Sort of she is, right? I mean, if Mike hadn't died . . ."

"Been killed."

"Okay, if Mike hadn't been killed, you'd have been married, and Makena would have been your legal stepdaughter." He laughed again, holding his side and sliding down in his seat. "Okay, okay, I'll concede on the details. This makes you almost a *step*grandma. How's that?"

"Shut up, Walter. Just shut the hell up." She was in no mood. "I'm telling you all this because I could use some actual help figuring out what to do. You're the one with all the kids. How is this supposed to work? Did Nina do something special when she was pregnant with your girls?"

He wiped his eyes and sat up a little straighter. He pressed the button that automatically rolled up the windows, then looked carefully in his rearview mirror and out the side windows before easing the car from its parking space.

"Well, yeah, but Nina is healthy. Woman won't even take an aspirin when she has a headache. And you know how she insists on all the food that comes into the house being organic. Free-range mangoes and all that."

Kali was silent. She knew that Makena's diet too often consisted of what she could harvest from garbage cans, or steal off store shelves. "I made an appointment for her to get a checkup at the clinic," she finally said, "and also to see what she needs in general."

"Good," said Walter. "I remember that Nina was big on those prenatal vitamins. And she was always going off to some kind of yoga class that was for pregnant women, to help make the delivery easier. Maybe you should call her."

"I will. Right now I'm trying to figure out how to get Makena to this appointment. If I tell her about it, she'll probably refuse to go."

"You want me to help?"

It was Kali's turn to laugh. "I hate to be the one to break the news, but you're not exactly her favorite person."

Walter grimaced. "And you are? I was more or less volunteering to put her in cuffs and give her a ride in the squad car. Your call, but just know that I'm happy to provide the transportation."

Kali's mental image of an outraged Makena exiting the back seat of the police car to an audience in front of the medical clinic was supplanted by a more sobering one of Makena giving birth to an underweight child with underdeveloped organs, or poor motor skills, or fetal stroke—or maybe even all of these problems. Each scenario was highly possible. The condition of prenatal methamphetamine exposure was a terrifyingly real problem among children who were born to meth mothers. Ironically, the drug itself was to blame, at least in part, for the growing number of pregnancies in young female users because of its inhibition-lowering effects.

She stared out of the passenger window. Her beautiful islands might be wrapped in birdsong and the perfume of a billion flowers, but they suffered from the same problems as any other place on the planet. Through the glass, she could see the litter that had accumulated along the road's edge, and knew that a multitude of empty plastic water bottles could be found abandoned along her favorite paths. She closed her eyes briefly. Maybe it was simply her training as a detective that meant she would always look more deeply than a casual observer to peer below the surface of everything she encountered, but she didn't know how to shift her perspective. It was simply who she was.

Even as the thought crossed her mind, she glimpsed an empty plastic shopping bag dangling from the branches of a tall bush along the side of the road, and felt her stomach tighten with anger and despair. Surely anyone could see the ugliness of the discarded bag.

Just then, a convertible filled with young people passed them, their music blaring, seemingly oblivious to the fact that the vehicle they'd just passed was a police car.

Walter swore, and flipped on his siren.

"Just give them a lecture, okay?" said Kali. "I have a strong feeling that it's going to be a bitch of a day."

One of the passengers in the convertible looked back at them as the driver pulled over, then dropped a plastic bottle and a crumpled paper bag onto the road verge.

"Ignore what I just said," said Kali, reconsidering. "Give them a nice fat ticket, and I'll fill them in on criminal littering in the meantime."

Walter grinned as he pulled up behind the convertible. The car eased over onto the verge, and Walter pulled in behind it, cutting the engine. "Are you going to use your scary voice?"

"You bet I am," she said, pulling out her badge and hanging it around her neck. "Plus, this will give me something constructive to do to take my mind off the pineapple-field bodies while I'm waiting for Tomas to get back to me."

"About the disappearance of Matthew Greene?"

"That, and whether his father-in-law, Bill Bragden, was seriously an official suspect."

"How could he not have been? He seemed pretty sure his daughter was the victim of domestic abuse."

"Yeah, but I can't read him. He's old now, and it's hard to picture him killing someone, even in revenge."

"How many killers have you met that were obvious from the beginning?"

Kali considered his question. "You're right. But this guy . . . I don't know. Piano teacher, lives in a fussy house with too many vases and candy dishes, takes good care of his garden . . ."

Walter shook his head. "Classic, high-functioning psychopaths sometimes have nice gardens, too."

"We should bring him over to Maui for questioning. Get him out of his comfort zone."

"Agreed."

"Lots to think about."

"Yeah." He looked at the idle convertible on the road ahead of them, its wheels straddling the verge.

"But first them, I guess." He turned toward her, brow raised. "Before I give them a ticket, you want me to throw in a speech about drugs and a warning about the consequences of unprotected sex?"

Her eyes narrowed. "Sure. Be my guest." She undid her seat belt and opened the door. "Then you can buy me lunch before we talk to the rooster guy."

* * *

The post-traffic-ticket stop for lunch was brief. They pulled into a roadside parking area where a food truck was selling fish tacos, and ordered *ono* tacos topped with slaw and avocado. After enjoying their meal at a picnic table in the shade, they made the twenty-minute drive to the Kahanu Garden on Ulaino Road. Inside, they followed a pathway that opened into a green area and past the colossal rock structure of Pi'ilanihale Heiau. The ancient edifice had been created from basalt lava rock, and was spread across several acres that included multiple terraces and platforms. Once, long ago, the *heiau* had been a place of worship and cere-mony, where gods were offered sacrifices, and people gath-ered for moments of significance within their community.

Existing within the garden's borders was an expansive na-tive *hala* Pandanus forest, which bore the distinction of being the largest existing forest of its type within the Hawai-ian Islands. There were extensive collections of native plants and flora that had been introduced to Hawai'i from other parts of Polynesia, and they walked among them, eventually coming upon a grove of breadfruit trees where they found Angelo Mendoza tinkering with the engine of a riding lawnmower. He was surrounded by a small sea of manicured, freshly cut grass. When he saw Walter and Kali approach, he stopped fiddling with the mower and removed a wide-brimmed hat, then wiped his forehead with the back of his hand.

"Angelo Mendoza?" said Walter.

"That's me." He looked inquisitively at Walter, then turned his attention to Kali, recognizing her.

"Hi there, Angelo," she said.

"Oh, it's you. I got something you cops need?" Angelo di-rected the question to Kali, his voice unfriendly.

"We'll have to see," she said.

"Tell me about your big rooster show, Angelo," said Walter.

Angelo scowled. "Ain't no roosters here." He spread his arms wide, indicating the vast green lawn. He looked at Kali, bemused. "Not that I can see, anyway. Maybe your holy detective thinks she can see invisible things."

They ignored his attempt to engage a confrontation. "You cured of your cockfight betting problem?" said Walter. "Word on the street is you're the top dog when it comes to handicapping fights."

Angelo threw back his head and laughed. "Now, who on earth told you such a thing?" he asked. He waited, clearly expecting Walter to share his source.

Walter merely smiled. "There's a police rule: no kissing and telling," he said. "What you can do is tell me when and where the big fight is supposed to go down."

Angelo feigned surprise. "Big fight, huh? Guess no one told me. Not that I'd be interested, of course."

"Some people think you're the guy pulling all the strings," said Kali.

He regarded her with contempt, directing his answer to Walter instead. "Who's 'some people,' huh, brah? You just wanna start trouble. That's all you cops ever wanna do."

"Maybe we just want to make sure laws don't get broken," said Kali.

He swung on her, his voice betraying his disgust. "Whose laws? Roosters doing battle—that's part of our history. You would know that if you were a real Hawaiian, not some sell-out with a badge."

"You know I'm local, Angelo," she said.

He was combative. "You no Hawaiian. You just some bleached-out version." He spat on the ground.

"Am I?" she asked him.

"How far back you go?" he asked in response, now clearly belligerent.

"All the way," she said, remaining calm. She looked toward the grove of trees. "You know anything about these *'ulu* trees? What we use them for?"

He looked derisively at the fruit hanging from the branches of the tree closest to him. "Breadfruit is food. You stupid or something?"

She shrugged. "Sure. Food. Medicine, too—the sap is good for sprains. But it's also what the old canoe builders use to seal the joints in their boats."

"You read that somewhere, lady cop?"

"Where's the fight, Angelo?" asked Walter, interrupting the direction the exchange had taken.

"Told you, there ain't no fight."

"Would you like to come down to the station and make a formal statement to that effect?" asked Walter, growing stern.

"Only if you got a warrant that says I have to," offered Angelo. He put his hat back on, pulling it firmly toward his ears. He turned toward the mower, reaching into the engine. "Otherwise, this law-abiding man's got work to do, and you're wasting my valuable time."

"That's fine for right now." Walter smiled. He winked at Angelo, who glared in return. "But I expect we'll be seeing you around."

"Oh yeah? When's that?"

"When the cock crows, pal," said Walter. "That's when."

CHAPTER 14

It was still dark when Kali woke the following morning. The transition from deep sleep to full consciousness was abrupt and instantaneous. One second she was floating above a placid dream lake, perfectly in harmony with the shimmering surface just beneath her; the next, she was sitting upright, heart pounding. She pushed aside the sheet tangled around her legs and swung her feet to the cool, rough floorboards.

She did a mental check: There was no scent of smoke, no sound of an intruder moving furtively through the adjoining room, no storm wind beating against the roof or walls of the house. She moved quietly across the room and into the hall, peeking into the guest room where Makena lay sleeping, undisturbed.

There was nothing obviously out of place, but something was nevertheless amiss. She saw the outline of Hilo standing at the window, watching her with interest. A soft, hopeful whimper left his lips, indicating that he would be more than happy to accompany her, even at this early hour, if she was interested in going for a walk.

She sensed what had shifted in the atmosphere. The Kilauea volcano on Hawai'i Island was going to erupt. She stood beside Hilo at the window, looking toward the sloping hill that ran downward to the beach. There was nothing to be seen—the volcano was on the southeastern side of Hawai'i Island, and both the width of the archipelago's largest land mass and the wide 'Alenuihāhā Channel separating the other island from Maui provided a visual buffer—but she knew that by daylight, the roar beneath the surface of the earth would have released its pent-up molten core, and that smoke and ash from Kilauea's howling mouth would have formed a thick cloud above its head that could very well become visible as it drifted with the wind currents.

She moved quickly through the house to the front door and down the steps onto the lawn. Hilo padded behind her as she jogged parallel to the ocean, searching in the darkness for the short path through the hill's vegetation that led to the water. The sea was deep in this spot, and there was very little here in the way of beach. To the left where the ground curved away was the small, natural cove and the short dock where the *Gingerfish* rested, held fast by her anchor. The thought triggered a mental image of the tiny charms decorating the lonely skeletons on Lāna'i. She shook her head, frustrated.

Farther off, to the right, the hillside dropped steadily to where a jumble of lava rocks formed a crude breakwater, running steadily downward in elevation to a curved arm of wild beach. One long, flat piece of lava rock jutted out from the stack of boulders supporting it. She made her way to it, stepping carefully onto the surface, Hilo close behind.

When she'd been a child, this rock had been her imaginary flying ship—part of a larger universe she'd created where she and a band of cohorts that included her grandmother's cat launched themselves to other parts of the world, where they were then transformed into heroes who helped those in need. Now, she crouched on the rock, her bare feet pressed against the wet surface. She closed her eyes, bent her head, and clasped her knees. Breath after breath, she became still, sensing through the soles of her feet the tumultuous act that was about to take place.

She lowered herself onto the rock and sat there for the better part of an hour. Hilo lay next to her, his long body taking up the empty space beside her, his ears alert. Kali shuddered, but not from cold; seconds later, warning alarms rang on the far coast, undetectable by her ears from this distance, but nevertheless known. She felt the volcano's wild release.

As the spray from the sea grew in intensity as the tide moved in and the water level rose, she took a deep breath, lying back on the rock next to the dog, feeling the water droplets make contact with her exposed arms and legs. She drifted off for a while, half-dreaming, until the light made a subtle change. Sunrise was imminent. Slowly, she stood and faced the east, stretching her arms over her head. "*E ala e, ka la i kahikina*," she chanted, greeting the sun and the new day. "*Arise, for the sun is in the east.*"

The darkness shifted toward gray light, and the thin red and amber line separating the sea and sky became more pronounced. As the crown of the sun came into view, she climbed carefully off the rock and back to the hillside, followed silently by Hilo. When she reached the steps of her lanai, she sat down again, enjoying the view of color rising from the thin horizon; the light growing steadily on the earth below; the tall damp blades of grass gaining definition; and the sound of the morning birds singing and sharing whatever news birds shared with one another.

Then the image of skeletons in the fallow field intruded,

dimming the enjoyment of the dawn's light. She rose and stretched. Hilo watched her, waiting for some further indication of her intentions.

"Come on, fella," she said to him, leading the way up the steps and into the kitchen. Makena stood in the doorway, looking sleepy and confused.

"Where did you go?" she asked.

Kali looked at her. "Didn't you feel it?"

Makena shook her head, not understanding. "Feel what? The kid?" One hand reached down, touching the small, almost imperceptible swell above her sharply defined hipbones. "I think it's too soon."

"No, not that. The volcano."

"What the hell are you talking about?"

Kali tried to be patient. "Kilauea. It's erupting."

Makena rolled her eyes and scowled. "And you *felt* it? From all the way over on the other coast of Hawai'i Island? You are so freaking weird. Of course I didn't feel it, and neither did you or anyone else unless they were standing next to it." She looked around the dim kitchen. "I'm going back to bed. Hilo can come with me."

She walked back into the small bedroom, followed by the dog. Kali watched her, saying nothing. She waited until the door was closed, then went to the counter and lifted the electric kettle from its base and filled it with water. She switched it on, and as the water heated, she measured coffee beans into a grinder, then poured them into the glass press. When the water was hot, she poured it carefully over the ground beans, relishing the scent of the coffee as it filled the small kitchen space. She opened the fridge, removing the loaf of raisin bread that had garnered George's disapproval at the market, and placed two slices in her old toaster. She filled a mug with coffee, and reached into a cabinet for a small plate. By the time the toast popped up and she'd buttered it and carried the plate and her coffee mug to the table, her dark mood had begun to dissipate.

The printed list of missing persons was on the table. She read through it as she ate, frustrated that the list would have to be expanded significantly to include the new discoveries. So far, there was little in common between any of the people described on the current list: a middle-aged banker, a high school science teacher, two car mechanics from different parts of the country, one ballroom dancing competitor, and a mix of other professions that seemed completely unlinked to the pineapple industry. There were several workers missing, but they didn't appear to match the age and height range suggested by Stitches.

She considered briefly that the location of the bodies might be unrelated to the victims themselves, but dismissed the thought. The carved pineapple was too much of a direct link. She pictured the burials, considering the differences and similarities. The first body had been placed in a container, while the others had been wrapped and placed directly into the ground, their shrouds long-disintegrated. One had been beheaded, at least one had a broken neck, and the trio of bodies had been laid carefully side by side. Except for the infant, each person had been buried with their hands folded over their chest. The most obvious and important connection was the small anchor found in each grave. That was a similarity that proved there had been a relationship between the burials. Even if the silent, hidden dead had been strangers to one another, it seemed a given that they had each known the same killer.

She picked up a pen from the table and sketched the anchor in the margins of her printed list. Then came a buzzing sound, and Kali reached for her phone. The voice of Stitches emanated from the speaker.

"Very sorry to have disturbed you at home, Detective. You weren't at the station when I called."

Kali bit her lip. "My apologies, Doctor. You apparently begin the day a little earlier than me."

"Quite all right. I'm calling because I have the preliminary report for you on the four new bodies, and some news on the first. I called Walter, but there was no answer, so I left him a message. I'm sure he's still enjoying breakfast somewhere and doesn't wish to be disturbed."

Kali smiled involuntarily. Walter's love of breakfast food—in all its incarnations—was well-known, and Stitches was probably correct in her assumption. Kali imagined that her uncle was most likely seated at his favorite table at the Ranch Restaurant, dousing a plate of coconut pancakes with sweet syrup, and polishing off his second or third cup of coffee. For a moment, she wished she were with him.

Stiches shattered her placid imaginings. "Meanwhile, it's getting quite crowded over here. I've just had a couple of traffic fatalities delivered, and I'm running out of tables and storage units. But about our latest pineapple-field finds: There was enough hair on each of the adult skulls to collect DNA samples," she informed Kali, her voice crisp. "They're with the lab, awaiting comparison from the DNA that's been provided by Matthew Greene's relatives. To summarize without a firm identification yet: From the latest dig, we have one adult female with long, blond hair; one female infant, and two males—one with dark hair, who was found next to the female, and the other buried alone, who had brown hair and lots of dental work, and was about six feet three inches in height. I would hazard a guess from the fact that there's significant wear on the remaining natural teeth and an impressive collection of fillings, extractions, and other fun things, that this man will have left behind significant dental records."

"You mentioned the neck was broken."

"Yes, technically an occiput-C2 fracture—but a cervical fracture doesn't necessarily mean death, unless the spinal cord was severed. Since many people recover from broken vertebrae, we can't assume this was the cause of death."

Kali remained silent, waiting for Stitches to continue.

"As for the rest, our family burial consists of an adult male and adult female with skull damage consistent with being struck on the head with a heavy object, and also one very young female infant. All with their skulls present, but the infant has a misshapen skull consistent with fetal hydrocephalus. When untreated, that condition can certainly be fatal, but we don't know yet if that was the reason for death in this particular case."

"Hydrocephalus? What would cause that?"

"Many things. Poor spinal development, genetics . . ." Stitches took a deep breath. "As for the headless man, we've sent the body over to Oahʻu, where a forensic anthropology team connected to the Joint Base Pearl Harbor–Hickam is working on the remains. We're in the midst of preparing the other bodies and will send them over as well."

"Do you—"

"Please," said Stitches, cutting her short. "You know better than to ask me how long it will take. I have absolutely no idea. Perhaps by the time I have those answers, you and Walter will have come up with some possible names to connect to the bodies."

"We're working on it," said Kali, trying to keep her voice from betraying her own frustration.

"Yes. That's what we're doing as well. Enjoy your day, Detective."

The call ended, and Kali dropped the phone onto the table. In her mind, she saw the little metal anchors lined up in a row, shiny and silent. Calling cards. She knew they meant something. If she could work out that part of the puzzle, maybe it would lead her to a killer who had found it necessary, or at least convenient, to take a man's head and end the lives of four other people—and then leave behind nothing but a wooden carving of a fruit, and a tiny, shining charm.

CHAPTER 15

Chief of Police Leo Pait stood in the doorway of the Hana station, his tall, narrow figure somehow managing to block most of the light. He had one hand on each side of the doorframe, giving the impression that he was holding up the building. He leaned inward slightly, peering around the main room with obvious interest. Kali, Walter, and Hara were clustered around Walter's desk, looking at an image on Walter's computer screen. Kali held a sheet of paper.

"Goodness," said Pait. "Must be six or seven years since I was actually inside this station." He looked at Walter and winked. "Not much in the way of ambience, I have to say. Redecorating my own office has turned out to be one of the best moves I've made in the last few years. New paint. New furniture. Very uplifting. I had someone come in to feng shui the whole place. Enhances the flow of energy, you know."

Kali could sense that Walter was about to say something that not only he, but she and Hara as well, were likely to regret. She spoke before he had time to say anything.

"Chief Pait." She made an effort to smile in a convincing way. "It's quite a surprise to see you here today."

"Out in the wilds, yes." He walked into the room, lifted a

stack of papers from the corner of Hara's desk, and placed them carefully next to the computer keyboard, then sat down on the newly cleared edge. Even seated, he seemed taller than the others. "But I'm not here to discuss the psychological boost to cognitive processes that the right combination of paint colors and textiles can deliver. I've had a great idea, and wanted to discuss it with you in person. Two great ideas, actually."

There was an immediate increase in the tension level in the room, moving like a wave between Kali and Walter, who had each lived through several of Chief Pait's great ideas in the past. Even Hara, who had heard stories, looked apprehensive.

"Oh?" said Kali, continuing to force a smile. She folded the piece of paper she'd been holding and placed it in the back pocket of her jeans. "Well, we're all ears." She looked encouragingly from Walter to Hara. "Aren't we?"

They nodded slowly in response, their eyes glued to Pait's face.

"Here's the thing, team," Pait said, leaning forward as though they were all co-conspirators in some undefined game. "We've got a lot of work to do to repair the image of our islands as havens of serenity and safety. Mass grave sites and a killer on the loose for years—perhaps even decades— taints the illusion of tranquility we all strive so hard to maintain. Sunsets and whales leaping through the blue waves into the blue sky. Music and aloha—that's what we want the tourists to be focused on. All of that."

Walter shook his head as if to clear it. "How about boiling lava spewing from the core of it all? Drugs and alcohol abuse? Domestic violence?"

"Exactly," said Pait, looking fondly at Walter. "That's it exactly. It's opposite the image the tourism board wants to promote. So let's give our visitors a little extra aloha, shall we?"

Kali's eyebrows rose. Hara looked down at the floor.

"The *tourists*?" repeated Walter, his voice rising. "What about the hardworking, tax-paying families that actually live here?"

"Yes, yes, them too, of course," said Pait. "In fact, what I have in mind will make them happy as well. Make them see us as one of them." He fumbled over the awkward sentence. "Or them as us, and vice versa." He threw up his hands. "You know what I'm trying to say. It's all about connection. And we have you, Walter, to thank for part of my brilliant plan."

Everyone in the room except Pait held their breath. The chief turned to Walter, his leg banging against the front of Hara's desk. Pait didn't seem to notice.

"I heard through the department grapevine that you'll be taking part in that ukulele competition at the Fire Garden Cultural Festival that's coming up. Got me to thinking about making it a department-wide activity. There's a wonderful opportunity here for community outreach. Connection. There's great talent in our ranks: Joe Keahi over in Evidence, Joyce Hale and Tutu Kalani in Patrol, Walter on his little guitar. We'll play up the public relations angle of officers as bona fide locals."

Walter made a small, unhappy sound. Kali turned toward the window, hiding a smile.

"Now, just a minute, Chief—" Walter began, but Pait cut him off.

"And Detective Māhoe! Not only an extraordinary sleuth, but a genuine Hawaiian priest to boot!"

Kali's smile vanished. She swung around to face Pait, her face reflecting her dismay.

"I'm not a priest," she began, but the chief wasn't through.

"I've been told that hula dancing is part of your cere-monial procedures, and that you happen to be quite adept at the art. Happily, there's a hula demonstration component to the festival."

Kali's expression darkened. "Who, may I ask, told you that?"

Pait waved one long, pale hand in the air. "Oh, one of the officers I expect. Can't recall exactly who at the moment. But that's not important. What *is* important is that we band together for the people, yes?"

Kali took a deep breath, then spoke. "Actually, Chief, it might be more effective—"

"Good, that's settled, then," said Pait as though she hadn't spoken. "I've already signed you up for a hula demonstration." He turned to Hara. "Officer . . . ?"

"Hara, sir," said Hara, his voice filled with trepidation.

"What's your gift, son—singing? A musical instrument, perhaps? I'm sure you have some talent to share from your . . . what is it? Japanese-Hawaiian heritage?"

Kali shook her head in despair at Pait's questions and comments. "You can't say that, Chief," she said, but he was oblivious.

There was a pained expression on Hara's face. "Yes, Japanese-Hawaiian. I practice traditional Japanese drumming, sir."

Kali and Walter turned to Hara in surprise.

"Well, then. There you have it." Pait rose from the corner of the desk. "I'll leave you to decide if Japanese drumming is Hawaiian enough, then. Someone from my office will be in touch to coordinate. Meanwhile, carry on. We have unsolved crimes to deal with, don't we?" Pait gave a thumbs-up to the others, then turned toward the door, making his way out of the building. They heard him say goodbye to the duty officer seated behind a counter near the entrance.

Lost for words, Kali, Walter, and Hara slowly drew apart. Hara walked back to his own desk and rearranged the papers Pait had moved, then sat down in his chair. Walter began rummaging around in the top drawer of his desk, swearing softly under his breath. Kali walked over to the coffeemaker.

"Just double-checking," she said. "There's nothing stronger than coffee in this building, is there?" No one answered. At his desk, Walter swore again, still searching through the detritus that had accumulated in the drawer.

"Anyone seen my bottle of aspirin?" he asked.

"No, sir," said Hara, his voice subdued.

"Small drawer, bottom right side," said Kali.

Walter abandoned his search of the top drawer and turned his attention to the smaller one Kali had indicated. The aspirin bottle was there. He took it out, opened it, and shook four tablets into his palm. He stared at them for a moment, then slammed them in his mouth and tossed back his head to swallow. Kali watched him from her vantage point of the counter, then chose a small glass and poured it half full from a large plastic bottle of water resting next to the microwave. She brought the glass to Walter, placing it next to his keyboard.

"Drink this," she directed. "Those pills are going to dissolve in the back of your throat and the taste will be awful. I think the day is already bad enough."

Walter picked up the glass and drank from it.

"Bet it was Roger Sanoe in accounting," he said, scowling. "He saw me buying new strings for my ukulele last weekend and I mentioned the festival. Filthy bastard. Think I might shoot him in the foot."

Hara looked up, alarmed.

Kali smiled at Hara reassuringly. "He doesn't mean it." She turned to Walter, her look conveying that she wasn't absolutely sure. "Your problem-solving skills could use some tweaking," she said, moving closer to the window. Outside, the edge of the parking area was visible. Pait's car was just easing out of its spot when the brake lights flashed and he pulled back in. Kali watched as he climbed out of the front seat, slammed the car door and sprinted back to the office. The sound of the door banging open followed, and they saw him once again standing in the doorway.

"I nearly forgot my second plan," he said, slightly breathless. "That fellow with the podcast show, the one that starred in that great television series, something about lights and Maui. Let's get one of you on there as soon as possible. Dispel any fears about a serial killer, talk to the public; make a plea to anyone who might be able to help us with some information about the missing people those bodies belong to."

Kali made a choking sound. She stared at Pait, then turned to Walter, speechless. Walter spoke into the void.

"Excellent idea, Chief. We'll figure out who should do it." He looked sideways at Kali. "Since he's already blabbering about the discoveries on Lāna'i, and the newspaper coverage has people looking over their shoulders, worried about becoming the next victim, it would be a good opportunity to offer some assurance. Maybe even motivate somebody to reach out to us to offer a possible identification."

"Excellent!" Pait turned away again. "Carry on, everyone!"

A moment later, Kali could hear the sound of gravel crunching beneath the wheels of Pait's car as it pulled away. She turned to Walter. "Toss me those aspirin."

Hara watched Kali and Walter nervously.

"Captain," said Hara, hesitant. "I don't understand . . ."

"What just happened?" Walter laughed, but the sound was humorless. "We used to call it the Pait Effect. The man can turn any scenario into a political maneuver. Genius, really." He sighed. "Get used to it, kid."

"That's right," said Kali. "Escape from a Pait plan is not only improbable, it's likely impossible." She patted her back pocket and turned to Walter. "For the record, I refuse to deal with Chad. And I've got the address for the farm worker

Hara tracked down. He's up-country over in Makawao. I'm going to go talk to him."

Walter swiveled his chair to face her. "You just said escape was not an option."

Kali took her canvas messenger bag off the back of her chair where it hung, then crossed to the door and opened it. "Escape? Hell, I'm flat out running away."

CHAPTER 16

K ali followed the quiet main street of Makawao past its row of shops and galleries for the third time. The address she was looking for wasn't where her directions indicated it would be. There was one main intersection that linked four roads leading away from the small town's center, and Uphill Street wasn't one of the names on any of the road signs.

She slowed the Jeep and pulled into a space painted diagonally on the pavement in front of the Star Shop. The cheerful, wood-shingled building was slightly dilapidated, with a wide, sagging front porch and glittering windows, the light reflecting off glass objects hanging from the window frames inside. It was unfamiliar to her, but it had been years since she'd spent any time in the small town.

She could hear singing as she walked across the threshold, her day bag swinging against her side. It was a woman's voice, soft and caressing, the words to her tune sung in what Kali recognized as Spanish. She stepped into a space filled with gifts. There were small glass stars dangling from transparent strands of fluorocarbon fishing line attached to hooks in the ceiling above her head. The stars shifted slightly in the breeze, and the sunlight moved through them to create random prisms. Charmed, Kali smiled, and called out in greeting.

"Aloha," she said, and the singing stopped. A slender, elderly woman with black hair streaked with silver came into sight from behind a display, holding a tray. Several glass kaleidoscopes rested on its surface. They looked handmade to Kali, and she caught her breath involuntarily at their beauty.

"Aloha," said the woman. She saw Kali's gaze had taken in the kaleidoscopes. "Pick one up," she said, smiling. "Go ahead. Look out the window with it."

Kali reached forward, choosing one that had a triangular tube base constructed from small, opaque glass panels. It felt substantial as she lifted it, filling her hand. At the end, there were more glass panels fastened on a central pin that allowed them to move in a circular pattern. She looked through the small viewing spot on one end, and spun the moving panels at the other end with one hand. Inside, small colored glass beads tumbled, unfolding in beautiful patterns against an interior mirror.

Kali lowered the kaleidoscope and replaced it carefully on the tray. The woman waited, then moved toward an empty space on a shelf next to a row of stuffed toy animals, and slid the tray onto its surface. She turned back to Kali.

"They're extraordinary," said Kali.

The woman smiled in gratitude. "Thank you. I've been making them for a very long time. Not so many anymore. But still. Some each year. They bring me great pleasure."

Kali gestured toward the stars. "And these?"

"My little corner of the universe. A safe place filled with light and beauty. You have to create your own, you know. The forces of the world expect you to make an effort."

Kali nodded. "Yes. I agree with you. But it seems the effort is overwhelming for a lot of people. I think maybe some of them just don't know where to start."

There was a momentary stillness as each woman considered what had been said. Then Kali spoke. "I'm sorry, I think I've been distracted by all of this beauty. I'm trying to find an address, but the road seems to be missing. It's called Uphill Road."

The woman laughed.

"That's what local people call the Olinda Road." She pointed behind her. "Because it goes uphill, you see. Into the high country. Who are you looking for? I know most of the houses in that part of town."

"Manuel Raso. Do you know him?"

A small, shadowy frown swept across the woman's face.

"Oh. That one." She looked away briefly, her eyes brushing the small, barely moving constellations above her head. "I think he is a lonely man."

Kali wondered at the comment. "Do you know his house?"

"Yes. You'll follow the Olinda Road for about three-quarters of a mile, and his house will be on your left. White, I believe. But you can hardly miss it. There is a short driveway with a mailbox shaped like a large pineapple."

Kali started. "Did you say a pineapple?"

"Yes, very garishly colored if you ask me. But since you didn't, I'll keep my opinion to myself." Her eyes twinkled.

Kali said nothing, but her mind raced. "Well, thank you," she finally mustered. "And thank you for letting me look through the kaleidoscope. I'll have to come back soon." She hesitated. "The stars—are they for sale?"

"Not the ones already hanging," said the woman. "But there are more. You can choose your own." She walked behind a counter where an old cash register sat, bending slightly to lift a square wicker basket from a lower shelf.

Kali moved closer, drawn by the small shiny glass stars visible inside, each fitted with a long piece of clear fishing line.

"Feel free to look through them," said the woman. "See which one wants to be yours."

Kali reached in, gently lifting a blue star, turning it over, then replacing it. She looked back into the basket. Each star was between an inch and an inch-and-a-half across. The hues were subtle, running the full range of the rainbow. Her eye caught a star that seemed to be made from a pale green glass that grew slightly more intense at each of its points, but was nearly clear in the center. She held it up to the light, delighted by the color.

"This one," she said with confidence. She glanced toward the shelf and the row of stuffed animals. "And that small stuffed pony. The white one with the blue polka dots and the brown tail, please."

The woman smiled. "Children?"

Kali hesitated. "Yes, but not mine."

"Well, someone will be pleased."

Kali handed the star to the woman.

"Would you like me to wrap this for you so that it doesn't become chipped?" the woman asked.

Kali shook her head. She reached into her bag, pulling out a cloth wallet. "That won't be necessary," she said, placing a twenty dollar bill on the counter.

The woman counted out some change, and placed it on the counter next to the stuffed horse and the pale green star. As Kali moved her purchases to her bag, the woman met her eyes. "I hope this star shines happy light on you," she said. "And the little horse brings a smile to someone's face."

"Thank you," said Kali, pleased. She looked up at the woman, a sudden thought occurring. "You know, while I'm here, I'd like to show you something." She pulled out her phone and scrolled through her images until she came to one of the little anchor, then held it out so the woman had a clear view. "Have you ever seen anything like this? It's about half the size of these small stars."

The woman took the phone and looked closely at the image. "Hmmm," she murmured. "Yes, I have seen something like this, but it was a while ago. It's an anchor, yes?"

Kali nodded.

"Well, we do live on an island. Chances are I saw it on a sign or a bumper sticker." She handed Kali's phone back to her. "Maybe a shop selling jewelry might know? It would make a pretty pendant if there was a chain or a cord attached to the little hole."

Kali put the phone back into her bag. "Yes, it would. Thanks for looking." She left, walking quickly across the porch and down the steps to her parking spot. She started the engine of the Jeep, but before she pulled away, she hung the little star from her rearview mirror, where it immediately caught the sun.

The road, true to its nickname, ran upwards, twisting as it went. After a half mile, Kali began watching the left side, slowing as the pineapple mailbox came into view. She wasn't sure what she'd expected to see, but the mailbox was hardly a duplicate of the pineapple found resting on the dead man's shoulders. Instead, it was a kitschy, heavy-duty plastic monstrosity positioned on its side on top of a short post. The lid resembled the green, spiky crown of the fruit, and could be pulled open to insert or remove mail. Kali couldn't help but think that whoever it was that delivered the mail here must hate having to open the prickly lid.

She parked in the driveway and sat for a moment, allowing anyone inside to take note that company had arrived. She had deliberately not called ahead, but had learned that too much surprise could sometimes be a bad thing. Then there was a brief movement in the front window of the house, and a curtain pulled back to give someone inside a better view of the Jeep. Kali opened the door and slid from the seat, her bag looped over one shoulder. She walked slowly up the short length of the dirt driveway to the front door. By the time she reached it, it was open, and a heavy man in an old pair of trousers and a stretched-out T-shirt was standing in the frame, watching her.

"Aloha," she called, her voice friendly.

"Aloha maybe," the man said, his voice neutral. "If you're here to raise money, beg for money, or sell me something for money, you can leave and take your aloha with you."

"None of those things," Kali answered, displaying her badge. "I'm with the Maui Police Department. Detective Kali Māhoe. You're Manuel Raso, yes? If you have some spare time, I wanted to ask you about the old pineapple plantation on Lāna'i."

He nodded in affirmation, but looked surprised all the same. Kali watched the expression on his face change from one of caution to mild interest. From what little she'd been able to find out about him, he hadn't worked steadily since Shandling Fruit had ceased production, and was now well into his early seventies. She'd found that older people who were bored usually had a lot of memories they were willing to share.

She gestured back toward the brightly colored pineapple at the end of the drive. "That's quite a mailbox."

His face creased into a wide smile. "Grandkids gave that to me. Pretty special, isn't it?"

"Very," agreed Kali. "Do you have a few minutes to chat with me? An investigation I'm working on involves the old fields, and I'm trying to get a sense of the workflow that was involved with the production. I was told you were the head foreman for a number of years, and might be able to help me understand some of the day-to-day."

"That's right." He stood away from the door. "Come on in. Afraid it's pretty hot inside. If you don't mind sitting out in the back, I'll tell you what I can."

CHAPTER 17

Kali followed Manuel across the front room and through the kitchen, then out the back door onto a large lanai. It was shaded and much cooler there, and Kali felt herself relax. An assortment of mismatched chairs faced the trees leading up the slope behind the house, and a well-tended collection of plants in pretty pots had been placed on the wooden floorboards amongst the chairs.

Manuel chose a large metal deck chair lined with cushions, and made himself comfortable. There was a wood-slatted chair beside it, and Kali turned it slightly to face him. She sat down and placed her bag on the floor at her feet, reaching in and rummaging around for her notebook and pen. Manuel watched her, his face reflecting what appeared to be a mild suspicion outweighed by curiosity.

"You don't look like a cop," he said.

"Oh?" she said, her voice still friendly. "What is a cop supposed to look like?"

He laughed gruffly. "I mean, you aren't wearing a uniform or anything."

She glanced down briefly at her faded jeans and canvas slip-on shoes. The shoes had been a deep purple color when she'd purchased them, but repeated wear and washings had left them a pale violet shade. Her white T-shirt bore a logo showing a can of Spam. Around her neck was a leather cord, from which her small collection of talismans hung. She considered what Manuel had said, and had to agree. She probably didn't look anything at all like what most people assumed a cop should look like.

"Well, I'm not part of the uniform division," she said. "So I guess that might be confusing. But what I'd really like to discuss is the Shandling Fruit pineapple plantation on Lānaʻi. I understand it's been defunct since 1997, but it must have been a busy place before then."

Manuel nodded, even as a deep scowl consumed his face. "Greedy. That's what the Shandling people were. Greedy and heartless. Didn't care about the job losses, or how they would affect the people and families who worked the fields. All they cared about was how it would cost them less and give them bigger profits to grow their pineapples where it's cheaper. Costa Rica. Honduras. Ecuador. Thailand and India, too. Those places. Cheap labor, and more."

Kali noticed that his breathing had become more rapid. He began to drum the armrest of his chair with his fingertips, growing agitated. Clearly, he had still not come completely to terms with the shutdown of Lānaʻi's farms and production facilities.

"There was kind of an art to it, you know. Determining the pick point, when the pineapple was at its peak for harvesting, all brown and yellow. You could smell them when it was time—a kind of perfume that filled the air and your heart. One day, it wouldn't be there. The next day, you'd walk into the field and it was as though every fruit in the field had decided it was time to be full."

Kali watched his eyes. The light slowly growing in them was replaced abruptly with sadness.

"They told us we could find new jobs in the new hotels,

those two big resorts they built. What could we do there? Take out other people's trash? Bring them food on trays? Change their dirty sheets as if we were servants, trapped inside a big house?" He shook his head. "No, no. It was all wrong. We were strong men and women, meant to be outside, working with the earth beneath the sun." He looked at her. "When the business shut down there, it broke so many people. Their spirits and their hearts."

She spoke carefully. "There must have been a lot of anger when the announcement came that the shutdown was happening."

He looked at her, incredulous. "Anger? People's lives were being destroyed. And that wasn't the worst of it." He rose from the chair, the action labored. "Let me show you something," he said. As she began to get up to follow him, he shook his head. "Stay here in the shade. I'll be right back."

He went back inside, where Kali could hear him fumbling around. In a few minutes he was back, carrying a heavy photo album. He placed it on a small, glass-topped table that stood at one end of the lanai, brushing off a few stray leaves that had fallen on the table's surface. He dragged it closer to where Kali was seated, pulled his own chair up to the table, and sat back down.

"I guess these days, everyone keeps their pictures on their phones," he says. "But this is how we used to do it. Big books full of memories you could keep nearby and look through whenever you wanted to remember some other time or place. You could pick them up and hold them."

She watched as he opened the album and flipped through a few pages, each one of them a series of cellophane sleeves that held photographs. He removed a few, laying them on the table glass in front of Kali. He pointed to one.

"This was my crew, the people who kept things running all day. And me, in the middle."

She lifted the photo, inspecting it closely. There were five men—two on either side of a tall, strong version of Manuel that was far younger than the man across the table from her. They looked happy and fit, as though the photographer had caught them at the exact moment when they'd collectively gotten the punchline of a shared joke.

He gathered the remaining loose photos into a small stack and handed them to her. She looked closely at each one. The faces were Portuguese, Asian, Hawaiian, Black, Hispanic, Filipino, and White, men and women and a good number of older teens.

In one, a row of baskets sat on the ground, filled with what looked like green, sharp pineapple leaves.

"The fruit grows from the crowns," he told her. He sighed, as though remembering. "All planted by hand—long row after row of crowns shoved into the earth."

He leaned forward, reaching for the book and selecting another image showing a woman standing alone. He sat holding it for a moment, gazing at the woman's face, then handed the photo to Kali. The woman was wearing a hat to protect her face and head from the sun, but her shy smile was clearly visible. She was wearing what appeared to be a pair of thick gloves, and one hand was holding a large pineapple by its green, spiky crown.

"This is my late wife, Carolina. Made the best coconut cake in the world. She worked on the picking line, laying fruit on the conveyer belt. The fruit would end up in a truck bed, then be sorted and packed with the crown facing down to be transported to the dock for the barge trip to the processing plant off-island. The best-looking ones were left whole, to be sold at the markets." His face darkened. "After they were sprayed again, of course."

Kali was silent, waiting for whatever it was that he wanted or needed to say.

"No one wants to talk about it," he said. He looked through

the photos on the table, choosing another one. There were two men in the image, standing on the back of a large truck. "These guys both died a few years after the plants closed. Cancer. I think it was from the chemical sprays. My wife, too. She was only fifty-two."

All Kali could hear was the whirring of a small table fan set in front of an open window, blowing into the house from the lanai. Then she heard a car passing on the road in front of the house, a snippet of music from its radio momentarily lilting across the air, linking the listener in the car to herself. Once again, she sat, absorbing yet another story of loss told to her by a still-grieving stranger.

"I'm sorry," she said. "I've heard about the heavy spraying. Pesticides?"

"Fungicides, too. To kill nematodes. Mealybugs and the like. They sprayed those plants regularly, and the rest of us couldn't help but breathe it in or get it on us. They kept telling us it was safe. I got lucky, somehow. I don't know why." He looked at her. "There was even an extra spray treatment at the end of the harvesting for the whole fruits heading to supermarkets. As if no one ever made the connection that chemicals that killed one kind of life would of course have an effect on all the other life nearby. Those executives. Greedy, all of them. Gambling with other peoples' lives."

"The pineapple company people?"

He nodded. "Them and the chemical company people, working together. The bigwigs in their sharp suits, stopping by for a few days in the islands to get a tan and mingle with the natives." He lifted the heavy album and searched through it, peering closely at the images. Finally, he passed the album to Kali and pointed to a picture at the bottom of one page.

"Those guys are the ones we mostly dealt with. That picture was taken at a little awards dinner they held after some important harvesting record got broken."

In the image, three men stood together in a group in front of a banquet table. They all looked happy. The man in the middle held a plaque, and each of the men standing beside him was turned slightly toward it, each resting a hand on the shoulder of the center man.

Kali took it in, then turned the page, gazing at scenes from past growing seasons, and the faces and figures of strangers. Her eyes froze suddenly on a photo showing several ladies in the act of preparing food at a counter. To their left was a yellowish-brown refrigerator that looked very familiar. She slipped the photo from its sleeve and handed it to Manuel.

"Where was this taken?" she asked.

He held the photo up, studying it. "That was our new break room. Those ladies were some of the planters."

"Can you tell me anything about the refrigerator?"

He looked at her as though she'd just asked him to re-upholster her flying saucer, then gazed back at the photo.

"The refrigerator?"

"Yes. Was it new? Do you remember what year this was taken? Do you know what happened to the fridge?"

He sat back, still looking at her in confusion. "Well . . . let me see. It was a big deal when we got it, because the old one leftover from the previous pineapple company had been on the blink and we needed something to keep lunch things in. We were given three used ones, and this was the nicest one. We only got it just a couple of years before those of us who were still working all lost our jobs. So, summer of 1994 or '95 would be my guess."

"There were others? Were they the same as this one—brand and color, for instance?"

"No, the other two were small, old, beat-up ones that had

been donated at various times. I think they were both white. This big fancy golden one was a gift from the management people. They could have afforded to give us a new one, but we were grateful anyway. I have no idea what happened to it. When we all left on the last day, we just took our hats and lunch pails and locked all the doors behind us." He looked at her again. "Is that what all this is about? Did someone steal the refrigerator?"

She gave him a small smile, and stood up. "No, nothing like that. It would be very helpful if I could take these photos with me. I promise you they'll be treated well, and I'll return them unharmed as soon as our investigation is over. Would that be okay?"

He looked at her doubtfully, then picked up the photo of his wife from where he'd placed it on the small table. "All of them?" he asked.

Kali watched him and saw a look in his eyes that she had seen more than once in her own, gazing back at her from the bathroom mirror as she brushed her hair and prepared herself for the day in a house where only she woke up each morning.

"Not that one," she said. "Keep that beautiful photo of your wife here with you. I'll take the others, and the album, and bring them back to you soon."

His face brightened. He gathered the other photographs together and replaced them in their empty slots in the album, then handed it to Kali.

"That will be fine," he said. "When you come back, maybe you would like to hear more stories about the pineapples."

She took the album and nodded, moving toward the door. "I'd like that," she said. "Meanwhile, thank you for your time. You've been a great help."

She made her way back to the Jeep, placing the album gently on the seat beside her. The little glass star swung as she pulled her door closed and dug through her bag for her phone and punched in a number. Walter answered immediately.

"I've got something," she said. "I'm heading back to the station now. See you in about an hour."

CHAPTER 18

The photos loaned by Manuel Raso were spread across Kali's desk. Walter stood beside her, looking through them, lifting each in turn to study the details. He lingered long on the one showing the refrigerator, holding it up to the light of the open window for a better look.

"So," he said, "based on the fact that the fridge was still there when the pineapple plantation shut down permanently in 1997, we can eliminate our pineapple man going missing before then. Probably the others as well, as it's unlikely a killer would have used the field as a cemetery while workers were still coming and going."

Kali nodded her agreement.

They heard a chair push back. Hara stood up suddenly from his desk, nervously shifting his weight from one foot to the other. "Yes, sir. I've added that information to the calculations," he said, betraying his own excitement. "That leaves us seven males still unaccounted for, and four women that fit the general victim descriptions. And . . ."

Walter looked at him with a raised brow. "And what? Spit it out, Officer, before you explode. Or implode. Or possibly both."

"We have a definite link between two of the missing people and the pineapple plantation," said Hara, sitting back down, his excitement barely contained. "Reggie McCartney and Helen Stafford. An unmarried couple who fall within the physical parameters given to us by forensics for the male and female found with the infant. Went missing on Lāna'i in December of 1997. Helen Stafford was listed as a former employee at the pineapple operation."

Walter let out a low whistle.

"Any mention of a child?" Kali asked. She could feel her pulse quickening.

"No," said Hara, "but it looks like there's a sister in Reno, Nevada. Both her home and work numbers are here, with a note that she helps out afternoons at a senior center near where she lives. We have that number, too."

Walter's phone buzzed. He looked at the small screen, replacing the photo on the table. "It's Stitches."

Kali stood up, moving closer. "Put her on speakerphone."

Walter nodded, then answered the call. "Hello, Doctor. I'm here with Kali and Officer Hara. We have you on speaker. What's up?"

Stitches's voice reverberated throughout the interior of the office. "The dental records for Matthew Greene supplied by his parents are an exact match for the second skeleton," she said without preamble. "The parents also positively identified that sunburst belt buckle, which had apparently been a gift from the mother. DNA samples were also provided by the mother and father and are being compared to what we have here. Test results will be in later today, but I believe we have an identity: Matthew Alan Greene."

"One down," said Walter. "That's good. But we're not any closer to finding out what happened to Matthew, or why."

"*You* aren't any closer," corrected Stitches. "We are still evaluating the remaining unidentified bodies. I'll be in touch soon." A beep followed, then silence. Walter put his phone away and turned to the others.

"Thoughts?"

"More calls. What time is it in Reno?" asked Kali, walking across the room. She stood next to Hara's chair, peering at his screen, where the list of missing persons was displayed.

Hara typed rapidly on his keyboard, pulling up the local time. "Close to noon," he said, waiting for instructions.

"Okay," said Kali. "And what's the sister's name?"

"Marcia Woolsey," said Hara. "The number—"

"I see it. Let's try the home number first." She pulled her own phone out of her back pocket and dialed the number that had been entered next to the woman's name. She activated the speaker option on the phone, and all three of them listened to the sound of ringing on the other end.

Outside, a breeze moved the branches of the 'Ākia shrubs growing along the side of the building, stirring up the scent of the plant's small, yellow-tinged flowers, gently wafting through the widow screen into the air of the room. All the while the ringing continued, until a woman answered.

"Hello?"

Kali glanced at the others. "Marcia Woolsey?"

There was a faint hesitation, and Kali imagined the woman trying to determine if she'd just made the mistake of opening the line to a sales pitch or a plea for campaign funds.

"Yes. This is Marcia."

Kali spoke quickly, before the woman decided to hang up. "This is Detective Kali Māhoe calling from the Maui Police Department. If you have a moment, I'd like to speak to you about your sister, Helen Stafford."

This time the pause was longer.

"Miss Woolsey? Are you there?"

A deep sigh came in reply. "Yes, I'm here. I'm sorry, it's just that you took me by surprise. How can I help?"

Kali spoke carefully. "There have been some developments in the missing persons case that you filed here in Maui after your sister's disappearance. Our records show that when your sister disappeared, she may have been in the company of Reggie McCartney. One of the things I'm calling to check on is whether you've had any news of either of them since the last time you were in contact with the police."

"No, there's been nothing." The woman's voice grew wistful. "No word from anyone."

"I'd appreciate it if you could refresh me on the details, including any information you might have about the relationship between your sister and Mr. McCartney."

Marcia took a long, deep breath, then began to recount what she remembered. Kali listened as she described a carefree young woman and her college sweetheart, who'd dreamed of living in a tropical setting far from the ordinary cares of the world.

"They had a calendar on the kitchen wall in their apartment with pictures of Hawai'i. Helen had always hated Reno and the desert, the whole time we were growing up. She used to tell me she'd been born in the wrong place and time, and I think she may have been right. She was kind of a hippie. So was Reggie. Long hair and beads and tie-dyed shirts, you know? I used to tease them both so much." Marcia laughed, but then grew silent for a moment. "I wish I hadn't done that," she finally said. "I wish I had been nicer. She was my only sister. And Reggie was a really great guy. The kind of person that kids and animals just naturally followed around, like they instinctively knew he would always be kind."

Kali chose her words carefully. "And was it just the two of them?"

Marcia's voice sounded confused. "What do you mean?"

"Did they have children?"

This time, the silence was pronounced. Finally Marcia responded. "Why, no. I mean, they talked about wanting children, but in a kind of somewhere-down-the-road kind of way. They were just kids themselves. My sister was twenty-four when she disappeared, and Reggie was just a year older. Why do you ask?"

"If your sister had been pregnant, would she have told you?"

Marcia's voice faltered. "Yes . . . I mean, I think so. But maybe not. Our parents wouldn't have approved, and it would have been difficult to keep something like that from them. Of course, Helen and I weren't staying in touch as much as I liked after she moved to Hawai'i, so I can't really say for certain."

"And to your knowledge, was there anything worrying her? When you spoke with her, did she talk about her job with the pineapple company, or mention anything going on there that may have been troubling to her?"

"At the plantation? Goodness, no, not that I can recall. The police asked about that as well, but honestly, she seemed to love her job, and always spoke positively about the people she worked for, and the people she worked with."

Next to Kali, Walter leaned over the desk and scribbled on a piece of paper. He handed it to her, and she read the hastily scrawled words: *What did Reggie do?*

"You're being very helpful, Marcia. Can you tell me anything about Reggie? What was his job?"

"After they moved to Hawai'i, he was working mostly as a handyman. He'd actually been an architecture student, and I think his goal was to do some kind of artistic woodworking, but for the time being he was taking small repair and renovation jobs."

Kali hesitated. "Do you recall either your sister or her boyfriend ever mentioning anything to you about an anchor that may have been used as something symbolic in their lives?"

There was confused silence before Marcia spoke again, this time uncertain. "I'm sorry, I don't understand. You mean, like a boat anchor?"

"Yes, more or less. We're trying to determine the meaning of a symbol that may be connected to your sister's disappearance. As far as we've been able to determine, it's a stylized boat anchor, roughly the size of a penny."

"Not offhand, but there's no telling what she—what they—may have been connected to. I know she was always joining clubs and things. Organic gardening, holistic massage, supernatural watch groups. She was interested in everything, especially if it was offbeat or unusual. I know that Reggie shared her interests."

"There was a small commune on Lāna'i during the years that your sister was working for the pineapple company. It was led by a man called Abraham Waters, who marketed himself as a kind of healer. The commune was partly a church, operated out of a small farm called Eden's River. Does that ring a bell?"

"Not specifically," said Marcia, slowly. "But honestly, it wouldn't surprise me in the least. That's exactly the type of thing that would have attracted both Helen and Reggie."

Kali looked at the missing-persons list. "We don't have any contact information for Reggie's immediate family or any extended relatives. Would you perhaps have that information?"

"No, I'm sorry." Marcia's voice sounded genuinely regretful. "I have no idea."

Kali let the moment linger before asking her next question. "This may be a difficult request, but would you be willing to supply a DNA sample?"

"Oh dear." The woman's voice was immediately distressed. "Oh dear—does that mean you found . . . something?"

"We may have, I'm afraid. I don't want you to be alarmed; this is simply a request to help us narrow down a few things. You understand?"

Marcia's voice sounded shaky. "Yes, I do understand. What can I do to help?"

"Three things. Can you tell me what became of Helen's belongings after she went missing? And do you have access to your sister's dental and medical records? And lastly, is it possible you have anything closely related to her? I know it sounds odd, but something like an old hairbrush would be very useful."

Marcia considered the questions before responding right away. "I don't know what happened to the things she had in Hawai'i. They weren't sent to me, I'm afraid—but there are some of her old things here in my house. Winter clothes she didn't think she'd need. I'll look through them and see if there's anything mixed in with them." Her voice sounded sad. "I thought eventually Helen would come home, so I kept it all here, in the closet in my spare room."

Next to her, Walter gave a thumbs-up. Hara sat tensely on the edge of his chair.

Kali tried not to sound elated. "That would be enormously helpful. If you could get back to me, we can go from there. We can also give you instructions on how to provide a DNA sample. Our colleagues in Reno will help you with that, and send the results to us here in Maui."

"Yes, of course."

"Thank you for your help, Miss Woolsey. I assure you we're all very grateful. I'm going to pass you to Officer David Hara now. He'll explain to you how to reach us."

She passed her phone to Hara, and she and Walter moved to the far side of the room.

"I'll call Reno about the sample, and have Hara see what he can find out about Reggie McCartney while we're waiting for them to get back to us," said Walter.

"Got it. I'll track down whoever's living in the place that's listed as their last address," said Kali. "The landlord may have cleaned out the place and thrown away everything left behind by Helen and Reggie," she continued, "but we may get lucky and find out they stashed a box of their belongings somewhere."

"Some luck would be welcome," agreed Walter. "As long as it's the good kind."

Finishing up the phone call, Hara moved to the printer. He was replacing the standard copy paper with a heavy-duty laser photo paper. Kali watched from the corner of her eye as he went back to his computer and typed rapidly on the keyboard. The printer hummed to life. Hara walked toward them and thrust the newly printed pages into Walter's hands. "Photos of Matthew Greene, Helen Stafford, and Reggie McCartney," he said. "Last known driver's licenses, plus what we had in the records from the original missing-persons report."

Kali stood close to Walter, eyeing the photos curiously. Matthew Greene had a narrow face and brown hair parted on the side. He wasn't smiling for the camera. She set his image aside. The other photos showed a slender young woman with long, light-colored hair and a happy smile beneath a nose and cheeks sprinkled with freckles. Reggie McCartney was stocky, with dark, curling hair that reached well past his shoulders. To Kali, both people looked friendly and uncomplicated, faces that would have blended in easily to any group of tourists or young people gathered at a bar or beachside café. Besides the driver's license photos, there was another one showing Helen and Reggie together, seated side by side, shoulders touching. Each was wearing a plastic flower lei. They were standing in front of the arrivals hall at the airport in Honolulu, a stack of suitcases on the sidewalk next to them. Kali wondered if they'd asked a taxi driver to snap the image, overcome with excitement to be in Hawai'i.

"Here, you take these," Walter said to her, handing her the photos. "Good job, Hara."

Hara nodded. Kali could tell that he was pleased. She smiled. "Can you help me tape up these photos?"

Hara looked at the available wall space. "Maybe we could put up one of those crime scene whiteboards you see in all the television shows so we can spread out our information."

Walter lifted his brow. "Yeah. Like on Kali's favorite police show, *Lights Out Maui*. And then we can put up another one for every one of the other cases we're working on. We'll need to add on a few rooms pretty quick."

Kali looked thoughtful. "Ignoring the Chad Caesar reference, I *would* like to spread these images out," she said, looking around. At the end of the room, against the wall facing the outside of the building, a metal table was being used as a repository for miscellaneous books, papers, and stacks of nonessential folders. She walked toward the table and surveyed the surface accumulation. "Let's find somewhere else for all of this, at least temporarily," she said. "Hara, feel like giving me a hand?"

He joined her, making no attempt to disguise his eagerness. "I'll go and get a few of those big plastic bins from the storage room," he said, then hurried toward the door.

"Don't get too busy organizing, please. Remember that I need you later for rooster fights," said Walter as he watched Hara's retreating back. "I've got a hot date with a local champion tonight, though he doesn't know it yet."

"What's up?" Kali asked as she began to sort through the papers on the table.

Walter reached forward, gathering up a stack of safety

flyers intended for presentations at local schools. "Remember I told you about Bitty and Johnny Benga, the sister and brother we had in custody?"

"Had? As in past tense?"

"Couldn't hold them any longer," said Walter, his voice patient, restrained. "They have a lawyer working the native rights angle."

"Benga," repeated Kali. "I don't remember you mentioning their name before. Isn't that Samoan?"

"I think so, yeah. But because their families have been here long enough to be landowners, they're regarded as native Hawaiians, with all of the rights that go along with that. Their lawyer is arguing that cock fighting is a traditional sport and they have a legal right to practice it."

"Explain that to the roosters."

"Oh, right. Those cuddly, eye-gouging, flesh-ripping sons of dinosaurs?"

Kali shrugged. "Still kind of brutal, in my opinion. Especially when the birds get fitted out with those gruesome metal spurs. That's straight out of a horror movie."

"All I know is that organized cock fighting is breaking the law." His phone buzzed, and he put down the flyers and glanced at the phone screen before he answered the call. He held it up so Kali could see Chief Pait's name on the display.

"Hello, Chief," he said. Then he frowned, nodding as he listened. "Uh-huh. Uh-huh. Okay, got it, but I think Detective Māhoe . . . Right, understood."

He ended the call and looked at Kali. "Guess who's a featured podcast guest on Chad Caesar's show this afternoon?"

She backed away a few steps, eyes widening. "No. Absolutely not. There is no possible way I am——"

"Relax!" said Walter, laughing. "It's me. The chief wants me to appeal to the public. Guess I just have that special little something."

"Yeah. You can keep a handle on your temper in Chad's company, and I can't."

"True dat," said Walter, still grinning. He looked around, gradually giving way to a weary expression. "Not that I'm looking forward to it either. For the moment, I'll have to leave the paper sorting up to you and Hara." He sighed and reached into his pocket, jiggling his car keys. "Feel free to call and interrupt at any time if you find anything here that we need to move on. Other than that, I'll see you this evening. Wear shoes you can run in."

Kali watched as he left, consumed with relief that it was Walter and not her who had to answer Chad's questions. She picked up an armful of paper files and walked into the hallway and down a few doors to the building's single supply room. It took several trips back and forth until the table was cleared. She left Hara in the storage area to organize the papers and flyers into separate plastic bins.

She stood in front of the table in the main station room, holding Manuel Raso's photo album. She placed it on the table and turned the pages, removing a selection of photos and making a small pile. One by one, she spread them out on the surface, clustering those of Helen and Reggie in one corner, and placing the photo of Matthew Greene on the far side. She added the crime scene photos showing the bodies and their graves, and placed a gridded map of Lāna'i in the center, already marked with the exact location of each discovery. As she stood staring at the display, Hara joined her, looking thoughtfully at the materials that she'd set out.

"What's next?" he asked.

"Now we connect the dots," said Kali, her mind already leaping between the past and the present, and all the places where monsters were likely to hide.

CHAPTER 19

Walter was clearly uncomfortable. He adjusted the bulky headset covering his ears, tugged at the collar of his police uniform, and glanced self-consciously toward a camera set on a tripod across from the table where he sat facing Chad Caesar. On Walter's left, close by, a smiling young woman was making a last adjustment to the camera angle.

The heavy wood table that separated Walter from Chad was an oval covered by a thick, polished slab of dark marble. A glass shaped like a goblet, filled with water, had been placed in front of Walter's chair, while an identical glass rested on the table in front of Chad. The wall to Walter's right, also visible to the camera, was covered from floor to ceiling with colorful artwork. He recognized it as the work of a popular, up-and-coming Hawaiian graffiti artist whose art had been featured on the sides of buildings in O'ahu. The bright backdrop was a swirling mélange of shapes and colors that surrounded a central cartoonish version of the famous Chiaramonti bust of Julius Caesar. Instead of Caesar's face, a stylized likeness of Chad peered into the room. Running horizontally beneath the portrait was a banner that had been painted to make it look as though the letters were etched from stone, bearing the words I AM THE RULER OF THE NEWS in a Romanesque font.

Walter reached into his pants pocket and pulled out a square of white paper. He unfolded it and placed it on the table in front of him, next to his phone. The young woman finished fiddling with the camera equipment and smiled encouragingly at Walter, then gave Chad a thumbs-up. She counted down from three on her fingers, and then mouthed the word "Live." Adjusting the microphone in front of him, Chad faced the camera, a huge smile on his face.

"Greetings, friends and followers! I'm both delighted and excited to tell you that joining me today is Captain Walter Alaka'i of the Maui Police Department." He briefly flashed his smile at Walter, then grew serious. "We're here, of course, to discuss the alarming news that there's a serial killer loose in the vicinity."

Walter twisted in his seat, trying to get comfortable. He glanced toward the camera, then back to Chad. "We're live, right? People can hear us now?"

Chad smiled patiently. "Yes, Captain, we're live. Viewers throughout the world have tuned in today, breathlessly anticipating what you have to share about the latest threat to our gentle life in Hawai'i."

Walter's look was skeptical. "I'm not sure that you and I are living in the same Hawai'i. And to our knowledge, there is no immediate threat."

"How can you be so certain?" Chad's response was quick, his voice taking on a tone of urgency. He leaned slightly over the table toward Walter, pushing the microphone forward so that it stayed in line with his mouth. "Dozens of bodies, all . . ."

"That's incorrect. We . . ." Walter's voice faded.

Chad gestured. "You have to keep the microphone close to your mouth, Captain. Speak directly into it."

Walter pulled the microphone closer. "I can tell you," he

said, over-enunciating the first few words, "that we have un-covered several individuals—not dozens—who we believe were left abandoned in an unused field on one of the old Lāna'i pineapple plantations some time ago, perhaps as long ago as twenty-five years."

"Absolutely terrifying!" Chad responded, the timbre of his voice growing dramatically deep.

Walter frowned. "Well," he began, but Chad interrupted.

"To think that all this time, a murderer has been walking among us," Chad said gravely. "Maybe the person standing in front of you at the grocery store. Perhaps someone you've sat beside in a movie theater!"

Walter tilted his head, searching Chad's face, trying to find any shred of genuine concern among the theater. "First of all, I should point out that there's a difference between murder and homicide. And whoever it was who committed these crimes may no longer be alive, or even be in Hawai'i," he said. "We have no way to tell at this time. That's why we'd like to appeal to the public for some help."

"I assure you, Captain, that my loyal—and highly intelli-gent—audience would love to help the Maui Police Depart-ment solve this mystery. Everyone is worried. We're all locking our doors at night."

"Well," said Walter, a slight frown on his face, "locking your doors at night is a pretty sensible thing to do in gen-eral."

"But this is our tropical utopia! Trust and love abound. No one wants to have to look over their shoulder, or put bars on their windows."

Walter sighed. "Statistically," he began, but again Chad cut him off.

"What can you tell us about the investigation?"

Walter took a deep breath. "We are doing everything within our power to identify the deceased and locate the per-son or persons responsible."

"How can we help, Captain? As you no doubt already know, I played an investigative journalist on *Lights Out Maui* and am deeply familiar with formal investigative procedures. I'm a professional, just like yourself. Tell us what we can do."

Walter waited. It was clear from his expression that he would have liked to comment on Chad's claims, that he was struggling to ignore that part of the discussion. "There are several things that would be helpful," he finally said. "First, anyone having any information about any adult males going missing from 1997 to 2000, or information related directly to persons by the name of Helen Stafford and Reggie McCartney, are asked to get in touch with us on a special hotline we've established." He reached forward, where the piece of white paper he'd brought rested facedown on the table's surface. He held it up for the camera. It was an image of the anchor charm, the outlines emphasized in heavy black ink. "Next, anyone with information about this symbol is likewise asked to get in touch with us."

Chad turned toward the camera. "This is serious business, folks. A matter—quite literally—of life and death. No pranks or frivolous calls, please. We want our local police force to respect us, and"—he flourished his smile first at Walter, then at the camera—"eventually *thank us* for our help."

Walter refolded the paper and began to rise from his chair.

"Wait just a minute, Captain. We still haven't talked about the details of the investigation."

Walter sank back into his seat, reluctant.

"So far," continued Chad, "the police search has been confined to one pineapple field on Lāna'i, but there are still hundreds of acres of fields that are no longer farmed. Will the search be expanded?"

Walter shook his head. "I'm afraid there are aspects of our

investigation that I'm not at liberty to discuss at this time."
As Chad made a small sound of protest, Walter continued.
"What I can say is that it's possible there's a connection be-
tween the deaths and the pineapple plantation itself."

Chad leaned forward, clearly very eager. "You mean the
land, of course. As locals, we know the terrifying stories
about the demons and bloodthirsty monsters that make their
home on Lāna'i."

"Those are unverified stories. Legends."

"Are they? Current events would suggest otherwise, don't
you think?"

"The legends you're referring to took place, if they took
place at all, a long, long time ago. And there was a happy
ending to those stories: The monsters were conquered and
banished from the island."

"It's a well-known fact that the Maui Police Department
employs a detective who's also a cultural expert in these
matters. Detective Kali Māhoe is also a bona fide *kahuna,*
isn't she? Has she determined a link between the monster
legends and the victims?"

Before Walter could respond, the door linking the studio
to an outer hallway was suddenly thrust open. He watched
as a large, longhaired tabby cat wearing a wide, fancy collar
studded with fake gems sauntered into the room and made a
beeline for Chad. In one smooth move, it leapt onto the table
and knocked over the goblet of water in front of him, then
began pushing its head against Chad's arm, purring loudly.
Unaware of the cat's approach, Chad jumped as the cat appeared in front of him and knocked over the water. He
turned to the girl at the camera, clearly flustered. He didn't
notice Walter lift his phone and take a photo.

"How did Cleopatra get in here?" he hissed. "That door is
supposed to be closed." The cat bumped Chad's face with
the top of its head, then burrowed against his neck, purring
rapidly. Gently, he reached up and scooped the cat into his

arms, where it instantly went limp and closed its eyes. Unable to help himself, Chad nuzzled the cat, making mock purring noises in return. He suddenly looked up, embarrassed, with the cat cradled in his arms.

Walter grinned. "Friend of yours?"

Arms wrapped around the cat, Chad rocked it slightly, then placed it gently back on the floor. He gestured to his assistant to put the cat into the hallway and to close the door. The cat resisted, holding on to the edge of the doorframe with its front claws, mewing loudly in protest.

"Oh, uh, just the studio cat," said Chad. "Kind of likes me, I guess."

"Sure does." Walter's voice was innocent. He was fully aware that Chad had lost his dominance over the interview. "Nice coincidence for you that the cat's name is Cleopatra. And that it lives in the studio attached to your house."

Chad's face flushed. He readjusted his headset and moved his chair back into position in front of the microphone. "As we were discussing," he began.

"I guess I didn't take you for the sentimental type," Walter continued, still focusing on the cat.

"I'm not at all sentimental," said Chad, eyes narrowing.

"Hey, what's that thing Julius Caesar wrote?" asked Walter. "Something about no one's so brave that they can't be disturbed by something unexpected?"

Chad pushed his chair away from the table slightly, and turned to the camera. He forced a smile. "Looks like that's all we're going to have time for today, everyone. Remember—stay safe, which means don't take candy from strangers; and if you think of anything useful, call the Maui Police Department's hotline." He looked back at Walter, his trademark blend of sparkle and arrogance having evaporated. "Um, thanks for joining us today, Captain. Tell Detective Māhoe hello for me, won't you? Perhaps we can have her on the show next time."

"I'll be sure to ask her," said Walter. "And thanks for your help with the investigation. This has been a lot of fun."

The ocean breeze lifted the faded curtains at the kitchen window, making its way across the room and stirring the papers on the table. Kali grinned, then closed her laptop and leaned back in her chair. Then her phone buzzed. She answered, and Walter's voice came through the speaker.

"Turns out the high-and-mighty Chad Caesar was conquered by a fifteen-pound cat," he said.

"Yeah, I saw that," she laughed. "Somehow, it makes me like him a little bit. Just a tiny bit, but you know. More than before."

"It's wearing a collar that looks like jewelry."

"Did you get a picture?"

"You bet I did."

"Good job! As thanks, I won't bitch too much while we're on rooster patrol tonight."

"I'll make sure you remember you said that."

After Walter hung up, Kali opened her laptop again, scanning the podcast site still on display. She dragged the time bar back a few seconds, then watched again as the cat leapt into Chad's lap and began to purr loudly as it snuggled into his neck. She watched it three more times, then got up, laughing, to make herself something to eat.

CHAPTER 20

The pathway led between a barn with peeling paint and a dilapidated, wood-framed house. It was dark, an inky blackness that seemed to move on its own in the slight evening breeze. What was left of the waning moon was obscured behind a thick layer of heavy clouds that had settled, bloated with rain, just above the surface of the world.

Gun drawn, Kali slipped quietly along a path of uneven brick pavers that had been laid out in a ragged, narrow line in the sandy ground between the buildings. At the end of the path on her left, a thin shaft of light reflected on a row of bushes, emanating from a cracked doorway in the house. She stood frozen, listening. From inside the barn to her right, there were muffled shouts and cries.

She moved to the end of the path. There was a field spread out below the barn, sloping downward between a row of grassy hillocks barely outlined in the night. Faint glints of moonlight on metal showed that the field was filled with vehicles.

She turned, waiting as Walter slipped along the path just behind her. As she halted in the shadows at the corner of the house, he caught up, speaking quietly. He reached up and fingered the earpiece he was wearing.

"Vice says hold back a minute," he whispered. "They'll signal when to go."

Kali nodded. She could see other figures now, moving against the side of the barn among the darker areas created by the undergrowth and shadows. She could tell from their thickened silhouettes that the moving figures were wearing bulletproof vests and helmets.

"This body armor is making me nervous," she whispered back, tugging at the straps holding her vest in place. "Did someone forget to tell us something?"

"Just hang tight. We let them go in first." He adjusted his own padded vest and nodded toward a smaller door directly across from them, located on the side of the barn. "Keep your eye on this exit."

They watched as the vice squad moved into position in the front, outside of the barn's huge main double doors, spreading out in a wide fan. There was an imperceptible movement from the figure closest to the doors, then a silent rush as the doors were pulled open and the team streamed inside. Sounds of people shouting and animals screeching could be heard clearly now. Seconds later, the side door across from Kali and Walter was flung open, and three people came running out, heading away from the car park into the darkness on the far side of the house.

Kali and Walter leapt forward, pointing their guns.

"Freeze!" yelled Walter. "Police!"

"Hands on your heads NOW!" shouted Kali. In the light of the open door, she could see that there were two men and one woman. One of the men looked familiar.

"Hey there, Angelo!" called Walter.

Angelo and the other man came to a halt, but the woman pivoted on her heel and turned in the opposite direction. She was large and heavy, and was carrying something in the crook of her arm that made her look larger.

Kali trained her gun on the woman and moved to intercept her, impressed that the woman was so nimble. "Stop where you are, ma'am!" she yelled. "Drop whatever you're holding! DROP IT NOW!"

Instead of dropping it, the woman took a half step forward and flung her arms at Kali, hurling into the air the large, angry rooster she had been holding. As the woman turned and fled, the bird splayed its taloned feet, its flapping wings spread wide. It screeched as it was released, an ungodly shriek that filled the night. Instinctively, Kali raised one arm to protect her face. The rooster's spurs ripped through the sleeve of her shirt and through the skin on the back of her arm.

"What the—!" she cried out, trying to recover her sight line. She knocked the enormous bird aside and sprinted down the path past the spot where Walter was holding the two men at gunpoint. She ran down the slope toward the parking area, stumbling in the darkness on uneven footing. As she passed the first row of cars, she saw movement above her. She turned just as the large woman launched herself from the bed of a pickup truck, tackling Kali and bringing her to the ground, knocking the gun from her hand.

The woman was spitting and snarling, her weight holding Kali pinned on the soft ground. Again Kali was struck with her agility, and twisted beneath her. As the woman leaned forward, lips drawn back, teeth exposed, Kali contracted as far as she was able and slammed her head upwards just in time, headbutting the woman as hard as she could from her position.

It was enough. The woman's trajectory was interrupted, giving Kali the time and momentum necessary to twist out from beneath her. She scrambled on her knees to where her gun could be seen lying by the truck's rear tires. She grabbed it and turned, holding it with both hands, and pointed it at the woman again.

"Right now, lady, I really want to shoot you, so I suggest you DO NOT MOVE AT ALL," she warned her. Over the woman's shoulder, she could see Walter jogging toward her, followed by another officer holding a wide-angle flashlight.

Walter slowed his pace as he drew close. He was grinning. "I see you've met Bitty Benga," he said.

"Bastard!" shouted the woman.

Ignoring her, Walter nodded to the officer holding the flashlight. "Give me a little light over here, if you will. I want Detective Māhoe to have a good view as the cuffs go on."

As Walter fastened the handcuffs around Bitty's wrists, Kali holstered her gun. She rolled back the torn, bloody sleeve of her shirt and surveyed the cuts on her arms. There were two gouges, both bleeding. She winced as she examined them.

"I hope you bleed to death!" snarled Bitty.

"You should be worried about your pet rooster," said Kali. "I might make a soup out of him. I'll bring you some. It will help break up the monotony of prison food."

Bitty was enraged, her face twisted with fury. She lowered her head and rushed one more time at Kali, but was stopped short by Walter, who grabbed her joined arms behind her back and jerked her to a halt.

"Enough of that," he said, sternly.

"That was Elvis Feathers, my champion rooster!" yelled Bitty. There was real distress in her voice. "Don't you dare hurt him!"

Walter nodded to the officer beside him. "She's all yours," he said, watching as the officer led Bitty away.

Kali looked from the woman's retreating back to Walter,

incredulous. She glanced again at the cuts on her arms, wiping at the congealed blood.

"*Me* hurt *him*? Is she nuts?"

"You have mud in your hair," said Walter.

"That crazy bitch tried to bite me, you know."

Walter looked at the cuts on her arm. "Then you got off easy. I'll take the rooster claws any day. And you might want to put something on those scratches."

"Yeah," she said. "So we get bulletproof vests, but nothing to protect us from birds."

"Well, you should have let the bird hit you in your middle. Bad judgment on your part, seems like."

She glared at him. "Funny. So who was the guy with Angelo?"

"Bitty's brother Johnny. They weren't too happy to see me."

She rubbed at the blood on her arm as they walked back toward the barn. The place was brightly lit now, and the doors stood propped open. A large group of people milled about just inside, surrounded by uniformed police and members of the vice squad. As she and Walter neared the opening, Kali could see the interior space. There was a large open area on the lower level, surrounded on three sides by an upper balcony that rimmed the hayloft.

They made their way inside, pausing at the edge of the dirt floor space, where a shallow, circular pit had been dug roughly in the ground in the middle of the opening. Someone had located the main light switch, and the illuminated scene was depressing. There were loose feathers everywhere, and the noise from a long row of caged birds in the back of the space created a chaotic atmosphere.

"You ever been to one of these?" Walter asked.

She shrugged. "Sure. Growing up, you know? Not everyone thinks it's a bad thing."

"Yeah. A lot of people are quick to point out that roosters

naturally fight one another anyway, and who are we to tell them they're misbehaving?"

Kali frowned. "This is orchestrated violence, though. Fights to the death, not little scuffles over who gets to jump the pretty hen."

"You're right about the footwear," said Walter. He walked over to the cages. Clipped to the outside of one of the mesh containers was a pair of fighting spurs made of razor blades. "Like these," he said. "Pretty gruesome. Just as sick as people who get their kicks out of watching animals shred one another to death. Very messed up." He turned to her and grinned. "Watching them in a farmyard, though. Can't say I don't enjoy a bit of testosterone-driven courting."

"You're such a romantic," she said.

He ignored the sarcasm. "Regardless, it's against the law, and so is the gambling that goes along with it." He looked over toward the group of people who had been assembled for questioning. "Looks like at least three underage kids in the spectator group, too, from what I can see. Maybe nine, ten years old. And we took a pistol off of Johnny Benga. So, we've got gambling, firearms, minors, and animal cruelty just for starters. Bitty kept her office here in the barn, in the back, so there are probably gambling records, too. We know that's Angelo's specialty."

They stood, looking around the barn with curiosity. A vice squad officer was leading a small group of handcuffed individuals toward the entrance. One of them was an older man with a straggly beard and muscular arms emphasized by his shirt's rolled-up sleeves. As the group began to pass the spot where Kali and Walter stood watching, the bearded man halted, peering closely at Walter's face.

"Hey! It's you, the cop from the podcast today," he said. "Big star, right?"

The officer walking behind him gave the bearded man a

small push. Walter shook his head at Kali, ignoring the comment.

"Wait!" the older man said to the vice officer. "Slow down a minute. I gotta tell that big cop something." He twisted backward, speaking louder, directing his words toward Walter. "I got some juice for you, brah. About those plantation killings you was talking about, you know? I was gonna call you tomorrow, and here you are!"

"Here I am," said Walter. He signaled to the vice officer to stop, then spoke to the man in handcuffs. "You've got one minute. Go."

"What's the reward, man?"

"*Less* than one minute. I'm already losing patience."

"Just saying, you know? Information like that, there should be a reward."

"You'll feel good. Plus your karma will improve. Thirty seconds."

"Okay, okay. I'll take some good karma." He looked over at Kali for a second before elaborating. "That anchor? You should talk to the Eden's River people."

Kali walked closer. "Eden's River?"

"Church group, kind of a well-being place. Eden's River. At first, seemed like mostly a bunch of women and organic food. I checked it out, you know? Being a single guy and all."

"Do you know the location of this church?" asked Kali.

"It was on Lāna'i. Not in a building, like with a pointy steeple showing the highway to heaven. More like a free-love farm."

Kali and Walter exchanged glances. "Do you think it was a commune?"

"Yeah! That's the word. Grew all their own food and dressed funny and everybody slept with everybody else."

"Did you know the person who was in charge?"

"Guy named Abraham was the dude. Creepy as shit." He

grinned. "Turned out the women were spooky, too. Not as much *honi honi* as I expected, so I got out of there."

Walter stepped closer. "Where, exactly, on Lānaʻi?"

"On a farm down near Kaunolū, the old royal fishing grounds. You know it?"

"Do you know where Abraham and his followers are these days?"

The man shrugged. "Heard some stories they moved here, to Maui, but I never saw any of them around. I don't know where, like an address or anything."

"What's your name?"

"Alan Lee."

"You have anything else to share, Mr. Lee?" Walter asked.

"Yeah, a few thoughts on roosters. Birds love to fight more than they love to eat. I love to watch them fight. It's a win-win. It's our Hawaiian right, man!"

"On behalf of the Maui Police Department, I thank you for your help and your opinion." Walter's face was a stone. "You'd get the Good Samaritan award for today, except for the handcuffs and the animal cruelty charges." Walter turned to the vice officer. "You can escort Mr. Lee, please."

Kali and Walter watched them walk away, listening to Alan Lee's voice as he cajoled the vice officer at his side.

"Eden's River again." Kali shook her head. "The name still sounds more like an outdoor adventure outfitter or some kind of yoga retreat than it does a church."

They walked from the barn into the open space outside. Someone had turned on a floodlight that partially illuminated the parking lot. Kali did a quick calculation, and estimated there were about ninety vehicles, parked in makeshift rows and clusters. They stood watching as the team from the vice squad finished rounding up the last groups of people.

"I'll get Hara to add in a records search for anything about Abraham Waters and his cult that Bobby didn't already share," he said. "Just in case there's more. Somebody's got to know where he is now."

"Call me in the morning?"

Walter looked at the sky. "I think, technically, it *is* morning."

"Yeah." She rubbed at her arm again, then closed her eyes and took a deep breath. "Then don't call me at all. I've probably already got some crazy rooster disease and won't be able to crawl to the phone anyway."

"You shouldn't have pissed off the rooster god."

"He was a *kupua* that belonged to a king. Nothing to do with me."

"Shapeshifter god, right?"

"Yeah. And mean. Could take on a ferocious human form, or a terrifying rooster that was a master fighter that killed his rivals and won every fight."

"Guess there's a lesson there." He took her arm, looking closely at the gashes. "Go home and wash your arm and put something on it. Maybe you should get a tetanus shot or something. Those scratches are pretty deep."

"I'll be fine. Battle scar." She grimaced, poking at the blood dried along her wrist where it had trickled from the wound. "Someday we'll laugh about it."

"Sure. Maybe you can add another tattoo. Bitty's face around the scar. You know, kind of a tribute."

Kali shivered involuntarily at the image. She already had enough nightmares in her life. What she needed was a good night's sleep.

CHAPTER 21

The sound of Hilo barking happily wafted through the open window of the kitchen. Kali looked out, and saw him rolling in the long grass. A few feet away, she could see Makena picking a mango from one of the many fruit trees in the yard. She was reaching upward into the branches, studying several plump golden fruits, each of them tinged with crimson. As Kali watched, Hilo climbed to his feet and began running around the tree, inviting Makena to chase him or throw a mango for him. The scene was oddly domestic, and Kali felt an unfamiliar surge of something close to contentment.

She reached for her ringing phone, losing the moment. It was Stitches, who wasted no time on pleasantries.

"We have a positive ID on the couple. The adult female body is Helen Stafford. Her sister, Marcia, found an old sweater in Helen's belongings, mixed in with the things she had stored at her house in Reno, all of which she turned over to the local authorities after you spoke with her. The Reno forensics team found several hairs on the sweater and were able to get an exact DNA match with the sample taken from the hair on the female skeleton."

Kali sucked in her breath.

"Reggie McCartney's family was traced to California," continued Stitches, "and familial DNA samples combined with medical records and general physical characteristics are enough of a match to confirm identity."

"Anything else?"

"Yes. Both adults have smashed skulls, as mentioned before. Based on that, I think it's safe to assume that Matthew Green's neck wasn't an old injury, but also the cause of death since his own skull is fully intact. The killer, or killers, may have acted on opportunity, rather than a modus operandi that was consistent from one killing to the next."

"What about the baby?"

"Ah . . . now that's something interesting. The baby appears to have been stillborn, and not quite to term. I estimate around thirty-two weeks. And, as we noticed when the body was uncovered, it had a deformed skull."

In her mind, Kali pictured the infant nestled close to the woman's body. She wondered if the mother had had any inkling that her own life was about to end, and whether the loss of her child had left her depressed and distracted, allowing the killer to take advantage of her. Her mind leapt to the body in the refrigerator, and to Matthew Greene. She asked herself how these people had been connected, and what had made each of them a target of their killer.

"Right. I don't suppose there's any news on the pineapple man?"

"Nothing definitive yet," said Stitches. "A male somewhere between eighteen and twenty is the best estimate so far. Other than the missing head, of course, there is no obvious cause of death. He could have been shot, had his throat slit, been poisoned, died of asphyxiation, or had any number of unpleasant endings. Or, like the others, he may have died of a broken neck or a blow to the head. Without the rest of him, I'm afraid we may never know."

"Any luck on ethnicity?"

"The Honolulu team is working on that now."

After she hung up, Kali considered what had been learned. Out of five bodies, four had been identified. That wasn't too bad, considering. But the fate of the pineapple man, and the story of who he had been, continued to nag her. She pushed back her chair, ready to head over to the station, when the phone rang again. This time it was Walter. He sounded breathless.

"Found him," he said.

"Waters? Where is he?"

"Right here on Maui."

"How'd you track him down? Tax records?"

Walter snorted. "Hardly. Turns out he's got a brand-new venture since the Eden's River scheme caught up with him, though he's using the same name. He may be a surgeon, but he's clearly an idiot. He's living up-country on an old farmstead. So far, he's kept it pretty low-key. There's nothing officially going on as far as a registered retreat or church of any kind, and to all appearances he's dropped any reference to whatever shenanigans he was up to on Lāna'i, but there's a complaint on file from a local woman that her daughter was lured up there under the pretense of a yoga and wellness weekend with seminars and camping."

The daughter, explained Walter, had emptied out her bank account and given away all of her belongings, then moved into the new Eden's River. "A later interview with the daughter, who was in her early twenties at the time, quoted her as saying that Abraham was a 'divinely inspired healer' who helped her get her life on track."

"Is that it?"

"There was a call-in from another woman, who says she was seduced by Abraham and abandoned her husband and two kids to go and bask in his holy light. Her words, not mine. She eventually came to her senses and went home, but so far she hasn't had anything really bad to say about the commune or about Abraham—just that it turned out to not be her thing. She declined to make an official statement."

Walter texted her the current address for Abraham Waters, and Kali noted that the latest version of Eden's River was north of Hana and west of Pali Village, about a half hour away. She gathered her things, prepared to head out. She couldn't wait to meet him.

Kali drove slowly through a set of open gates. They were built of wood, and the paint had long ago worn away. A close look revealed remnants of a dark blue tint still embedded along the edges of the posts supporting the gates, suggesting they'd enjoyed a former, far more colorful life.

The dirt track was rutted and muddy. She followed it for about a hundred yards as it wound deeper into the *mauka* side of the road away from the sea and towards the distant slopes of Haleakalā volcano, its slowly eroding exterior blanketed by verdant vegetation.

The Jeep bounced along. There had been no attempt to control the dense foliage encroaching from either side of the road, and a wild profusion of branches and shrubs, many of them in flower, created a sort of tunnel-like portal that gave way suddenly to a wide, sloping field. She slowed to a halt in front of a collection of low buildings that were scattered across the field, mentally calculating the dimensions. The visible complex seemed to cover about three acres of land. The buildings were mostly in poor repair, and she could see that one small area of no more than a quarter of an acre appeared to have been cultivated, with stakes supporting tomato plants.

There was movement near the closest building, so she sat, waiting, as a youngish man and two women stepped out from behind the structure. The man was pushing a wheelbarrow full of soil and plants. The plants were upside down, their roots showing. All three people stopped suddenly as they caught sight of the Jeep. As Kali watched, the man turned to the women and said something. One of them nodded in response, placing her hand on the other woman's arm. The man let go of the wheelbarrow handles and began to walk toward Kali.

As he drew closer, she saw that his jeans were covered in dark stains, and that there were multiple soil smudges on his short-sleeve shirt. As he walked toward her, he pushed back his shoulder-length hair, which curled over his forehead, smiling in a friendly way. She noted that the smile did not extend to his eyes, which regarded her with caution.

She opened the door and slid off her seat onto the ground.

"Aloha," the man said. "Can I help you?" He gestured behind himself. "I don't know if you're aware, but this is actually private property."

"Is it?" she asked. "Who is the owner?"

The man looked uncomfortable. "That would be Abraham Waters," he said. He turned briefly, looking toward a path leading in the direction of a building set upon a rise among the trees.

"Is that where Mr. Waters lives?" she asked.

"Yes, but . . . he doesn't like to be disturbed."

"Are you related to him?"

The man frowned. "I'm sorry, but you're asking a lot of questions, and you still haven't explained what you want."

"Answers," she said. She pulled her badge out from beneath the loose, short-sleeve cotton shirt she wore unbuttoned over a tank top. The badge glinted in the sun. "I'm Detective Kali Māhoe, Maui Police. According to public records, this is a leasehold property. Mr. Waters may own the buildings, but he doesn't own the land. So, let's try this again. Who are you?"

He looked taken aback. "Sorry. I'm Jake. I just work here, taking care of the garden for Mr. Waters." He looked meaningfully at the house in the distance. "I can tell you that he doesn't like it when people just show up."

Kali raised an eyebrow. "Oh, is that so? I'm not interested in what he likes or doesn't like, so I'd appreciate it if you'd show me where to find him."

A wave of uncertainty washed over Jake's face. He led the way across the lawn, toward the left of the building where the two women were still waiting, staring openly at Kali. They smiled shyly as she and Jake passed near them. Kali saw that they were both wearing jeans that were partially covered by long, flimsy cotton dresses that fell to mid-calf, and that they both had long blond hair. She estimated them to be in their early twenties, and pregnant, by the looks of them. The way they were dressed reminded her of the women she'd seen on the ferry, the very same who'd been holding signs in the field with Chad and his group.

"They work here too?"

Jake didn't bother to turn around. "They help with the garden."

"Is that some sort of uniform they're wearing?"

"God demands modesty. They're dressed appropriately for outdoor work," he said.

Kali waited, but he didn't elaborate. She picked up her pace so that she was walking abreast of him, rather than behind. "My understanding is that Abraham Waters disbanded his church a long time ago."

Jake laughed. "God doesn't require a building, you know."

She looked up sharply, but kept her voice even. "How many people live here besides Mr. Waters?"

Jake looked straight ahead. "If there's anything else you want to know, you'll have to ask him yourself."

He hurried forward across the grass to the front door of the house. It was modest in size, and set back beneath the trees. Like the gates leading into the property, the wood siding on the structure had seen better days. There was a wood-slatted porch swing hanging at a slight angle from hooks in the ceiling of the covered lanai. A cat was curled into one corner, lifting its head and yawning lazily as they came up the steps and stopped in front of the screen door. Instead of knocking, Jake called through the screen into the dark, shaded recess of the entrance.

"Father? You have a visitor." Shifting side to side, he added, "There's a lady here from the police. A detective. I'm sorry to bother you, but she insists on speaking with you."

Kali heard the sound of someone moving across a wooden floor, presaging the arrival of a man in the door frame moments later. A shorter, much younger man stood behind him, looking out. She recognized the taller of the two men as Abraham Waters, though an older version than the photo she had seen. He looked at her, his gaze steady. She couldn't help but notice that he was still quite handsome, or that he seemed to be appraising her.

"Welcome," said Abraham. His voice was melodious, as though singing might come more natural to him than speaking. He directed his gaze toward Jake. "Open the door, please, Jacob. I'll speak with our guest inside where it's cooler. You may return to the garden."

Jake held the door open, and the young man behind Abraham stepped back. Kali walked inside, waiting for her eyes to adjust to the dim interior. She could hear Jake's footsteps retreating on the stairs, fading as he reached the grassy lawn.

"Did I hear correctly that you are a detective?" Abraham smiled at her, his hands resting easily by his sides.

"That's right." She looked him over. He struck her as strong and virile. Though the information gathered on him indicated that he was sixty-nine, his skin was tight and oddly undamaged by the sun. There was nothing frail about him. He wore his thick hair long and loose around his shoulders. He was slender, but she could see through his short sleeve jersey that his shoulders and upper arms were toned, defined.

"Well, I can't say I've ever actually met a detective before." He reached out to shake her hand. "Abraham Waters, but I expect you already know that. And this," he said, gesturing to the silent man standing behind him, "is my grandson, Nathan. How may I be of service to you?"

Nathan was about twenty, as far as she could tell. There was something childlike about him, unfinished and undefined. She regarded him with interest. The muddy brown of his eyes and his judgmental expression stood out in sharp contrast to the bright, curious light in Abraham's blue eyes. Kali noted the way his eyes kept darting from her face to the edge of the tattoo encircling her upper arm.

"Did I hear Jake address you as his father?" she asked, remembering that records showed he had a daughter, but that there had been no mention of a son.

"It is a term of respect and familiarity," he said.

"I see. I understand that you ran a private church on Lāna'i from 1993 until around 2000. You operated it as a commune, correct?"

Abraham smiled again, spreading his arms wide. "A wellness retreat center. Commune has such a negative connotation, doesn't it? Perhaps you're asking if I shared a small farmstead with other members of my family, and if I preached the Good Word to those whose hearts were open to hearing God's message?"

"I'm asking you if you accepted financial and other donations from people not related to you, and if those people also lived with you on your farmstead."

"We are all related. You are both my daughter and my sister."

She returned his gaze, unblinking. "I am neither of those things."

"Then you are a heathen, and you're going to hell. You

have carved your body with the marks of the devil!" It was Nathan who spoke, his voice thick with venom. He raised his volume, pointing at Kali's arm in condemnation. *"You shall not make any cuts in your body for the dead nor make any tattoo marks on yourselves: I am the Lord. Leviticus 19:28."*

"It's all right, Nathan," said Abraham. He reached up and placed his hand gently on the boy's outstretched hand, pushing it down so that it was no longer pointed at Kali. "Not everyone has heard the laws set forth by God. We must be generous and patient." He turned to Kali. "My grandson is passionate about the teachings of the Bible."

Kali felt her skin crawl. She thought of all the crime and pain and fear she had seen in the world that had sprung from the arrogance of those who felt entitled to judge others, or to disregard the sovereign rights of those around them. When the arrogance was rooted in religion, she found it particularly repugnant. She also knew it was generally a waste of time to point out to any kind of fanatic that there was almost always more than one viewpoint to be considered.

"Have you reestablished your commune here on Maui, Mr. Waters?"

"As I've just explained, what you refer to as a commune is, to me, a home where my family dwells."

"Then tell me, please, who *dwells* here besides you?" She met his eyes, tilting her head slightly, ignoring Nathan's glare.

"My wife, Ruth, and our daughter, Abigail, share this place with me."

"And the farm? Jake and the two young women helping him today? Where do they *dwell*?"

Abraham smiled. "Elsewhere."

She felt her temper flare. "Elsewhere on the property, or elsewhere on the island?"

"I'm afraid I don't feel compelled to keep track of the comings and goings of those kind and generous souls who come to help with picking fruit and harvesting the crops from our gardens." He leaned forward slightly. "If you like, Nathan would be happy to show you our little patch of lettuces and herbs. The basil is doing especially well right now."

She was careful to not look at Nathan, or to let her voice reflect the distaste she felt at the idea of him acting as a tour guide. "That won't be necessary," she said. "However, I'd like to speak with your daughter while I'm here."

He nodded. "Of course. Abigail is home. If you follow the pathway just past the gardens, you'll see her cottage."

Again, she ignored the boy. "And Abigail is Nathan's mother?"

"Yes. Though we take a more village-based approach to raising our children."

"*We?*"

"Those of us who have gathered as a community."

His voice was lulling, seductive. *Trickster*, she thought, imagining the Hawaiian god Kaulu whose powers included killing with a song, and ensnaring young goddesses. Kaulu possessed a powerful and deadly combination of immortality and a predilection for violence. She watched Abraham as he spoke. His eyes were steady and unblinking. She shook herself, breaking the spell, understanding how he had successfully lured others into trusting him enough to surrender not only their possessions, but also decisions about their lives and families. Instead of being disarmed, she felt repelled.

"Ah," she said. "Well, it certainly sounds as though your—shall we say *program*—has enjoyed a revival since your time on Lāna'i."

Abraham shrugged. His eyes suggested he recognized that she would not easily be susceptible to his efforts to charm her.

"We'll talk more," she said. "Soon. Meanwhile, enjoy your day."

She closed the screen door firmly behind her. As she walked down onto the lawn in search of the path mentioned by Abraham, she was aware that Nathan was framed in the doorway, watching her as she walked away.

CHAPTER 22

The path crossed a small stream that was spanned by a long, wide plank of wood. Kali stepped carefully, crossing the makeshift bridge and approaching the cottage. It was in poor repair. She found herself mentally criticizing Nathan for not being a better, more useful son when it came to his mother's safety and well-being.

She knocked, and the door opened slowly. Abigail was wearing an apron of faded, flowery cotton that had a narrow bib across the top, held up by two strips of fabric that tied behind her neck. There was a row of drooping ruffles adorning the bib, with an identical row along the hem of the skirt. Kali couldn't tell if the apron was handmade, or if it was a new one in a retro, 1950s style, but the effect was the same: a sense that the person wearing it wasn't being ironic, but was simply caught up in a story from the past they'd never actually lived through. Beneath the apron, she wore a now-familiar blue cotton skirt that brushed her ankles.

Kali studied Abigail carefully before she spoke. Her mostly dark blond hair was streaked with gray, pulled back severely from her face, causing the skin to draw away from the corners of her eyes. It looked uncomfortable. She struck Kali as being deeply weary. Perhaps, considered Kali, the apron merely indicated an intense, all-night baking session that had resulted in a lack of sleep.

"Abigail Waters?"

"Yes, that's me," said the woman. Her voice was soft, unpretentious. "And you are . . . ?

"Detective Kali Māhoe, Maui Police Department." Kali removed a card from her wallet and handed it to Abigail. "Do you have a few minutes to spare?"

The woman looked slightly confused.

"You're here to see me?"

"Yes, I have a few questions concerning a current investigation. I thought you might be able to help. I've already had a chat with your father, and he suggested I stop by to speak with you before I left."

The woman hesitated, then stepped back, away from the door.

"If you spoke to my father, then I suppose that would be okay," she said, glancing nervously in the direction of Abraham's house. She turned and led the way into a dimly lit kitchen area, gesturing to a round wooden breakfast table. "We can sit here if you don't mind. I haven't vacuumed the parlor yet."

Kali made a mental note of the word "parlor." It struck her as old-fashioned, out of place. It was a word her grandmother might have used.

"Thank you." She chose a chair that would allow her to see the other woman's face as clearly as possible. Abigail sat down opposite her, her back straight, her hands folded primly in her lap. Kali glanced around the room. It felt worn and tired, as though reflecting Abigail's lack of energy.

"I understand that you used to work in the pineapple fields on Lāna'i."

The woman looked startled. "My goodness. That was a very long time ago," she said. She looked away, slightly past

Kali, as if reaching back into the past. She placed Kali's card on the table. "I was just a girl then."

"You were a child when your family moved to Maui and you began working there, correct?"

"Well, not really working. I accompanied my mother to the plantation at first, and then later, when I was a little older, I had a part-time job. At first it was just on the weekends, and sometimes after classes if I was needed."

"You went to the Bible school your father ran?"

"Yes."

"And at the plantation, you worked outdoors, in the fields?"

Abigail nodded.

"In the beginning I did. Later, I worked on the production line, sorting fruit by grade." She looked down at her hands and sighed. "All these old scars on my hands are from handling the fruit." She laughed suddenly, the sound more rueful than joyful. "To this day, I can't stand the smell or taste of pineapple."

Kali smiled, noting the lack of a wedding ring on the woman's hand. "It's not my favorite fruit, either," she said. "But the reason I'm here is to find out if you remember anyone suddenly going missing during the time you worked for the pineapple company."

The woman looked at her, befuddled. She frowned at Kali. "I'm not sure I understand. Missing?"

"Suddenly not showing up for work. Never coming back."

Abigail thought for a moment. "Well, a lot of people took the job and then decided it was too much and left after just a few days or a few weeks. They didn't always say goodbye. Some of them left without getting paid for the short amount of time they actually did work. And there was a lot of casual day labor. You might see someone every day for month, then never see them again."

"Even on an island as small as Lāna'i?"

"Who's to say they were all from Lāna'i? I know that at least some of them worked on Maui, in the sugar cane fields. They'd get tired of one place and go to another for a while."

Kali felt discouraged, already aware of the transient nature of the workforce in Hawai'i's agricultural world. She took a deep breath, then stood up. "Well, thank you for your time." She tried to smile encouragingly. "I may need to speak to you again at some point. Is this the best place to find you?"

Abigail nodded, then stood up as well. Kali reached the doorway, then turned back in afterthought. "Do you live here in the cottage with your son and husband?"

The other woman stared back. "With my son, yes, though he spends more and more time at my father's home, in order to help him."

"And your husband?" asked Kali, persisting.

"I have no earthly husband. I am married to the church," said Abigail, as though this information should have been self-explanatory.

With an effort, Kali kept her voice neutral. "I see. Isn't that a very Catholic concept? A vow taken by nuns?"

"It's not the same at all," said Abigail, her frown returning.

"I'm sorry," said Kali. "I don't actually know the exact ideology of Eden's River. Perhaps you could tell me a little bit about your beliefs?"

"You only need to read the good Word of God to understand," said Abigail. The soft quality of her voice had taken on an edge of sadness. "We live together in peacefulness, and in righteousness, and in humility without possessiveness. We tend the earth and bring forth food. We comfort the sick—those who are physically ill, and those whose minds have fallen into the dark trough of evil that is the world. We strive to save those souls we can from eternal damnation."

"Sounds like that must keep you pretty busy," said Kali.

"Darkness likes to creep in, taking little steps that go un-noticed, until only the children of God can help those whom it has chosen to devour."

"I see," said Kali again, though she did not. She looked at Abigail's clothing. "The blue skirt you're wearing. It's such a lovely shade. Is it a kind of uniform? I noticed the young women in the garden were also wearing them. And I may have seen them somewhere else as well."

Abigail smiled. "We make them. My mother started the tradition a long time ago, when we first came to Hawai'i. God demands modesty, of course. And the color reminds us of the pure waters created with the forming of the Earth."

Kali nodded. "Blue seems like a nice choice, then." She reached into her pocket, pulling out the small anchor charm. "And is this a talisman also connected to the water theme of your . . . church? Something perhaps used by members of Eden's River to help ward off evil?"

Abigail's eyes grew wide. She reached out slowly with one hand toward the anchor. Kali could see that her fingers were trembling. Abigail touched the surface of the metal gently, then looked up at Kali.

"Who gave this to you?" she asked.

"No one," said Kali. "It was found with the skeletal re-mains of a man discovered in the old pineapple fields on Lāna'i."

Abigail's hand withdrew, the movement swift. She stared intently for another few seconds at the anchor, then stepped back. Her lips twitched. "The anchor is the symbol of our church, keeping us steady in the midst of earthly tempta-tion."

"And did this particular anchor belong to anyone you knew?"

The woman looked away. "It's a common enough symbol in Christianity. There were many of these anchors. I'm afraid I can't say."

"*Can't* say or *won't* say?"

"I think you should leave," said Abigail. Her voice was low, almost a whisper. "If you have any more questions, you should address them to my father. As the head of our family, he will be most helpful to you."

Kali didn't press her further. For the moment, Abigail had told her plenty.

She pulled the Jeep back onto the long driveway, slowing once she'd passed through the wooden gates, easing to a halt. She dug out her phone and called Walter.

"I'm at the Waters's place. There's definitely something wrong here. Can you get someone out here to check the buildings? I'm pretty certain he's restarted his cult."

"You mean his commune."

"Cult, commune, compound—call it what you like, it's creepy as hell here. While I was talking to him, I got the impression he could have killed everyone we found and convinced everyone around him he was doing something important and meaningful. A couple of Frontier Barbie doll clones in prairie skirts look as though they've had lobotomies. They're pretty young, too, and they're both pregnant. I'd say they're in their early twenties. Plus one guy, maybe a few years older, who says he's taking care of the gardens. I'd like to know what they're growing and how many people are living there besides Abraham, the daughter, and the weird grandson."

"What's weird about him?"

"Everything, as far as I can tell. He's got to be at least twenty, but he may have been living under a rock for his entire life. Everything that comes out of his mouth is some sort of biblical decree. Gave me a bunch of grief about my arm tattoo."

Walter chuckled. "Taking it personally?"

"It was meant personally. I guarantee it."

THE BONE FIELD   189

"Okay. I'll take Hara and a search warrant with me and check it out. You get the sense that something dangerous or illegal is going on?"

"I don't know about proving that immediately, but I'd like to get a better idea of the living situation here. Nathan, the grandson, would have been too young to have been part of anything, but someone here knows what the hell happened, and how those bodies found their way to the pineapple field."

"Agreed. Hara's been digging stuff up. Waters is listed as the leaseholder on the Maui property, after a real estate transfer that was made by someone who was identified as one of his followers."

"He likes to use the term 'family.' It's a good-sized piece of land, and I'm getting a strong sense that there's been at least a partial revival of whatever nonsense he was running on Lāna'i. I spoke with the daughter, Abigail. When I asked her how many people were in residence, she avoided my question."

"Right. I'm on it. You heading back here to the station now?"

"Yeah. I want to look through those photo albums that Manuel shared with us and then drive over to talk to him about Abraham and whether or not they ever crossed paths. Manuel may have known Matthew Greene as well."

"Good idea. We can compare notes later."

Her voice was quizzical. "Great. Afterwards, maybe you can explain why all these people insist on lying while they're quoting Scripture and talking nonstop about God."

"Aren't you supposed to be the one with all of the spiritual insight?"

"Yeah, right," she said, her voice dark. "I keep forgetting."

CHAPTER 23

Walter was waiting for Kali when she got back to the station.

"The coroner called. We've got news from Honolulu," he said by way of greeting. "Some details on the pineapple man. The tests they ran in Honolulu strongly suggest that he was no more than seventeen or eighteen years at the time of death, and that he was roughly five feet six." He grimaced. "According to the report, the head was not hacked off in a rage, but cut cleanly, probably after he was already dead. It looks like storing the wooden pineapple in a bone saw box may have been prescient of me—or maybe just ironic, depending upon your point of view."

"Well, at least it's something." Kali watched as Walter checked the time.

"We should have a search warrant for the Waters's place by the end of the day tomorrow," he said. "In the meantime, I've got to deal with the details on the cock-fighting bust. I assume you can do without me for a little while."

She smiled. "Sure." She looked around the room. "Where's Hara, by the way? He can help me sort through these images again."

"I'm here, Detective Māhoe," said Hara, stepping through the doorway. He was holding a bag. The aroma of grilled onions emanated from it. "The captain sent me out for a snack."

Kali looked questioningly at Walter. "Pretty close to dinnertime for a snack, isn't it? I'll bet Nina won't be happy if you don't have any appetite for whatever she's cooked up."

Walter grumbled. "She's off at a recital with the girls. Lara and Beth are dancing, and Suki is singing. Long story short, I have to fend for myself tonight." He walked past Hara, taking the bag from his hand. He opened the top and looked in. The onion aroma was joined by the scent of pulled pork and barbecue sauce. It filled the air, and Walter grinned in happiness. "Thank you, Officer. Excellent work." He raised the bag in a salute to Hara, then left.

Alone in the room, Kali and Hara placed the thick album beneath the light on the long table. Kali began to slowly turn the pages. As she'd already noted, there were numerous images of the day-to-day production in the fields and farm buildings, and many photos of individuals who must have meant something to Manuel. Most of the photos with people showed small groups, with an occasional portrait, or a lone person doing something related to the production process.

She thought about Manuel Raso's generation, and how his job had likely been so much more than just the place where he spent hours every day. It had been a career for not only him, but for so many of the other people working for the pineapple company—their lives entwined with bringing the sweet fruit to maturation, their moods affected by the amount of daily wind or worries over lack of rainfall, their time measured out in volume and numbers and slow ripenings.

"There," said Hara suddenly, pointing excitedly. "It's the girl. Helen Stafford."

Kali looked closely at the image, then removed it from the

cellophane sleeve and examined it more closely under the light. Hara was right. Helen Stafford was standing next to a table where several pineapples were on display, along with a stack of wooden transport crates visible in the background. She was smiling, making the "hang loose" shaka sign with the fingers of one hand, her thumb and pinky extended, her three center fingers curled against her palm.

Kali set the photo aside, and continued to turn the pages in the album. She was just about to move on to another page when an image caught her attention. It showed several women and a young girl, all wearing the long blue skirts that she had seen Abigail Waters and the women on the ferryboat wearing. She removed those images as well, and placed them in the small pile she had made that included the photo that depicted the harvest-gold refrigerator.

She stood up. "Feel like taking a ride?"

Hara nodded willingly. "Bring the album?"

"Yes, and this stack of images I pulled from them. Keep those separate."

They took the Jeep, making a quick stop at George's Island Market to pick up a coconut cake to bring to Manuel as a gift. Kali and Hara listened as George shared news from a tabloid headline that warned residents of Hawai'i that the oddly shaped clouds some of them had reported were cloaking devices used by a superior alien race to hide their spaceships. Kali tried to hide her concern that Hara seemed genuinely alarmed, and turned the conversation to the investigation.

"What do you know about a group of people calling themselves Eden's River, who used to have some kind of combination commune, farm, and church over on Lāna'i, George? The leader was a guy called Abraham Waters. It was billed as a Christian wellness retreat, but a lot of the people who came to participate wound up living there together."

George tilted his head in thought. "Commune and church? Sounds kind of like a cult."

"That's our thought as well, though we can't find a lot of information about what exactly was going on, other than allegations of young girls being involved."

George's face flooded with alarm. "How young is young?"

"Not sure yet," said Kali. "Late teens, early twenties is what we've heard so far. Whatever was going on there, enough of a problem was developing that the program—or whatever it was—got shut down on Lāna'i. We have reason to believe that he's trying to run the same show here on Maui."

"I'll keep my ears open," said George.

Kali nodded in gratitude, and handed the coconut cake to Hara, who carried it to the Jeep. They made their way through the tourist traffic moving slowly along the southern end of the Hana Highway. When they finally reached the pineapple mailbox at the foot of Manuel's driveway, it was growing late.

Hara followed her up the walkway. By the time they'd crossed the short distance to the door, Manuel had come out and stood waiting. He smiled when he saw Kali.

"Aloha, Detective," he said.

"Aloha, Mr. Raso," she said. "This is my colleague, Officer David Hara. We've come with a few more questions about your photographs. I apologize for not calling first, but do you perhaps have some time to spare for us?"

Some small shadow of loneliness in the old man's eyes lifted.

"Of course—please, come inside," he said.

Kali nodded to Hara, and he extended the cake box.

"We've brought you a little something," she said. "Coconut cake. I'm sure it's not as good as the ones your wife used to make, but we hope you enjoy it."

Manuel's face lit up. "My goodness! That's very gracious of you. I'm sure it will be delicious. Would you like to have a slice? I could make coffee."

Hara looked hopeful.

Kali smiled. "No, but thank you. I'm afraid we can't stay that long. We'd like to ask you about a few of the people who appear in your photos to see if you can tell us anything about them, but then we need to be on our way."

Manuel placed the cake carefully on a table in front of his sofa and led the way through the living room and out the back door to his shady lanai, where Kali had sat with him during their first meeting.

After they made themselves comfortable, she placed the small stack of individual photos on top of the album. Hara pulled a notebook and a pen out of his duty belt and sat attentively, waiting to jot down any information that Manuel could add to the investigation.

"When I first spoke with you, you told me about the chemical companies spraying the fruit crops. Do you remember a company representative by the name of Matthew Greene who had been sent here to experiment with some new sprays to control bugs and other things that might have damaged the crops and reduced the yield?"

"Do I ever." Manuel's eyes grew dark. "Greene was a bully. Liked to throw his weight around, and was especially aggressive with the women. Worse, I think he knew those sprays weren't safe. Too bad he wasn't around to answer for all the illnesses and cancer cases that eventually popped up."

Kali looked sideways at Hara, who was fidgeting. She tilted her chin towards him, and he turned to Manuel.

"Do you know where he went?" Hara asked.

"He skedaddled is all I know," said Manuel, still frowning. "One day he was there, and then he was gone. The guys in suits were quiet about it. The few of us that were still around to close up the facility thought maybe he got fired, but I always thought he just got on a plane and went back to some big, showy house on the mainland. He used to brag about how big his swimming pool was. Too blind and ignorant to see the enormous ocean right at his feet."

"And did you know anything about his wife?" Kali continued.

Manuel looked blank. "No. Can't say I knew he was married. She must be a saint to put up with his arrogance and tormenting. If they're still married, of course."

"They aren't," said Kali. "The wife, Lily Greene, died after a prolonged illness, and Matthew Greene has been missing for a number of years. All accounts suggest he never left Lānaʻi."

This seemed to interest Manuel. He stared off into the distance for a moment, then turned back to Kali. She passed him the photo of Helen Stafford.

"What about this girl?" she asked, trying to keep the hope from her voice.

Manuel studied the image, turning it toward the light.

"Yes. I think that's the girl who used to choose the display fruit—a few especially large pineapples with bright colors that would go to the grocery stores to be placed beside the product displays." His brow wrinkled as he searched his memory for details. "Hannah, maybe?"

"Helen," said Kali. "Helen Stafford."

Manuel sat back slightly, smiling. "Oh yes—Helen! That's right. A nice, friendly woman. Always smiling."

"Did she work at the plantation for very long?"

"No, not that long as I remember it. She had a friend who helped with planting the crowns. Maybe her boyfriend, come to think of it. I can't recall his name, but I remember that his hair was kind of long. He looked like a hippie, but he was nice."

"And these girls?" asked Kali, showing him the photo of the young girls in the long blue skirts.

Manuel peered at the image, frowning. "Oh, those girls from the church. The Garden of Eden or something like that. Sure, I remember them. They were always dancing around instead of working. Most of them were only there for a short time. I think they'd run out of cash and come to work in the fields for a few days or weeks." He took the photo from Kali. "Except the little girl. She was there longer. I think she was part of the family who ran the church. One of those other women in the picture was her mother. She worked there part-time, and used to bring the little girl with her to the plantation. She used to encourage the little girl to run around, telling everyone happy stories about their church and inviting them to come for a visit." He thought for a moment. "Lots of people brought their kids with them, though. A couple of the kids—that little girl included—got after-school jobs when they got older."

"What can you tell us about the people from the church?" asked Kali, watching as Hara wrote in his notebook. "Did you ever run into the founder, Abraham Waters?"

"Abraham Waters? Oh yes. I went there once to see what it was all about. It was after my wife passed away. Everyone was talking about it—a retreat that was about getting closer to God, and how the message was all about how to live in harmony with the events of your life, without allowing grief to cripple you. That appealed to me at the time. But that's not what it was all about. And Abraham Waters? Now that's one seriously crazy man."

"Could you be a little more specific?"

Manuel hesitated. "Well, for starters, it wasn't really a church. Not like a little white building with a steeple and a bell tower. It was more like a commune, or like a nice cult with yoga and live music. People all lived together on one piece of land. Waters didn't own it, but I believe I heard that he leased it from someone who bought it way back in the 1960s when the counterculture was taking hold in San Francisco, and a lot of people who identified with the hippie movement began moving here to the islands."

"Were there a lot of local people there?" asked Hara.

Manuel shrugged. "I don't know. What's 'a lot'? The day I was there, there were maybe thirty people, tops. You'd see them in the shops sometimes, too, but I think they grew most of their own food. For a while, they were around in the town, knocking on doors. Trying to get people to join their club, I guess. After I'd seen what was really going on, I mostly ignored them. What's it to me, right?" He laughed. "Maybe if their music had been better, I'd have taken them more seriously, but it was all noise—tambourines and bells."

"What about rumors that there may have been odd things going on at their farm?"

"Well, it's true that some of the locals were pretty annoyed that the Eden people would wander into the old ruins for some of their ceremonies. The commune people thought the Hawaiian beliefs were evil, so they used to bring holy water into the site and throw it on the old stones and pray over them."

"For what purpose? To bless them?"

"To cast out what they saw as things tainted by the devil." Manuel shook his head and sighed. "That's the problem, right? Convincing yourself that only your own personal beliefs are the right ones."

"That's part of the problem," agreed Kali. "But we're more concerned about claims that underage girls may have been targeted by Abraham Waters."

Manuel considered her words. When he spoke, he gave

off an uneasy air. "After a while, they started to keep to themselves. It's hard to say what was really going on."

Kali reached into her bag and pulled out the little anchor. "Have you ever seen anything like this before?"

Manuel leaned forward, reaching out to gently take the charm from Kali. He held it in his palm, turning it over several times. "A little anchor," he mused. He sat up suddenly. "Oh, yes. I remember. The anchor bracelet. The little girl— Abby, we called her, the little girl who was in the photo we just looked at—she had a bracelet with these little charms on it. A dozen, at least. She used to wear it all the time, and you could hear the jingle when she was around."

Both Kali and Hara tensed. "Are you certain?" asked Kali.

"One hundred percent," said Manuel. "I know, because the clasp broke one day and the little girl asked me if I could help her mend it. She was awfully upset. It had been a gift from her daddy, she told me, and he would have been furious with her if she lost it."

"Furious if a little girl lost a bracelet?" asked Kali. "That doesn't sound much like peace and love."

"Well, those kinds of people—setting themselves apart and making up their own rules. It's never really about peace and love, is it? It's always about something else." He laughed cynically. "Usually money or power, in my experience. Love? That's just the bait."

CHAPTER 24

K ali and Hara listened as Manuel talked some more about his days working in the pineapple fields. It was acutely apparent to both of them how much he missed the purpose and the work, and the people with whom he had shared those experiences over the years.

They assured him that the album would be returned as soon as possible. Afterward, Manuel walked them to the door. He thanked them again for the cake and reminded Kali of her earlier promise that she would return some time to visit when the investigation was over.

"Let me know if there's anything else I can tell you," he said, waving as they climbed back into the Jeep.

They'd pulled out onto the street when Hara turned to her.

"You know," he said, "I've studied cults a bit."

She regarded him with disbelief. "Firsthand?"

He smiled, suddenly shy. "No, not exactly. I didn't belong to one or anything. But one of the courses I took on criminal profiles delved into the topic a bit, and I found it really interesting, so I've read a lot more on the topic than the curriculum required."

"So tell me," she said encouragingly. "Give me the short course on what you learned about successful cult leaders."

"You probably know a lot of this," he said. "And the names of the famous cult leaders like Jim Jones, but there are certain personality traits that are consistent with the kinds of people who—well, you know, choose it as a career."

She laughed. "Okay, so we've got our Jim Jones and Charlie Manson and my favorite—Marshall Applewhite and his comet riders." She looked at Hara, weighing her observation. "I guess the big ones are all men with something to prove, or some need for adoration."

"Yes—and they were, or are, generally very charismatic, at least when it serves their goals. On the inside, though, there's often a lot of abuse and subjugation."

"Sexual?"

"Definitely."

"From what we've learned about Abraham Waters, would you say he's a classic example?"

"I would," he said. He stumbled over his next words. "I know you've been trained to be a traditional wisdom keeper, and that your role involves knowing a lot about spirituality. I don't mean to be disrespectful to you . . ."

"You shouldn't be the least bit concerned about that. We're two colleagues, having a professional discussion about personality types that may help lead us to a serial killer. That's a discussion worth having, don't you think?"

"It's just that I go to church," he said. "I don't think most people who have religious beliefs want to hurt others."

She thought about his words. In her estimation, religious institutions were places where evil often hid in plain sight, but that didn't mean there was nothing more. She kept her thoughts to herself and listened as Hara explained the profile of many of the famous cult leaders who had been tried and convicted. In addition to an inflated ego and unrealistic sense of personal power, the leaders he mentioned often believed themselves to have been divinely chosen by a higher power or authority to rule over others, a vantage point that allowed them to make unreasonable demands that included humiliation and sexual services—always in the name of good.

"An important characteristic of the people I studied is that they would systematically reward the followers who worshipped or venerated them, and got rid of anybody who challenged them or their absolute authority," said Hara, warming up to his topic. "It's how they keep control, by removing any kind of threat to their position."

"The location is important, too, isn't it? Keeping people away from their friends and family?"

He nodded vehemently. "Seclusion is key. Not only physically, but keeping people from listening to the news or watching television or having access to visitors or outside influences like computers." He stirred it all over in his mind. "Seems to me like Eden's River is pretty textbook."

By the time Kali got home, the sun was going down. Shadows sprang up in the yard, and the evening songs of birds filled the air. She sat on her front steps for a few moments, enjoying the tranquility of it all, then walked to the clearing in her yard. She kicked off her shoes and cued up her phone to a music selection, then laid it on the ground with the speaker volume turned up. The song she'd chosen was "E Ho 'i I Ka Pili," composed and sung by Keali'i Reichel, one of her favorite performers.

The rich layers of Reichel's voice filled the air. Kali wished that she could just sit on the steps in the shade and listen, but the coming performance at the cultural festival was weighing on her mind. Practicing was unavoidable. The last thing she wanted to do was disgrace the tradition, even if she had been pressured to appear instead of having made the choice herself.

Instead of swearing at Pait, she began to move, at first slowly and with hesitation, then more strongly, her body embracing the music through dance, the ancient form of hula that was sometimes said to have been gifted to the Hawaiian people by the goddess Laka. Kali danced the old form, the *hula kahiko* that existed long before outsiders arrived on the islands' shores and missionaries proclaimed that the practice was fraught with evil. Later outlawed and made *kapu*, or taboo, hula had quietly been kept alive until a less rigid sensibility was restored and it was again allowed to be danced in public.

At the *hālau* hula school she'd attended as a girl, the instructor had been an impatient woman who had been critical of Kali's natural skills. Her constant running and jumping, the instructor had told her, had given her tomboy muscles unsuited to the graceful movements that defined the dance. Kali had struggled particularly when it came to the lessons on rain. The strong muscles in her young arms had developed in response to hanging from trees, throwing balls, and doing backflips, and her teacher was unimpressed with Kali's efforts to suggest raindrops falling gently from the sky.

"You have thunder in your arms!" her teacher had admonished. "Think of the rain landing lightly on the leaves and grass, not pummeling them!"

Kali could still remember the hot, red flush that had filled her cheeks. She watched the other girls and boys, growing vexed and impatient. Try as she might, none of her efforts seemed to please her teacher. When her grandmother asked her later that day if she had enjoyed her lesson, Kali had only scowled, declaring that she was through with hula forever, and would learn to fish instead.

Her grandmother had merely smiled. She waited patiently

as Kali sat down, sullen, on the steps leading down from the lanai to the lawn, shoving her bare feet into the deep grass.

"I understand," said Pualani. "When I was learning hula I used to go to the left when everyone else went to the right. One boy who was learning with me said that if I was told to follow a path into the mountains, I would end up in the sea instead."

Kali had been skeptical. "You're only saying that to make me feel better."

"I'm afraid it's quite true. Of course, because it was challenging for me, and especially because I wanted to prove that boy was wrong, I made it a point to learn every hand movement and every step—when to bend and when to raise my arms. But that's just how I am. When someone tells me I can't do something, it only makes me want to do it more, and do it better."

Pualani looked out across the lawn at the shimmer of light that rose from the place where the sunlight met the surface of the sea. "Why don't you help me in the garden today instead?" she asked Kali. "It needs weeding."

Kali had agreed, and followed her grandmother to the side of the house where tomatoes and long beans grew on trellises next to a small, landscaped bed of flowers. Over the next hour, Kali and Pualani knelt and pulled weeds from the beds, reached and pinched suckers from the trellised plants, and bent to tidy the ground around their roots.

Later in the day, they walked down to the beach to gather shells and stones and bits of coral. They each filled a bucket and then carried their treasures back to the garden while the contents clanked against the metal sides. They poured the shells and other things onto the grass, spreading them out so they could see clearly what they had to work with. Then, side by side, they formed the things they'd collected into flower shapes in a border around the flower bed, filling the spaces between each stony bloom with round black lava pebbles, polished smooth by the sea.

"Let's have something cool to drink," suggested Pualani when they were through. "Then we'll bless the beautiful space we've made."

They sat in the shade offered by the lanai and sipped tall glasses of chilled water from a pitcher. Pualani had added several thick slices of mango to the water, infusing it with the sweetness of the fruit. When she'd finished, Pualani set down her glass and smiled at Kali. "Come, Granddaughter. I will need your help. We will thank the earth for supplying us with the means to create this beautiful space in our garden."

Pualani stood facing the broad flower blooms they had shaped with their stones: round ones in the middle, with pieces of coral fanning out from the center. The small, dark stones surrounding each bloom made them stand out clearly. Pualani began to chant with closed eyes. Her voice rose and fell, and Kali listened to the familiar words, feeling the song resonate in her bones. Pualani began to move, adding small movements of the sacred hula dance to the words of her prayer. She opened her eyes and smiled again at Kali.

"Now, help me, please."

Kali hesitated, some of her earlier sullenness returning. "I don't know this dance."

"But you do. We have already practiced it, and we will make it up as we go along, just the two of us."

"When did we practice it?"

"Just now, as we worked in the garden. We bent to weed, and we reached to tend the higher plants—just like this."

Pualani demonstrated, dipping as though she were reaching for weeds, and mimicking the motion of planting seeds. At first hesitantly, and then with growing assurance, Kali did her best to replicate the movements.

Now, in the growing shadows, she imagined her grandmother's graceful form beside her, teaching her with infinite patience the arm and hand movements and what each meant—when to move her feet or bend, and when to reach into the sky.

"Fill yourself with rain, Granddaughter."

Kali cleared her mind, then did exactly that: She filled her thoughts with rain, and what it meant to the earth, picturing the drops falling steadily from the sky, downward onto the ground, slaking the thirst of the trees and grass and flowers. She imagined the touch of the rain on her face, and moved her arms and hands to imitate the flow.

"And can you be like the wind?" came her grandmother's voice again, cradled in memory.

I can be like the wind, she thought, and her arms filled with the moving air. She bent and rose, then moved her hips in a smooth *'ami*, just as she'd been taught as a young girl.

"The sea, Granddaughter. Sense the sea and the waves and the currents. Let the tide pull you in and out."

And she did, all through the song and into the next, her movements becoming more sure as the familiar motions took hold. She felt the soft ground beneath the soles of her feet, the tickle of the grass as she moved through it. There was movement on the lanai, and she turned to see Makena standing next to one of the tall posts supporting the lanai roof. She was watching Kali, but when Kali waved, inviting Makena to join her on the lawn, Makena merely turned away and disappeared inside. Kali sighed. At least she had gotten in a practice before the performance that was coming up at the cultural festival. She felt herself tense involuntarily at Pait's scheming, but then reconsidered her response. Maybe it was a good thing she'd been pushed into revisiting this important part of who she was. She flexed the arm that had been scratched by the irate rooster, then reached down to massage her left calf muscle. It had been a while. Served her right if her legs were sore.

CHAPTER 25

The timbre of Hilo's whimpering became a distressed, drawn-out whine. He stood in the bedroom doorway, and spun as he saw Kali sit up in response to his cries. There was another sound, resting just beneath Hilo's voice—a soft moaning.

Kali bolted from her bed, lunging through the doorway into the hall, turning immediately to the left where Makena's door stood partly open. Hilo was already there, rooted anxiously by the girl's head.

"Makena—what's wrong?"

There was another moan, and Kali reached for the bedside lamp, switching it on. She drew in her breath in alarm. The light revealed Makena, lying curled on her side, the sheet below her waist soaked in blood. Her hair was damp with perspiration, spread out in dark tangles across the pillowcase. Kali knelt beside her, pushing the hair away from the girl's face.

Makena's eyes fluttered open. "Kali—what's happening to me?" she asked, her voice betraying fear. She attempted to sit up, but a spasm of pain crossed her face, and she fell back against the mattress, groaning.

"Stay still. Don't try to move. I'll be right back." Kali darted back to her bedroom and grabbed her phone from the bedside table, quickly punching in 911. She identified herself and gave her address, then moved quickly to the bathroom and pulled a towel off the drying rack beside the shower.

She went back to Makena's side, flipping on the overhead light as she passed the light switch next to the door. The bed-cover was jumbled around Makena's feet, and she pulled it gently away, trying to determine how much blood had been lost. Makena was clutching her stomach, and Kali reached out and placed her hand on Makena's forehead.

"I'm afraid, Kali," Makena whispered, her breath hot.

"You don't need to be afraid. I'm right here, and help is on the way." Her voice was gentle; she did her best not to convey her own fear. She sat back, kneeling beside the bed. "When did the bleeding begin?"

"Last night. Just a little bit. I fell asleep, but I had cramps." Makena took a deep, shuddering breath. "I didn't think it was anything important."

Kali bit her lip, struck once again by her conviction that this girl was ill-equipped, in every way, to be a mother. The wail of sirens could be heard in the distance. Hilo grew more distressed, running from the bedroom to the front door and back. Kali got up and called to him, leading him to her bed-room. "It's going to be okay, fella. Stay here." She patted his head. "Be a good boy." She shut the door, hurrying back to Makena.

The sirens drew closer, and soon the flashing lights of the ambulance could be seen reflected in the window glass.

Makena's eyes grew wide and frightened. "What's happening to me?" she asked again, her voice breaking. "Why does everything hurt so much?"

"Please try to be still," Kali answered, not knowing what else to say.

Makena began to cry. Kali reached out and took her hand. There was no resistance. Kali noted the delicate fingers—long and slender, joined to her arms by tiny wrists. When she had been much younger, Mike had called his daughter his little hummingbird. Kali remembered his face, suffused with love and pride, as he'd watched his small child happily running along a hiking path. She squeezed Makena's hand and stood up, gazing with worry at the small, damaged hummingbird curled into the sheets.

"I'll be right back," she said. She made her way to the front door, switching on lights as she went. The paramedics were already on the front steps. Kali recognized them both.

"Mark, Katie—thanks for getting here so quickly." She turned toward the bedroom. "She's in here. I think she's miscarrying."

"How far along?" asked Katie.

"Best guess, second trimester, but we don't know for sure."

Katie nodded, and Mark led the way into Makena's room. He halted in the doorway and spoke quietly to Kali.

"Is that . . ."

"Yes. Makena Shirai." Kali stepped aside, allowing Mark and Katie the space they needed to get to Makena. Katie remained next to the thin, groaning figure. Mark spoke to her, checking her vital signs. As he lifted her arm to gauge her blood pressure, he saw the map of needle scars on her skin. He made a quick examination, then signaled to Kali that he'd like to speak to her privately.

"She's hemorrhaging. We need to get her to the hospital. Is there anyone you should contact?"

"There's just me."

"Okay. We're going to get her ready for transport. She's lost a lot of blood."

"And the baby?"

"Can't say, but it's not looking great."

Kali nodded. She watched as Makena was moved to a stretcher and taken to the ambulance. Makena's face had lost some of its terror. Instead, her skin had taken on a dull grayness, and once again Kali tried not to relay her worry. "I'm going to be right behind the ambulance, Makena," she said. "I'll grab a few of your things and meet you in the hospital. Please don't worry. Everything will be fine."

Makena's eyes flickered. She made a small movement with her head that might have been a nod. The paramedics completed the process of safely securing her, and as the ambulance pulled away, Kali ran back to the house and up the steps. She let Hilo out of her room, and found her small travel duffel on the closet floor. Inside Makena's room, she pulled open a drawer to find a fresh change of clothing, and was surprised to see the little polka-dot horse sitting atop a soft green infant's outfit still attached to a plastic hanger. The price tag was still fastened to it. She didn't know if Makena had purchased it, stolen it, or received it as a gift, but she suddenly didn't care. The fact that it was here, tucked away and waiting, said volumes.

She located a clean shirt and a pair of faded jeans among the girl's scant belongings, surprised once again when she saw that they were neatly folded. She found some underwear, and pulled Makena's toothbrush from a glass on the bathroom shelf. Even after she'd packed everything, the duffel felt light and forlorn.

Kali checked that Hilo had food and water in his bowls, then slipped her feet into her faded purple slip-on shoes and hurried to the Jeep. The ambulance could no longer be seen, but she could hear the siren's urgent notes, its energy, both alarming and comforting at the same time, reaching back to her through the cool predawn air.

The hospital waiting room was freezing. Kali sat up, cold and bleary, and stretched her neck to relieve the crick in the muscle connected to her shoulder. The bright artificial lights glared, highlighting the threadbare armrest of her chair and the worn patches on the square of carpet that partially covered the sterile linoleum floor between the row of chairs where she was seated and the identical row across from her. When it was new, she reflected, the carpet's indiscriminate blue and beige pattern may have softened the hard edges of the room to some extent—but in its present stained and fraying state, it only offered a level of subtle despair.

She checked her phone screen for the time and any messages. It was a few minutes before six o'clock, and she was thankful it was still early enough that there were no calls to deal with.

Twenty minutes passed, and she was just about to go in search of coffee when the wide double doors on one side of the waiting area opened and a doctor entered. He was dressed in scrubs, and his glasses had been shoved up over the surgical skullcap he wore. He smiled briefly as he approached her.

"Detective Māhoe?"

She stood up, his countenance making her feel hopeful. "Yes. How is Makena?"

"Resting," he said. "She lost quite a bit of blood, but is stable. I'm afraid there was no way to save the pregnancy." He looked her in the eye. "She was in her second trimester. I would estimate thirty weeks. However, there was significant underdevelopment, and I'm sorry to say there were clear signs that life had ended several days ago."

Kali looked away. She felt a sense of sadness, and wished fervently that Mike was here, so he could help his daughter navigate the world in a way that she had been unable to do in his absence. She looked at the doctor and nodded in understanding. "Her health hasn't been . . . well, good, for several years."

"No. That's clear. I'd like her to stay for the day and possibly tomorrow."

"May I see her?"

"She's a little woozy, but yes." He regarded her with sympathy. "You can notify the father, if he's part of this equation."

"He's not," she said. She picked up the duffel bag from where she'd placed it beside her chair and followed the doctor through the big double doors and down a corridor. The room was marginally warmer and brighter. Makena took up a strikingly small amount of space in the bed. She appeared to be sleeping. Kali moved quietly to a chair for visitors that had been placed along one wall. She put the duffel on the floor, and was about to sit down when Makena spoke.

"I know you're here." Her voice sounded weak. "You don't need to stay."

"I'm here because I want to be. How do you feel?"

"I don't feel anything."

There was silence. Kali thought about Makena's words and wondered if they were true. She didn't know how to respond. She wasn't given to reciting platitudes. The truth was far more important, even though it was almost always more difficult.

"Do you mean you don't feel any pain, or that you don't know what you feel about the miscarriage? That's to be expected. It's only just happened."

"Oh, give me a break. I didn't want the kid anyway." Makena turned her head away and closed her eyes.

Kali didn't know whether or not to believe her, but it was neither the time nor the place to go very deeply into a discussion. "My concern is for you," she said.

"Then go away and let me sleep."

Kali hesitated, then moved toward the door. "Okay. Rest

is a good idea. I'll check with the doctor and find out when I can pick you up." She pointed to the visitor's chair. "I brought some things from home. They're in that small bag over there."

"Home." Makena's voice was faint.

Kali waited, but there was nothing more. "If you think of anything else I can bring you, please just let me know." She turned, and was standing in the doorway when she heard Makena speak, her voice barely audible.

"Tell Hilo I miss him."

"I will. Feel better. I'll see you soon." Kali walked down the corridor and took the elevator to a lower level that led through the hospital's main lobby and the exit doors. In the bright, warm morning, she walked slowly toward her parking space, feeling a sense of loss that she didn't even understand. The image of the stillborn baby in the pineapple field suddenly invaded her thoughts, along with the doctor's reference to the father of Makena's baby. She felt the hair on the back of her neck prickle. She needed to speak to Stitches.

CHAPTER 26

"Kali? Tomas Alva here. Any chance you have time to come over to Lāna'i this afternoon?"

Kali stood in the hospital parking lot and gripped the phone, preparing herself for more bad news. "Don't tell me there's another body," she said apprehensively.

"No," he said. "This is good news, I hope. Out of all the so-called tips that have been coming in since Chief Pait's press conference and Walter's podcast appearance, I think we finally have a good one. A lady here phoned in and said she's willing to talk about her time living at Eden's River. She's offered to meet us out at the site where it used to be. Seems like a good idea for you to be here."

Kali's mood lightened. "I'll be there," she said, trying not to hope too much that there was finally going to be a break. After leaving a message for Stitches and another one letting Walter know where she was heading, she called the main station and was told the launch would be waiting for her as soon as she could get to the harbor.

The drive to the dock was blissfully free of pig carcasses, and she made good time. As promised, the small police launch was waiting for her, and the boat sped smoothly across the channel waters. Tomas was waiting on the other side, parked near the dock on Lāna'i. Kali was surprised to see that instead of his police cruiser, he had come to pick her up in a four-wheel-drive truck. As they drove away from the harbor, Tomas filled her in on what he knew about the former member of Eden's River they were on their way to meet.

"She lived there for two years, after she was initially invited by another woman who had left a brochure on her doorstep."

"What's this woman's name?"

"Originally, it was Anita Chambers, but she changed it—legally—to Anita Waters once she'd bought into Abraham's baloney. Guess she never bothered to change it back."

Tomas explained that Anita's first experience had been to attend a healing seminar offered at the commune. "She said she'd suffered from lower back pain for years, and that after Abraham laid his hands on her during a healing massage session, she was cured."

"Spiritual massage. Really? Nice angle. Has the pain come back?"

"Interestingly, she claims it hasn't. Her disillusionment with Eden's River had more to do with the demands that Abraham was increasingly making on the women members."

"Sex?"

"What else? Apparently he wanted them all pregnant. I guess that's one way to increase membership."

"Sexual demands seem to be one of the calling cards of a cult leader," said Kali. She looked out the window, noting their location and how close they were to the pineapple fields. "Where is it that we're meeting her?"

"Just down the road from here," said Tomas, flipping on his blinker and easing the truck onto a rough track south of the Palawai Basin and the old pineapple plantation. He drove for about a mile along a turnoff that led to Kaunolū, an ancient fishing village that was regarded as an important sacred site. Instead of continuing all the way to the historic landmark, he turned onto an even narrower track that led in a northeasterly direction.

"Guess I know why we're in this truck and not your cruiser," said Kali, holding on to her armrest as the truck jolted along the rutted path.

"Yeah. No grading back here, at least since the last heavy rains. Looks like most of the surface washed out, then dried into these ruts."

The area ahead of them became smoother and greener. The truck slowed, and Tomas eased to a stop beside a stand of trees. There was another vehicle parked there, an older, beaten-up SUV. A woman stood leaning against the driver's door. Kali estimated her to be in her forties. She was tall and angular, and her auburn hair was cut short. Her jeans and cotton shirt, the latter with a row of gleaming buttons, struck Kali as being sensible, and she wondered what it was that she had expected to see—a woman in rose-colored glasses and jumbles of glass beads wearing a tie-dyed T-shirt with some old hippie slogan?

"Aloha," said Tomas. "You're Anita Waters?" The woman nodded, and Tomas indicated Kali. Tomas held up his badge, and Kali lifted hers from where it was suspended at the end of the cord around her neck. "This is my colleague, Detective Kali Māhoe. She's also part of the team looking into Eden's River."

"Eden's Abyss, more like," said the woman dryly. She turned to Kali. "Nice to meet you both."

"Same," said Kali, smiling. She looked around. "So this is where Eden's River was located?"

"Through here," replied Anita, leading the way toward a bend in the path that revealed an opening in the foliage, and a glimpse of a wide meadow on the other side. There was a crumbling post-and-rail wooden fence running up from each side of the field to the gap in the greenery.

Kali and Tomas both halted in astonishment as they reached the opening. There was a taller post on each side where the fence ended at the gap. Old, rusty hinges hung from them. There was no sign of the missing gate, and the post on the left had rotted and broken off near the top. It was the post on the right that had caught their attention—the top of it was decorated with a large, carved wooden pineapple. Its surface was weathered from exposure, but it was all too familiar in its size as well as the detailed carving.

"Well, I'll be," said Tomas.

Anita looked at him in confusion. "What's that?" she said.

"The pineapple," said Kali, pointing to the fence post.

"Oh yes. Pretty, isn't it?" She frowned. "There used to be two. One on each side. I think the other one came off when the post began to rot. I wonder what happened to it."

Kali and Tomas exchanged glances, but refrained from commenting; it didn't stop both of them from picturing the missing pineapple on the shoulders of the lonely skeleton. Not far from the entrance, a barn-like structure could be seen among the trees and thick brush. There were two smaller buildings behind it. Anita gestured toward the structures.

"Well, here we are." She looked more closely at the scene. "It's been years since I came out here. I must say, it all looks a little worse for the wear. Smaller than I remember. There used to be some nice gardens. And things didn't look so shaggy and unkempt."

"When did you leave the commune?" asked Kali.

"End of 1996." She turned to Kali, her face somber. "And I'd characterize it as a cult, not a commune—at least not in the strict sense."

They walked closer to the barn.

"This is where we all spent the majority of our time when we weren't cooking or cleaning or working in the gardens, or doing some other kind of chore," said Anita. She reached into the tall grass and extracted an old clay flower pot. "I enjoyed being outside with the others. There was always singing. Camaraderie, you know? A sense that we were all here for the same reason, and glad to be together, sharing the day." Her face clouded over. "But anything that seems too good to be true usually is, right?"

"Almost always," agreed Kali.

"Is this where all of you lived?" Tomas asked Anita, eyeing the old building.

"No, though I think some of us occasionally slept there. Most of us lived in our own tents or trailers here on the grounds." She gazed up at the barn. "We used this space for meals, and for lectures and seminars. And for services and healing work, of course."

There was a picnic table beneath a stand of trees at the edge of the meadow. Tomas led the way toward it, and they sat down. Anita ran her hand over the scarred surface, slowly tracing the outline of initials that had been carved there. She told them of rising early to plant and weed and harvest before the sun grew too hot, and of looking forward to joining one another in the large kitchen to prepare the day's first meal together.

"Abraham would always be there to lead us in prayer," she said. "While we ate beside one another at a long table, he'd share stories from the Bible and tell us their meaning." She frowned. "I remember that when people tried to ask questions, he would demand silence. But then, later, he would walk among us and talk in more detail about the morning lesson."

The afternoons, explained Anita, tended to be much the same. There was more work and another shared meal, followed by a break of several hours. It was during this time that Abraham would choose certain members who would receive healing work.

"Women?" asked Kali, revealing her suspicion.

"Mostly. But not always," said Anita. Her face brightened momentarily. "We all hoped to be among the day's chosen ones," she said. "But I realized at some point that he had his favorites. He always seemed to favor the youngest girls, though I sometimes wondered how he could tell them apart. They all seemed to be identical—starstruck eyes, long hair, childlike bodies."

Kali felt a shiver.

"Was there ever any violence?" asked Tomas.

"No . . ." she said slowly. "Not violence, but I would say there was definitely abuse. It didn't start out that way, at least from what I can remember. There were couples here, and everyone seemed pretty happy. Gradually, things got . . . well, stricter, I suppose. And couples were discouraged." She smiled wryly. "At some point, Abraham decided that the only person anyone would have sexual relations with was him."

Tomas nodded imperceptibly to Kali, and she looked directly at Anita.

"Do you think you could be specific about the things you saw—and perhaps experienced?" Kali waited. "If you feel comfortable sharing the details with us, of course. And what would be truly helpful would be for you to give us a signed statement about all of this."

Anita looked off into the distance, then focused her gaze on the nearby buildings. "Sure. I can do that, though what good will that do? It's been so long. The first time I came here, I was so excited. I'd received one of the brochures that was being distributed, and it spoke to me—you know, like it touched on things that I already believed in, and it promised that if I was willing to commit myself to the idea of existing peacefully in God's love, that I would have no earthly cares. I could surrender to just *being*, and that would lead to healing on a deep and profound level."

Kali stared at the other woman. "Do you mean physical healing, as from an injury or illness?"

Anita met her eyes. "Yes, but it was more. It went deeper than that. Maybe this will sound strange to you, but Abraham taught that if you have something wrong with your body, it's probably because you have something wrong in your mind or deep in your heart."

Kali nodded. "It doesn't sound strange to me at all. There's a similar concept in Hawaiian healing traditions, and also embedded in the traditions from many other cultures. I think even modern medical science has come to recognize that holding on too long to strong emotions, like stress or anger or grief, can literally make you sick."

Anita looked at her gratefully. "It's true. For me, it was debilitating back pain. I had a session with Abraham the first afternoon when I visited, after he showed me around. He asked me to lie on the floor, where there was a blanket and a cushion already prepared. I remember how warm and strong his hands were when he placed them on my back. He began to ask me about myself, and somehow, in the midst of what was taking place, I told him all about how much anger I felt toward a man who had been a big part of my life, who had chosen another woman instead of me, even after leading me on with the promise of marriage and a family. I started to cry, really hard, and Abraham's hands were pressing gently on my back, and his voice was so soothing—the prayer he said over me seemed so personal. I felt blessed. Truly blessed." Anita's eyes had filled with tears. "I felt as though I had been led to this place by something more powerful than I'd ever experienced before. That I was home. It was as though a powerful current jolted through me from my head to my toes, and the pain was gone."

Kali and Tomas waited for Anita to regain her composure. She looked up suddenly, smiling ruefully. "But I wasn't special at all, as it turned out." She got up from the table and began to walk toward the barn. She paused beside it, pointing to the small house in the rear.

"Abraham lived there," she said. "After I expressed interest in being an official member of Eden's River, I was told that I would have to address him as 'father' from that point on, and that his house was off-limits. There was a gradual shift that began to take place, like my energy was being absorbed into the group. Once, when I asked a question about the day's Bible lesson during our lunch break, Abraham chastised me in front of the others, and one of the senior members of the fellowship took my plate away from me. I was made to sit and watch the others eat, as if I had committed some minor crime. After the meal was over, I was told that to question Abraham was to question God himself, and that my arrogance was a danger to our family."

"And by 'family,' you mean the commune group?" asked Tomas.

"Yes, exactly." Anita went on. "There was a lot that bordered on bizarre, though it took me a few months to realize that. Public spankings, for instance. Abraham would sit on a chair and make the person who was being spanked bend over his knees, like a child. Then his wife, Ruth, would deliver the spanking. Once, when a member was late for a meal because she'd fallen asleep out under a tree, Ruth struck her repeatedly until the member begged her to stop. No one watching, including me, dared to intervene."

Kali recalled Bill Bragden's story about his daughter being the victim of domestic abuse, and felt a wash of anger. She thought about Abigail's passive demeanor, and her obvious deference to her father. The thought rose, unbidden, of Abigail as a child being mistreated and humiliated. With an effort, Kali kept her voice free of inflection. "Did the violence escalate? During the time you lived there, did you observe a marked change in Abraham's approach to running things, or punishing people for challenging him?"

Anita looked uneasy. "He wouldn't have said so, I'm sure. But I believe he truly had himself convinced that we all belonged to him, like property." She looked away, back toward the house. "He said everything he did, all of his decisions, sprang from God's will, and though it might be difficult to understand at times, he had been chosen—just as we had—to fulfill a greater destiny."

Tomas shook his head. "And what was that?"

Anita leaned toward them, her voice intense. "To create a race of devout people who carried his divine seed and would change the world and fill it with love."

Tomas stared at her in disbelief. "You've got to be kidding. So he was going to impregnate every woman who lived here?"

"Oh yes," said Anita, very seriously. "When I understood fully what my part in that was going to be, I left." She shrugged. "Kids have never been part of my plan, even divinely conceived ones. I guess you could say it opened my eyes to what was really going on. The next time I was sent to run errands in the town, I headed straight for a friend's house and never went back."

"Surely there were other men living on the farm," said Kali. "Did they have sex with the female members of the group? It seems like it would have been hard to keep track of who was fathering which child."

Anita shook her head. "No. Only Abraham. His wife was part of it. She kept track of things, as it were. And she would prepare us—a ritual bath, braiding our hair, praying with us before we entered the chamber where Abraham was waiting."

Kali took a deep breath. "And the little girl, Abigail? His daughter?"

Anita hung her head. When she answered, her voice was barely audible.

"Yes. Abigail as well. I think she was about twelve or thirteen at the time. But honestly, I didn't know for sure until right before I left."

Kali felt sick. She walked, half in a daze, through the gate and past the lone pineapple on its peeling post and on toward the truck, leaving Tomas and Anita to discuss the details of her statement. She watched as Tomas thanked Anita, who climbed back into her SUV and drove away.

Tomas opened the door of the truck and climbed inside. He and Kali sat for a few moments in silence, digesting all that they had heard.

"The pineapple is a solid link to Eden's River and the body in the refrigerator," said Kali. "And we have Manuel Raso's identification of the anchor charms connecting them to a bracelet worn by Abigail Waters when she was a child doing her dad's dirty recruitment work at the pineapple farm alongside her mother. That's enough to bring him in, plus some."

"No argument here," said Tomas. He turned to her. "I feel exactly what you're feeling. But keep this in perspective: It doesn't mean he killed anyone. It just means that he's a depraved lunatic. There were other men living here too— plenty of people who knew about the wooden pineapple, and who could walk across the field to the old planation. Some of them may have even worked there for a time while living at Eden's River. And they all knew what was going on with Abraham and the women—and his daughter—so they're all to blame. There was probably a great deal of jealousy. I guess we all know how powerful an emotion that can be."

She felt her anger rising like a well of lava, threatening to spill over. "Sure. I know all that. But he's still a total bastard."

Tomas nodded in agreement. "I'll send a copy of Anita's statement along to you. We're getting close, Kali. I can feel it. Pretty soon there won't be a single monster left anywhere on Lāna'i—not even in the deepest shadows."

CHAPTER 27

Back on Maui, the air was humid. Kali ran the fingers of her right hand along the back of her neck beneath the collar of her light cotton shirt, feeling the dampness of her skin, realizing she should have opted for the air-conditioning rather than the open window next to her desk at the police station.

In her left hand, she held a sheet of paper. It was a printout of a report sent a few minutes earlier by Stitches in response to the question Kali had left for her before she'd gone to meet Tomas and Anita on Lāna'i. Kali stared at the report in disbelief. She read it once more, confused, unable to grasp the details laid out before her in black and white. Sparked by the emergency room physician's question to her about the father of Makena's child, she'd requested a report on the pineapple-field baby in order to satisfy her curiosity about whether the father of Helen's unfortunate child had been Reggie McCartney or Abraham, but the results of the DNA testing were unexpected. The baby carried Abraham's DNA, but not Helen's or Reggie's. In the notes included at the bottom of the report, Stitches had written, *Helen Stafford was not the mother of the infant found beside her in Grave Site*

Three. The DNA taken from the infant's body shows conclu-
sively that both mother and father had a close familial con-
nection. Neither Helen Stafford nor Reggie McCartney was
related at all to the child found with them.

The steady hum of traffic going by on the Hana Highway sifted through the screen of the window, punctuated with an occasional blast of conversation or a honking horn. The station was quiet. Walter and Hara were on their way to bring Abraham in for questioning, and Kali sat at her desk, staring at the paper in her hand, waiting for them to arrive. One of the small anchor charms, encased in its evidence bag, rested on the desk surface beside a half-full coffee mug. Absently, she folded the report and reached for the evidence bag, shoving both into the pocket of her jeans.

The coffee was cold. She stood up and stretched, then wandered toward the table where the photographs and notes surrounding Eden's River and the pineapple-field discoveries were laid out. Her mind was racing. The smiling faces of Helen and Reggie stared back at her from the table's surface. The image of the anchor hung above them, and she peered closely at it, imagining it dangling from a bracelet worn by a child who was too young and innocent and brainwashed to know right from wrong. The now-familiar driver's license photo detailing Matthew Greene's long, stern face filled the photo beside the one of the harvest-gold refrigerator with the skeleton still nestled inside it, crowned by the carved wooden fruit that occupied the space where the skull should have been. Just beneath this image was a picture of Bill Bragden, as well as the smaller photo taken from Manuel Raso's album, displaying the refrigerator in the employee break room at the pineapple plantation.

Hara had already added the photos of Eden's River that she'd taken during the morning excursion with Tomas. Kali ran her finger along the edges of the images in a wide circle, striving to see the connection that would explain why five people had died without anyone knowing why. The answer seemed to be close, but it was still out of her reach.

The sound of Walter's car pulling up outside interrupted her reverie. As she waited for Abraham to be ushered inside, the sound of a second vehicle could be heard, followed by the slamming of a door and a raised male voice, which she recognized as Nathan's. The voice grew louder as Walter opened the door and ushered Abraham inside into the small reception area, where a wall with a counter and a window of bulletproof glass laced with wire separated the space from the interior of the station. The duty officer looked up, taking note of the small parade.

Behind Abraham and Walter, Hara had blocked the doorway, preventing Nathan and an older woman from entering the room. Nathan was still shouting what sounded like Bible verses. There was a look of annoyance on Hara's face, and he turned toward Walter, looking for direction.

"Captain, what would you like me to do?"

"I would like," said Walter, standing next to Abraham, "for you to remind this citizen that this is an official police interview, and unless he would like to spend the next hour in a holding cell, he should wait quietly outside the building in his vehicle."

"You have no authority over my husband," interrupted the woman, scowling menacingly.

"Am I to understand you are Ruth Waters?" asked Kali, stepping past the counter. She had imagined a gentle, passive woman—not the angry, rabid one in front of her.

"Yes, that's my name," Ruth snarled. "My family and I answer to a higher power."

"Well . . . that may be true eventually," said Walter, keeping his cool. He looked directly into Ruth's eyes. "However, in the present moment, you, your husband, and your grandson will all answer to the Maui police authority. Now, I need to hear verbal confirmation from both of you that you will not cause a disturbance while we're interviewing your husband. Have I made myself clear?"

Ruth looked toward Abraham, who gave a brief nod.

"Fine," said Ruth. "My husband has graciously indicated that you may speak with him. We will wait." Her eyes swept from Kali and Walter to Hara. "My grandson and I will pass the time praying for each of you, that you may see the True Light."

Walter's eyebrows rose. Kali could tell from the way his lips moved that he was doing his best not to laugh out loud.

Hara looked at Ruth in disbelief. "Captain, should I . . ."

"Not necessary, Hara," said Walter. "These people will wait outside." Walter turned to the duty officer. "Should either of these individuals attempt to enter the building while I am interviewing Mr. Waters, they are to be placed under arrest for obstructing a police investigation. Feel free to interrupt me in the interview room."

Walter turned away without another look at Ruth or Nathan, and spoke directly to Abraham. "This way, Mr. Waters." He glanced at Kali. She followed them as they came through the barrier into the interior of the station and walked to the interview room. Walter led Abraham inside, directing Hara to get a glass of water for him. Kali stood just outside the door, fingering the tip of the coroner's report in her pocket, and watched as Walter checked the recording equipment. When Hara returned, Walter joined her outside of the interview room, closing the door behind him, leaving Hara to guard over Abraham.

"I'd like you to ask the questions," he said. "I'll jump in when I need to, but I think it will throw him off his game a bit to be questioned by a woman. Hara will be watching though the one-way glass so there's another official observer."

She nodded, then pulled the report from her pocket and thrust it into his hands. "Get a load of this," she said.

Walter read it, frowning. He looked up, his face clearing. He whistled through his teeth, the sound low and full of astonishment. "Damn," he said. "This is unexpected. What's your conclusion?"

"I'm not sure. But I don't want Abraham to know we have this information right now, so let's keep it to ourselves for the moment. Have you already offered him legal representation?"

"Yup." He snorted. "He says there is no legal authority in existence except for his partner in the clouds."

"Just checking all the boxes."

He nodded. "Have to do it. You ready?"

Kali nodded her assent. As they entered the interview room, Hara left to take his place out of Abraham's sight, behind the glass. Abraham looked up and smiled, his sparkling eyes unfathomable. Kali studied his blue shirt and his white linen trousers. She could see one of his sandals sticking out along the side of the table; his tanned foot matched the sun-browned tone of his face and arms. His silvery, coal-streaked hair was tucked behind his ears, curling over the neckline of his shirt. He looked comfortable, completely at ease. She felt sickened by his proximity.

"Nice to see you again, Detective," he said. His voice was caressing.

So that's how you're going to play it, she thought to herself. She was more than familiar with suspects who sought to dominate an interview in exactly this way—by speaking first and giving the impression that they were in control of the conversation. She ignored him, sitting down in one of the two chairs that faced him. Walter sat down beside her. He reached toward the voice recording device on the table, his finger poised on the switch that would activate it.

"We'll be recording our conversation today," said Kali. She signaled Walter, who turned on the recorder. Kali stated the date, time, and the full names and titles of all who were present. She read Abraham his rights again. Her voice was flat, without emotion. When she'd finished, she focused her gaze on him.

"We've heard a lot about your program at Eden's River, Abraham," she said, deliberately choosing not to address him as Mr. Waters. "I'm particularly interested in the relationships you developed with the women members of your cult."

He seemed to understand that her choice to use only his first name was meant to demonstrate a lack of respect. He looked up, head tilted slightly to one side, eyes unblinking.

"Cult? My goodness, such a dark word. Eden's River is a church, inhabited by God-fearing, God-loving individuals who seek to develop respectful, healthy lifestyles that lead to happiness and harmony." He shook his head gently, as though she were a child who had somehow disappointed him. "Shame on you, Detective." He turned his gaze to Walter. "You suggested we would be having a conversation— yet this feels more like an interrogation than it does an interview."

The musical cadence of his voice made the words seem almost like a song.

"Does it?" Kali said. "Let's talk about what's led you here. I understand that you are the surgeon who ruined the career of a young soccer player, destroying any chances for his future with a professional team."

"Stories always have more than one side," he said. "If God has meant for someone to excel at a sport, they will do so, led by Him."

Kali narrowed her gaze. "So you feel comfortable using your God as a scapegoat?"

His smile was enigmatic. "I realized when you came to my home and questioned me that you are a person without any faith."

"We aren't talking about me, Abraham. We're talking about you. Just you. You were quite active in your church in Chicago, and some of the wealthier members of your congregation apparently felt you were a good investment. A lot of money was funneled your way to set up and open your retreat on Lāna'i, and to keep you going for quite a few years. Your members turned over property and financial savings to you. What is it that they received in return—other than personal ruin and the destruction of their marriages and families? Is your God proud of you for all of your hard work building a pedestal for yourself?"

There was a flicker across his brow. "All that I do, all that I have done, all that I shall undertake in the future, is for the glory of God."

"The glory of you, you mean. Accumulation of wealth and real estate, control over other people, adoration from your followers that feeds your distorted sense of self-worth. That's not about any God. That's about Abraham."

"Every worldly possession and every donation received by Eden's River has been used to further our ministry."

"Well, I'll admit to being impressed that you didn't use it to build yourself a mega-church complex, or to buy a fleet of private planes, or a castle, as so many successful evangelists have done before you. At least you've kept it simple in the material goods department. But what about the lives you've taken control of and destroyed? Perhaps you could attach a rough estimate to what they've been worth?"

He looked at her, appearing genuinely sorrowful. "You are blind. Everything you've mentioned has been freely given. Gifts directed by God."

"Have I hurt your feelings, Abraham? I didn't take you for the sensitive type. Tell me about the punishments you meted out, the spankings and humiliation. Did you sleep with all of the female residents of Eden's River, or did you have some kind of age restriction?"

Abraham shrugged, still outwardly composed. "Isn't it considered rude to ask a woman her age?"

Walter shifted in his chair. Kali could feel the heat from his body, as though his temperature were rising in response to Abraham's closeness. She knew that Walter was most likely thinking of his own three daughters.

"Are you saying you are unable to make the distinction between a woman and a child?" she continued, keeping her voice calm. "Or are you saying you are simply unwilling to make that distinction?"

Abraham leaned forward. "I have done nothing wrong. Are you arresting me? If so, please explain the charges. You asked me to come here to tell you about our community, and I have done so."

Kali ignored him. "Clearly, based on numerous witness reports, you were unconcerned with whether or not these women were of age, or whether they were married or in relationships with others."

There was a scrape of metal on the cement floor of the interview room as Abraham sat back in his chair. He regarded her solemnly. "When I was a young medical student, I had a revelation. A vision, you might say. I saw myself saving lives and healing people. I was able to do that through my work as a surgeon, but it wasn't enough. I knew my calling was higher, that my reach needed to be wider. The idea of the Eden's River community was born of the desire to serve my God. I do not expect you to understand that, or to respect it. Nevertheless, it is the truth. I believe that those lost souls who come to me are led by a divine spirit. I do not question their relationship status, or demand the details of their lives prior to our meeting. They share what they choose to share."

"Yet, you urged them to cast all of that away. Entire lives. Families."

"I ask nothing of the sort. Those who do so were and are inspired by something far beyond me. Far beyond you."

"Seems like your wife might have minded a little bit. All those beautiful young women with their lithe, smooth bodies. And there she was, aging in the sunlight right beside you. Is she a jealous woman?"

"She is not. She is a willing and generous servant of the Lord."

"Who likes to spank other women?"

"Discipline is a valuable teacher."

"You were quoted as saying you felt your God working through you when you performed surgery. Based on your performance history and that poor soccer player, it seems as though He may have taken a few days off now and then."

"Miracles cannot be explained," Abraham said. His smile was benign. He said nothing more, but sat looking at her.

Kali reached into her pocket and pulled out the tiny anchor charm. She removed it from the plastic bag and held it up, then pushed it across the table toward him.

"And what about this? Was this a good luck charm you carried in the pocket of your scrubs just in case God wasn't answering the phone?"

Abraham leaned forward, examining the small object. A look of absolute disbelief flooded his face. He looked up at Kali and Walter sharply, then moved his chair closer to the table. He reached forward and lifted the charm from the table.

"Where did you get this?" he asked, his voice losing its smooth cadence. Kali felt Walter shift beside her, and tried to hide her own surprise at the response. Abraham's reaction struck her immediately as genuine. Though his shock at seeing the charm appeared to be sincere, he clearly recognized it.

"Never mind where I got it," she said. She spoke her next words emphatically. "Do you know who it belonged to?"

The expression on Abraham's face had become guarded. His eyelids drooped slightly. He looked down at the charm again, then up at Kali. He had regained his composure.

"This is a common Christian symbol," he said. "As for whom it might have belonged to . . ."

"Perhaps a young girl, wearing a bracelet with tiny anchors dangling from it? Your daughter Abigail, for instance. We have reason to believe this anchor charm belonged to her."

Abraham shrugged, but Kali could see that he was disturbed. "Children's baubles. She had so many. I'm sure I can't say with any certainty."

"Perhaps you could say why this anchor and two others identical to it were found buried with human remains in the pineapple field just beyond the property line of Eden's River?"

His face tightened. Kali had no doubt that he was struggling to parse this information, and that he was troubled by it.

"How interesting," he said. "I suppose I should be grateful that these remains you mention were not found *on* the church property." He grew suddenly restless. "I assume that now I've answered your questions, I am free to leave?"

"Certainly," said Kali. She turned to Walter. "Is there anything you'd like to add or ask before Abraham gets on with his day? He must be very busy with the details of his new property on Maui, and with making sure he develops a sales pitch to attract a new batch of young women to colonize it."

Walter addressed Abraham. "Thank you for your cooperation, Mr. Waters. Please do not leave the island. I feel confident that we'll have more questions for you quite soon." He stood up, and Abraham rose to his feet. Kali remained in her chair, her hands folded in her lap, smiling up at Abraham.

"I look forward to chatting again, Abraham. Until then, enjoy your day."

Walter signaled to Hara at the glass, and he appeared in the doorway to escort Abraham out of the room. Walter and Kali listened as the front door to the station opened and closed. Hara rejoined them, and they sat back down at the table together.

"He was really taken aback to see the anchor charm, wasn't he?" said Hara.

Kali nodded. "Shocked." She looked thoughtful. "I'd like to get Bill Bragden in for more questioning. Let's bring him over here to do it. I'd like to get him away from his house where he'll be less comfortable."

"Will do," said Walter. "We'll bring him over first thing in the morning." He looked at Kali, a question in his eyes. "Why didn't you say anything to him about what's in that autopsy report you showed me?"

"I'm saving that," she said. "It might be more effective to show it to Abigail." She took the paper out of her pocket and handed it to Hara, who scanned it quickly.

Hara looked from one of them to the other. His face grew flushed and he fidgeted slightly.

Walter sighed and shook his head. "What is it, Hara?" he asked.

"I'm just wondering, Captain." Hara looked at Kali. "Detective Māhoe, does all of this implicate Abigail Waters in the killings?"

"I don't know if we can prove that she was physically there, or if maybe she was a small part of some ritual that involved the killings," answered Kali. "She didn't move a refrigerator on her own. But her bracelet was certainly there. And I think we can safely use the term *murder* now. None of this was spur-of-the-moment."

CHAPTER 28

Instead of going directly home, Kali drove to the hospital to pick up Makena. She was preoccupied with processing the things that Abraham had said, and couldn't keep her mind from speculating about all the things he hadn't said. There was little conversation on the drive. By the time she'd parked the Jeep and helped Makena up the steps and inside the house, the light was growing dim. Hilo had rushed out to greet them when she opened the door, and had followed Makena to the sofa. She reached out to scratch his back. He wriggled happily at her touch.

"Let me fix you something for dinner," said Kali, wondering if she had anything in the refrigerator to make up a meal.

"Oh, now you talk to me," said Makena. The testiness had returned to her voice. She leaned against the back of the sofa and glared at Kali. Hilo lay down by Makena's feet, panting.

"Sorry," said Kali. She realized too late that she'd hardly spoken to Makena throughout the drive. "I'm not ignoring you intentionally, it's just . . ."

"That you're trying to solve a crime, and that's more important," said Makena. She pushed herself off the sofa and moved to the table. She pulled out a chair and sat down. "No worries. I'm used to it. Dad was the same way. I know where I fall on the list of what's important and what's not."

Kali bit her lip. She opened the refrigerator and pulled out a bowl of eggs and a small plate that held half a stick of butter. She rummaged around in the crisper drawer that held a few miscellaneous vegetables and removed a half-empty bag of spinach and part of an onion that was wrapped in plastic.

"It's not like that," she said. She tried again. "Why don't you make us a pot of tea, and I'll make omelets?"

"Did you learn to cook?" asked Makena, making no effort to hide her sarcasm.

Kali froze, holding the bag of spinach in one hand, the onion in the other. She looked at Makena, then burst out laughing, unable to help herself. To her surprise, Makena began to laugh as well.

"You're thinking of those brownies, aren't you?" Kali said, recalling a long-ago afternoon when she'd attempted to bake brownies from scratch, using a recipe from a cookbook she'd found on one of Mike's kitchen shelves. The results had been inedible, and Kali had been appalled to see the level of disappointment reflected on the faces of both father and daughter when they'd bitten into the dry, crumbling squares of chocolate.

Makena got up and walked over to the counter where the electric kettle was plugged into a wall socket. "Yeah. That and everything else." She glanced at the food Kali was transferring to the counter. "Is there any cheese?" she asked.

Kali looked back into the fridge. "A little goat's cheese," she answered. "It's got herbs in it. Is that okay?"

Makena nodded. "Yeah, I guess so." She eyed the vegetables in Kali's hands. "But no onion for me. Gives me heartburn."

For the next fifteen minutes, the two women prepared tea and omelets. They worked mostly in silence, but the atmosphere was less charged than it usually was when they were together. Kali accepted that while the moment wasn't exactly companionable, it was at least unmarked by the swearing and angry remarks that usually defined their exchanges. She unplugged her computer and transferred it to the coffee table in front of her sofa, then set the table, realizing that it had been quite some time since she'd put out place mats and set silverware and glasses out to share a meal with another person.

After they had finished eating, they sat across from one another, content. Hilo had relocated to beneath the table, lying stretched between their feet. As Kali leaned forward, ready to get up and remove their plates, Makena spoke.

"I don't remember my mother," she said. There was a moment before she said anything else, as if she were trying to picture her mother in her mind. "Not even a little bit. You know, what her voice sounded like, or if she wore perfume." There was no grief in her voice; it was a simple statement, as though this fact had only just occurred to her.

"I didn't know her," said Kali slowly, unsure whether or not a response was desired. "I wish I had, but she died a long time before I met your dad."

Makena was holding a teaspoon. She looked down at the stainless steel outline, and at her fingers as she rolled the bowl of the spoon against the surface of the table. On impulse, Kali stood up. She glanced at the window, gauging the light.

"Come on," she said. "I want to show you something outside if you feel up to it."

Makena didn't appear especially interested, but she rose from the table all the same. Her slight figure was silhouetted as she moved past the window, and Kali sensed the fragility of her body. She followed Kali across the lanai and down the steps to the lawn, then toward the thicket of trees where Mike's canoe lay shrouded in its *hālau* shelter by the palm fronds that covered the roof of the small structure. They ducked inside the *hālau*, which was open at either end, Hilo darting between them. He sniffed the ground and lost interest, then dashed from beneath the shelter and across the lawn toward the drop-off to the sea. The two women watched him for a moment, then turned their gazes to the canoe.

"This is the canoe your dad was building," said Kali.

She pulled away the large canvas tarp she'd used to cover it, revealing the slender, unfinished wooden boat. Even in its current state, it was beautiful. Makena moved toward it. She reached out and ran her fingers along the edge from the centerline toward the exaggerated stern neck that had been left in place to transport it to its current location. The interior space was only roughly hewn, suggesting the narrow cavity that had been intended.

"He wanted it to be authentic," said Kali. "He said it needed to rest here for several years for the wood to cure properly before he could finish carving out the interior." She didn't bother to say what each of them knew—that his life had ended before he'd had the opportunity to complete his task.

"Why do you keep it?" Makena asked.

Kali pondered the question. How could she explain to this girl that it was a connection—something she could touch? There were good memories attached to the almost-boat. Even in its present form, it still represented possibilities that she just couldn't let go of. Not yet, at least.

"I guess I just like knowing it's here, close by," she finally said. "Maybe someday, I'll try to finish it myself."

"Sure. Whatever," said Makena. She seemed to lose interest and turned away. She whistled for Hilo, and he galloped up, holding a dead fish in his mouth. He dropped it in front of her, his tail wagging so energetically that his whole body swayed from side to side.

"*Ewww*," said Makena, wrinkling her nose at the rank

scent of the fish. She pushed Hilo's head away. "Thanks for the present, but you are *not* sleeping with me tonight," she told the dog.

Kali watched her. Makena looked tired, and she berated herself for not being more sensitive to the ordeal that the younger woman had just endured. She made one more attempt to connect. "You know, I got roped into doing a hula demonstration at the Fire Garden Festival. Maybe you could come?" She shuffled awkwardly. "It would be fun to have you there."

Makena shrugged. "Maybe," she said.

Kali knew not to push the invitation. "Well, it would be nice to have you there." When Makena made no response, Kali pulled the canvas tarp carefully back over the surface of the canoe. "Anyway, I've got some work to catch up on," she said. "Do you mind?"

"Why should I?" said Makena. "I want to lie down anyway. Maybe I'll get up later and watch some TV."

Together, they walked the short distance back to the house. Hilo followed, staying close behind Makena. After they'd gone inside, Makena disappeared into her room and closed the door. Kali waited, but there was no sound. She lifted her bag off the floor by the table and brought it to the wide space in front of the windows near an old blue armchair where a worn rug covered the floorboards. She took out her notebook and the report sent to her by Stitches, and spread them on the rug. She sat on the floor, leaning against the lower part of the armchair and read carefully through her notes. It was too soon to have a transcript from the interview with Abraham, but she thought over all he had said, mulling over his words, wondering what he was hiding about Abigail's bracelet.

There was no sense of falling asleep, but the next thing she knew, she was being jolted awake by Hilo's nose, indicating that it was breakfast time and he was hungry. She sat upright, stretching the cramp from her neck that had resulted from sleeping at an unnatural angle on the living room floor. The sun was fully up, and she heard the trilling of the tiny local *'amakihi* birds through the open kitchen window. She filled Hilo's bowl and placed it on the floor for him. The sound of the birds outside was joined by the rattling of Hilo's bowl as he devoured his meal; she saw him push the empty bowl across the floor as she went into the bathroom to wash her face and untangle her hair.

By the time she'd changed her clothes, cleared the kitchen table, and transferred her notes to its surface, there was a nebulous, half-formed idea floating around in her head. Restless, she started the coffee preparation and placed a couple of slices of raisin bread in the toaster. As the small kitchen filled with the scent of toasting bread and fresh coffee, she glanced at Makena's door, acknowledging to herself that she wouldn't mind some breakfast company. But the door remained closed, and there was no sound or other indication that Makena was even awake.

Kali's text alert sounded, and she glanced at her phone. Walter had left a message that Bill Bragden had been picked up and that Tomas had delivered him to the police launch. An accompanying officer would bring him to the Hana station for questioning. Kali replied that she'd be waiting, then sent a message to Tomas asking him how Bill had responded to being sent over for a further interview. He replied that Bill seemed unhappy and uncomfortable, but hadn't resisted.

She spent the rest of the morning organizing her thoughts. By the time she was ready to leave, there was still no sign of Makena. She left Hilo lying in a patch of sunlight on the floor, then drove to the station. Walter was there, but Hara was nowhere to be seen.

"Is he meeting the boat?" she asked. "I thought someone was driving Bill to us."

"Correct." He grinned. "Hara just took delivery of his own cruiser. He's out testing it right now, happy as a puppy with a new toy. I expect by the time he rolls in, he'll have written at least fifty traffic tickets."

She smiled. "Good for him. He's a nice guy, and he's shaping up to be a good cop. Clear thinker, doesn't get emotional, excellent eye for detail, and looks great in that uniform."

"I hadn't noticed," said Walter, looking at her and shaking his head. "Little young for you, don't you think? You should look closer to home. Like next door, where that blond guy is always out there with his shirt off, making sharp things."

Her mind jumped to Elvar. She looked away, walking toward her desk.

"Touch a nerve?" asked Walter, watching her with interest. "You know, Mike wouldn't have wanted you to just shut down, and he certainly wouldn't have wanted you to get old and creaky all by yourself. He'd have wanted someone to be around to put your food in the blender for you, and make sure you could find the glass with your teeth in it in the morning."

"Who knows what he would have wanted?" she said. She changed the subject. "Do we have a report on Bill Bragden's wife, showing cause of death? I want to make sure there was nothing weird there before we talk to him."

"I got the impression when we spoke with him it might have been suicide. Overdose of sleeping pills, something like that. A depressed, grieving mother unable to cope with the loss of her only kid."

"That's what I thought, too, so I didn't press him. At the time, it didn't seem important. I'd like to know the details, though."

He did a search while Kali looked over his shoulder. It didn't take long to find what he was looking for. He and Kali looked at the screen, then at one another. "Well, there's a conversation starter for you," he said. He hit the print command for the document displayed on his screen. The printer in the corner of the office whirred to life.

Kali rose and crossed to the printer, removing the waiting sheet of paper and folding it neatly in half. "Damn people," she said, glancing at the folded paper. "This is exactly why I prefer the company of dogs."

CHAPTER 29

Bill Bragden sat at the metal table in the interview room in the same chair that Abraham had occupied. Kali couldn't help but compare them to one another. While Abraham had been confident and relaxed right up until the moment when the anchor charm had been introduced to the conversation, Bill looked gray and shriveled and sorrowful.

This time, Walter took the lead. "We've begun recording," he said. "You've been advised of your rights. Let it be noted that William Bragden, aka Bill Bragden, has waived his right to an attorney." He turned to Bill. "Is there anything you'd like to change about the information you shared with us when Detective Māhoe and I interviewed you at your home on Lānaʻi?"

Bill shook his head. "I don't think so. To be honest, I don't know if I can accurately recall everything we spoke about." Kali could hear the high level of stress in his voice.

Walter looked unimpressed. "Is that so? Well, we can start all over from the beginning if you like. Tell us again about your daughter and your son-in-law, and how you came to be living on Lānaʻi."

Hesitantly, Bill recounted his earlier story of arriving in Hawai'i to visit his daughter and her husband, and of how quickly he found himself falling in love with the islands. His voice became thick with emotion as he once again shared the details of his daughter's illness and his suspicions that her husband was abusing her. He ended his story with Matthew's disappearance, then sat very still.

Walter waited a moment, but when Bill said nothing more, Walter leaned forward and tapped his fingers impatiently on the surface of the metal table. "Is that all?" he asked, his voice brisk.

Bill shrugged slightly and turned to Kali, as though imploring her to understand. She stared back at him, unsmiling. She reached across the table, handing him the sheet of paper she'd carried into the room.

"You lied to us about your wife," she said. "You told us she was dead. There is no death certificate, nor is there a divorce decree. In fact, the last public record we have for Linda Bragden shows that she legally changed her name in 1999 from Linda Bragden to Linda Waters."

Bill looked down, his sorrow palpable. "No," he said. "I never told you that Linda was dead. I told you that I'd lost her, which is the absolute, embarrassing truth."

"At the very least, you deliberately misdirected us in the middle of a police investigation," said Walter.

"What could my personal failure as a husband and a father possibly have to do with your investigation?" asked Bill.

Kali watched him carefully, considering his words. "The Hina legend," she said finally. "That's why you told me that you try to greet the moon's arrival each evening. Hina is your wife, stolen from you by Abraham Waters, just as Hina was stolen from the demigod Maui by the fierce eel god Tetuna."

Bill looked at her, his eyes portals into the deep sadness he carried with him. Walter turned to Kali, listening.

"Tetuna kept a horde of fearsome sea monsters as his allies," she said slowly. "To get back his wife, Maui had to go to battle against them, and then conquer Tetuna."

"Yes," said Bill, his voice faint. "Yes, Maui won back his wife, but I did not. And I believe that Abraham Waters was—and still is—a worse monster than Tetuna or any of his cronies. Waters preyed upon my wife in a moment of unbearable grief and darkness, when she was bereft. Linda has always blamed herself for Lily's death, for not finding the right doctor with the right treatment—and also for the mistreatment we both know that Lily suffered at the hands of Matthew Greene. She blames me as well for not giving credence to Abraham's supposed powers, or for not joining his followers in prayer for our daughter." He looked from Kali to Walter, his gaze intense. "If it was Matthew that you found rotting in that field, then perhaps there is a God after all. I only wish that you had found Abraham Waters there, too."

"She went looking for an answer," said Kali. "Something larger and more powerful than her sorrow."

"Yes. She longed for answers and comfort." He looked down again, avoiding their eyes. "For some reason that I still fail to grasp, she found it in that horrible man and his horrible cult with its false promises of healing and redemption, instead of finding her solace with me."

Walter glanced at Kali, waiting for some signal. She nodded.

"Did you kill Matthew Greene?" he asked, his tone even and without prejudice. "Or do you have any knowledge of who Matthew Greene's killer may be?"

Without looking up, Bill shook his head *no*.

"For the record," said Walter, "William Bragden has denied taking the life of his son-in-law, Matthew Greene, or possessing any knowledge of the person who was responsible for ending Matthew Greene's life."

Kali waited until Bill seemed to regain some measure of composure. "When did your wife become involved in Eden's River?" she asked.

Bill looked up. "It was while Lily was still alive, but clearly getting worse. There were some young women who stopped by. They were pleasant and seemed kind. After Linda mentioned Lily's struggle, they told her about Abraham and his healing powers, that he had been blessed by God to help those who were suffering, regardless of how serious their health concerns might be. They told us stories of miraculous things that they'd witnessed Abraham accomplishing." His voice grew bitter. "I told Linda that Waters was a con man, and whatever he was up to was nothing more than a performance designed to astound the vulnerable, and to encourage them to part with money—or more. But she was desperate to save our daughter."

Bill described how Linda had grown angry at his resistance to giving Abraham a chance, while becoming more and more enamored of what she heard about Eden's River.

"But before Linda could take her there, Matthew killed Lily," he said, his bitterness mounting. "I know in my heart that he pushed her down those stairs—that he was weary of being saddled with a sick wife, and that his final act of violence was to take her life."

"But you had no proof, and the medical examiner found no reason to see her fall as anything more than an accident," said Walter.

"So you took things into your own hands," said Kali. "I understand how distraught you must have been. You must have seen his death as retribution—perhaps a fair trade for the life of your daughter."

"No, no, nothing of the kind!" said Bragden, his voice rising in distress. "I didn't kill him, I swear!"

"Where is your wife now, Mr. Bragden?" asked Walter.

Bill put his hands over his eyes, leaning forward. "She's still with him. Living on his new farm, here on Maui."

"Have you been there?"

"No. I begged her to come home when the commune on Lāna'i was shutting down. I thought that by then, she would have come to her senses and realized what a sham the whole thing was—the miracle work, the fake healings, Abraham's using all those women as sex slaves."

Kali listened, wanting to believe him. She wasn't sure why, but admitted to herself that her dislike of Abraham was so strong that she was ready to give the benefit of her doubt to anyone who had been victimized by him. But it wasn't her job to judge. It was her job to find the truth. Once again, she removed the small anchor, encased in the evidence bag, from her pocket. She placed it on the table in front of Bragden.

"Can you identify this object?"

He looked at it, his misery apparent.

"No," he said. "Not this object. The anchor, however, was the symbol of Abraham's church."

She felt Walter shift beside her, and sat back. Walter stood, indicating to Bill that he should stand as well.

"William Bragden, I am placing you under arrest for obstructing a murder investigation and for providing false information to the police," said Walter. "You are also a suspect in the death of Matthew Greene. Please come with me."

"I think we should bring Abigail and Ruth Waters in next, along with Linda Bragden," said Walter.

Kali frowned. "I don't know about Abigail," she said. "She was a kid when all this went down, and even if she saw or heard anything, her memories are likely to be unreliable."

"Bet she'd remember if she was raped by her own father," said Walter. There was a look of profound disgust on his face.

"Would she? I mean, would she even regard it as rape? She grew up in a distorted reality, where Abraham's authority was an extension of their religious doctrine."

Hara walked into the room. Kali would have sworn that he was swaggering slightly, his happiness about the new police cruiser distinguishable in his body language. He stiffened as he caught the drift of their discussion, and regarded them with curiosity.

"Did I just hear that we have the cult guy in custody?" he asked.

"No, just a suspect," said Walter. "Bill Bragden. I locked him up to see if we can shake him up a bit."

"You know," said Hara, "not everyone who grows up surrounded by fundamentalist views turns out to be brainwashed, or unable to tell right from wrong."

Walter nodded slowly. "No, of course not. But we have a unique situation here. We know from witness accounts that Abraham used his daughter as a kind of recruitment officer, bringing people from the pineapple plantation into his flock."

"But that doesn't mean she knew that what she was doing was wrong," insisted Hara.

Kali listened to the exchange, surprised that Hara was standing up a little bit to Walter and offering an opinion. She wondered if being given his own car had affected a personality shift, imbuing the younger man with a new sense of personal power. She almost smiled.

"Hara's right," she said to Walter. "I think the amount someone can be brainwashed into buying a belief system depends entirely upon the individual. At this point, I don't think we should assume anything. I'd rather go easy with her right now, and focus on the older women, Ruth and Linda. One of them at least—and probably both of them— know something about Matthew Greene. If I had to bet, I'd say they also have information about the other bodies. And we still have no idea who the pineapple man is."

"Do you think," began Walter, speaking slowly, "that maybe Bill Bragden thought that if he killed Matthew Greene, Linda would be satisfied and would stay with him? What reason would Waters have for killing him?"

"The same reason, I'd guess," she answered. "Or possibly, Greene challenged Waters in some way. Two alpha males in competition." She briefly considered the facts, then made a decision. "I'm going to talk to Abigail again. Maybe I can get her to tell me about Helen and Reggie joining the cult. From what we've learned about her role at the plantation, Abigail was most likely the point of contact. Let me do that before we bring in Mrs. Waters and Mrs. Waters."

Walter tilted his head in agreement. "Tell her you're going to record what she says, though. We may need it."

CHAPTER 30

Kali drove home, intending to have a quick bite and check in on Makena before she headed back to Eden's River to speak with Abigail. A few enormous raindrops spattered on the windshield of the Jeep, splashing the dust that had gathered on the glass surface. Hilo was waiting on the front of the lanai, whining, when she pulled into her parking space beneath the trees. Instead of running down the front steps to greet her, he remained standing by the front door, his tail lowered into the half-mast position that was always a sign that he was unhappy.

"What's wrong, boy?" she asked, rubbing his ears. The sky had clouded over, and there was the rumble of distant thunder. She opened the door and went inside, wondering if the approaching storm was causing Hilo to be uneasy. The house was silent. Makena's door stood open, and Kali walked toward it, noticing that the bed appeared to be stripped. She stood in the threshold and looked inside. The sheets and light bedcover had been neatly folded. The pillowcase was on top, and the bare pillow had been placed just behind the stack of bedding. In front, leaning against the soft stack, was the little horse, and a dress she'd found that was too small for her, which she had left in the closet for Makena.

She walked slowly into the room, followed by Hilo, engulfed by a sinking feeling. There was a piece of paper on the top of the bedding. She lifted it, carrying it to a spot in front of the window where she could study it in the light.

The note was brief, written in Makena's childish scrawl: *I washed all the sheets and blankets. Here's your dress. I didn't want you to think I was stealing it. Take care of Hilo.* Nothing else. No indication of where she was headed, or how she'd get there. Kali reread the note, gazing out the window at the distant sea. She dropped the piece of paper onto the bed and picked up the small stuffed horse, turning it over in her hands, the softness offering no comfort. She placed it back in its spot near the pillow. Then, hating herself for doing it, she walked through the small house, looking for what might be missing—any small item that Makena might have carried away to sell or use to barter for drugs.

Everything was where she'd left it, including the few pieces of valuable jewelry she possessed. There was a pair of gold earrings with tiny sapphires that Mike had given her for a birthday one year, her good wristwatch, and her grandmother's wedding band. The ring was too small, and she'd always planned to take it to a jeweler to have it altered to fit her finger, but had just never gotten around to it. She turned it over in her hand, slipping it onto the tip of her finger, then placed it back into the ceramic bowl that served as her jewelry box.

Her phone buzzed, and she pulled it from her back pocket. She didn't recognize the number, but when she pushed the button to accept the call, the soft, now-familiar voice of Abigail Waters came through the speaker.

"Detective Māhoe? This is Abigail Waters. I wonder if I might meet you somewhere to talk?"

Kali tried to hide her astonishment. "Yes, of course. I was going to get in touch with you anyway. Can you come to the police station?"

She could sense the hesitation. "Could we meet somewhere less . . . official?" asked Abigail. "I'd like to talk, but I think I'd be uncomfortable there, and it would be best if my father didn't know."

"All right," said Kali, cautious. "But I'll choose the place, if you don't mind. There's a shave-ice stand on the road between where you are and where I am, with picnic tables set up around the food truck. How about there?"

"I know the one you're talking about. Near the turnoff to the market center?"

"That's the one," said Kali.

"Could you meet me there in about an hour?"

Kali glanced at her watch, agreeing on the time. She ended the call, wondering what it was that Abigail wanted to tell her that she felt unsafe saying in front of her father. She left a message for Walter, then took a banana from a bunch on the kitchen counter, and grabbed a light jacket.

By the time she'd driven within sight of the shave-ice stand, the sky had grown dark, and the rain was falling steadily. The heavy drumbeat of drops striking the Jeep's canvas rooftop was oddly lulling, and she pulled into the parking area of the stand hoping against hope that Abigail might actually tell her something useful that would lead to the discovery of who had left five people in unmarked graves in the old fruit field—even if the people responsible had been her parents.

She peered past the windshield wipers and eased across the dirt parking area, which had devolved into a borderless pool of mud. The stand was shuttered and closed, and the only other vehicle visible was an old pickup truck parked at an angle in the rear of the stand near a line of picnic tables. The truck had been backed into its parking spot, the bed partially extending beneath the overhang of trees that grew along the edge of the space behind it. The headlights were on, shining outward.

Kali backed in beside it and set the parking break. It was impossible to see into the truck's cab, so she waited, not completely sure that this was Abigail's vehicle. When it was clear there was no reaction to her arrival from anyone in the truck, she grabbed her jacket and opened the door of the Jeep, then climbed out and pulled the hood over her hair.

The driver's door of the truck opened slightly, and Abigail leaned out. She was alone. "I wasn't sure what you would be driving," she said. "Do you want to sit in here with me?"

The rain was growing more intense. Kali shook her head, pointing to the Jeep. "In here," she said. "The passenger door's unlocked."

She turned around, walking behind the Jeep toward her door on the driver's side, picking her way across the slick footing. She was looking down, reaching for the handle of the driver's door, when there was a sudden movement from beneath the trees. Kali was aware of a figure rushing out toward her. She spun to defend herself, slipping in the mud as the figure raised an arm. She was vaguely aware that it was a man, and that he was holding something. As her mind made this connection, he brought the object down with force, striking her on the side of her head.

Kali felt herself fall, and fall again, walled in by blackness and silence. She rolled, aware that there was no sense of the usual, nebulous boundaries of space and time. The silence was complete—there was no sound at all, not even the beating of her own heart. There was nothing but the dark, opening into a vast and shapeless void, wrapping around her. She moved into it, grateful to be free.

Walter paced back and forth across the station room. He glanced at the wall clock, and then back down at his phone screen, his trepidation growing steadily. Hara watched him, his own alarm evident.

"It's been four hours since I got this message, and she's still not answering," said Walter. "Text, phone, nothing. I'm going to call her neighbor, that knife guy, and see if he noticed her leaving and what direction she went in."

"Her message didn't say where she was going to meet Abigail Waters?" asked Hara.

"Just that she'd see her in about an hour. So she didn't drive all the way out to the farm or commune or church or whatever the hell that Eden's River place is. That would've taken longer." He turned to Hara. "What's that guy's name? The Icelandic guy that lives next door to her?"

"Elvar Ellinsson. There was an article in the newspaper about him."

"Yeah, I saw that. Can you find his number?"

"Got it," said Hara, typing rapidly on his keyboard. He read out the digits and Walter made the call.

Elvar answered on the fourth ring, and Walter let out his breath, running his hand across his brow. He had begun to ask Elvar to go next door, but Elvar interrupted him.

"I was just on my way there," he said. "Hilo's outside, barking like crazy. He's all worked up about something. I'm heading over to make sure everything's okay."

Walter felt his heart begin to pound. He gave Elvar instructions to call him back as soon as he got to Kali's. Less than a minute later, Elvar phoned, out of breath.

"She's not here, and the Jeep is gone." He hesitated, his tone unsure. "The thing is, there's a screen knocked out of a window in the living room where Hilo got out. She must have left it open, even though it's raining. And her front door is unlocked."

That news troubled Walter. It meant that wherever she'd gone, she'd done so in a hurry, and hadn't planned to be away this long. "You have no idea which way she may have gone?"

"I didn't see her," said Elvar. "With all the rain pounding on our roof, I didn't hear her Jeep start up or see the lights. What can I do to help?"

"We've got limited manpower available right now. Do you have a car handy?"

"Sure. I can borrow Birta's Volkswagen. Where should I go?"

Walter thought it over. "Keep your phone at the ready, and head south from your driveway. Keep your eyes peeled for the Jeep parked anywhere along that stretch for about a forty-minute drive. I'm heading out with Officer Hara. If you spot the Jeep, pull over and call. I'll do the same."

He hung up and radioed the main station, requesting that helicopter backup be readied in case a wider search proved necessary, cursing the remoteness of the Hana station and the lack of available assistance at short notice. "Tell them to make sure there's a medic onboard," he said, his apprehension steadily increasing.

Hara drove while Walter scanned the sides of the road. Neither of them said what each of them was thinking—they needed to find Kali as quickly as they possibly could.

His tall frame crammed into the driver's space of his sister's small car, Elvar drove along the Hana Highway, looking left and right in hope of spotting the Jeep. The road was fairly empty, as were the occasional shops and businesses he passed. He was growing discouraged when he spotted the Jeep pulling onto the road from the shave-ice stand. He instantly recognized it as Kali's vehicle. There was a truck following it closely.

Elvar pulled off the road into the parking area and rolled down his window, knowing that Kali would recognize

Birta's car and stop. Instead, the Jeep crept toward the main road, bucking slightly as though the person driving it was unfamiliar with driving a standard transmission or how to operate a clutch without stalling. As it drew abreast of his car, he saw an unfamiliar woman at the wheel. She was young, and looking intently at the road, ignoring him. She made her way onto the main road, and the truck pulled out behind her. Another young woman was driving, and she paid no attention to the Volkswagen.

Elvar didn't recognize either driver. He watched as the taillights of the truck pulled away behind the Jeep. He dialed Walter, who answered immediately, and explained where he was and what he had just seen.

"Follow them," said Walter, "but try not to let them know you're behind them. Anytime they turn off somewhere, let me know right away. We're headed your way, and the police helicopter's in the air and closing in on this area."

"What's going on?" Elvar asked.

"Kali's likely in trouble," said Walter. "That's all I can say for sure."

"You mean she's in danger," said Elvar.

Walter hesitated. "Yeah. We think she's in danger. And you could be, too, if the people you just described realize that you're tailing them. Be careful. Don't approach them. Just stay in touch. We need to know where they're taking the Jeep."

Elvar hung up and sped along the highway until he caught sight of the taillights ahead. It was still raining, though not as hard, and the drivers of the Jeep and the truck were being cautious on the slick road. He slowed down, keeping the truck just within his line of sight. In another fifteen minutes, the two vehicles made an exit from the main road, turning onto a side road to the right. The track was thick with mud, and the Volkswagen fought its way over potholes that had become obscured by standing water.

He followed slowly as they made several more turns, eventually making their way onto a dirt track leading to the wooden gates of Eden's River. Elvar turned off his headlights and eased to a stop, watching from the distance of the road outside of the gates as the Jeep and truck parked near a large barn. There was the sound of the truck door slamming, and the two drivers disappeared into the dark barn. A few minutes later, he saw lights switch on in the windows of two upper rooms. The figure of a woman was silhouetted against the glass of one.

There were at least two other buildings that he could make out. He called Walter back, describing what he could see.

"Stay put until we get there," said Walter. "We're not too far out, but I don't want to keep the siren on when we get close."

"She might be in one of these two buildings," said Elvar. "I don't think she's in the barn. I can see one of the women moving around in front of the window in one of the rooms where the hayloft should be." Elvar stared at the window, watching for any sign that there might be other people present. "It looks like she's brushing her hair."

He got out of the car, making his way carefully across the unfamiliar footing and through the gates. He followed the path that led to Abraham's house, but it appeared to be dark. Lights could just be made out in the smaller house farther along the pathway, so he crept along as quietly as he could. The diminishing rain still spattered against his face, and a restless wind moved the tree branches overhead and along the edge of the path, spreading the drops of water collected among the leaves.

He tripped when he reached the board over the stream, catching himself just before he fell into the water. The light he'd seen was emanating from low windows along the ground level at the base of the house. He crawled forward, using the shrubs for cover, and stared inside. There was a group of people standing together near a tall lamp. As one of them stepped away, he caught his breath. He could see Kali, tied to a chair.

Elvar drew back from the window. He retraced his steps along the path and across the stream back to the car, fumbling for his keys and phone. He dialed Walter's number, then opened the trunk, groping for anything he might be able to use as a weapon, berating himself for not having one of his own knives with him. His hand closed around the tire iron, and he pulled it out.

"Where are you?" asked Walter, betraying his fear.

Elvar described his location.

"That's Eden's River," said Walter, speaking to Hara.

"She's inside a kind of basement in the house to the rear off the main path," continued Elvar. "She's tied to a chair. There's blood all over her face."

"Don't do anything, Elvar. Leave it to the police. Stay by the car. The chopper should be there soon, and we're on our way. Is there a clearing?"

"Yes, a wide open garden space in front of the barn," Elvar said, already racing back up the path toward the house. Walter said something else, but Elvar had already shoved the phone deep into his pocket, freeing up the use of his hands.

CHAPTER 31

Kali made a mighty effort to open her eyes. For a moment, she was unable to distinguish between up and down. There was a swimmy, fluid sensation, and she instinctively tried to reach out to steady herself, to grab on to a surface with enough force to keep the world from whirling off its poles and off into infinity. She couldn't move her arms. It took her a second to realize that she was seated upright in a stiff chair with her arms tied tightly behind her back, and that the reason she couldn't see clearly was largely due to one eye having swelled almost shut. She lurched slightly, the sense of vertigo seizing her stomach, causing her to retch.

"I'm sorry that my son hit you so hard," said a woman's voice. To Kali's ears, the tone didn't sound nearly as apologetic as it should. She tried to turn her head to see who was speaking, but the room was in shadows, and moving only increased her sense of falling.

"My father says we need to help you, you see," continued the voice. "He says that your soul is in mortal danger, and that it is our responsibility to save you from damnation."

It was Abigail Waters. Kali made the recognition just as

the woman came into focus, stepping out from a corner of the room to her left and switching on a tall lamp.

"I know it's difficult for you to understand," Abigail said, her voice both soft and urgent, "because no one ever taught you any better, but you'll be grateful to us someday. When you see the gates of Heaven open to let you in, you'll understand."

Kali didn't try to speak. Behind her another light, brighter than the lamp, switched on. Then came a low cough as someone cleared his throat, and a man moved into view, joining Abigail. He slipped his arm protectively around her shoulders, regarding Kali gravely. Even in her compromised state, Kali noticed that Abigail seemed to stiffen at her father's touch.

"Hello again, Detective." Abraham smiled. Kali's gaze wavered and then settled on his face. She noticed for the first time the length of his front teeth, the sharply pointed canines revealed as his lips drew outward into a thin smile.

There was another male voice, and she tried to move her head to see who was speaking.

"Hello, Miss Māhoe. You remember me?"

It was Nathan. *Yes, I remember you*, she thought to herself. *You're the scary one.*

Nathan nodded at her, the movement brief. "I apologize for tying you up. You're probably finding all of this difficult to comprehend, and you probably don't feel much like speaking."

She didn't. The room smelled sour and dusty, as though it had been sealed up for too long without an open window to dispel the odors that had been trapped inside years ago. The side of her head throbbed, and her hands were numb. She flexed her arms, willing the blood to flow toward her fingertips, and was rewarded with the intense, prickling pain of renewed circulation.

Nathan moved closer to her chair. He pushed up the short

sleeve of her T-shirt to expose the warrior band tattoo on her upper arm. He reached out with one finger, tracing the outline of it, the movement gentle. Then he frowned and pulled away, staring her in the eye.

"*Or do you not know that your body is a temple of the Holy Spirit who is in you, whom you have from God, and that you are not your own? For you have been bought with a price: Therefore glorify God in your body*." He shook his head. "That's from 1 Corinthians. It means that this mark on your body is an abomination. It is witchcraft, and it will not please God." His gaze was intense. "Have you any others?"

Kali said nothing. She tried to keep her eyes locked on his, to not glance involuntarily toward her hip, where her other treasured tattoo could be found—the one she and Mike had chosen together years before. As she focused on Nathan, her eye caught the glint of metal from beside him. There was a small, rolling cart next to where he stood. It had several shelves, and on the top was a tray of what she assumed to be surgical tools and knives. Next to them were bottles of hydrogen peroxide and rubbing alcohol, and a stack of cotton bandages and pads.

She took a deep breath.

"My goodness." Her voice sounded weak. She looked from Abigail to Nathan. "Don't you mind that your grandfather has you doing his dirty work for him?" She focused on Abigail. "It's just like when you were a child helping at the pineapple plantation, convincing the people you met that your father was some kind of miracle worker instead of the con man and rapist that he really is."

Nathan stepped forward, arm raised. Kali held her breath as he hit her, the force nearly knocking the chair over.

"You will speak no word against my grandfather," Nathan said, eerily calm. "Do you understand? I won't have it. Everything we do is God's work. We are merely His servants."

Abraham stood silent. Kali felt powerless, and was filled with silent fury. She ran the tip of her tongue over her lip. The slap had split the skin, and she could taste the warmth of her own blood. She forced herself to look at the tray of knives resting on the surface of the stainless steel. A chill ran through her, and another wave of nausea roiled through her stomach.

Abraham ignored her and spoke to Nathan. "She will not be able to hear God until the marks of the devil are gone." Abraham came to stand beside Kali. He studied her tattoo, then spoke to Nathan as though instructing a group of young surgeons on procedure. "The fortunate thing about tattoos is that they are confined to the surface of the body, not like evil thoughts embedded in the mind. These marks of the devil can be removed, but the true work is not removing these offending symbols—it is to make certain that the mind has been purified as well."

Something clicked when Kali heard his proclamation. "The man in the refrigerator," she said. "You couldn't cleanse his mind, could you, Abraham? You couldn't force him to think like you."

Abraham turned to her, his face grave.

"That's it, isn't it?" she said. "It's why you cut off his head. You thought his thoughts were impure, and you couldn't decontaminate his mind. What was it that he was thinking about, Abraham?"

Abigail made a small, choking sound. Kali kept her focus on Abraham, but from the corner of her eye she could see that Abigail was becoming agitated. Abraham noticed it as well. He reached out his hand and rested it on his daughter's arm. Kali saw her cringe—the response was involuntary and subtle, but it was there nonetheless.

"I offered him the key to the doors to Heaven," said Abraham. "But his mind had been given over to evil and lust. He desired another man, you see. He was gormless and uneducated. What I did was for the benefit of his eternal soul."

"But he was my friend," said Abigail, her voice barely a whisper.

The tension in the room grew stronger. "He was your friend," repeated Kali, "and you couldn't bear to see what happened to him, to see what your father had done to desecrate his body. So you put the pineapple on his shoulders, and you left him with a charm from your bracelet. You meant it to protect him, didn't you?"

There was a look of terror on Abigail's face. Abraham paused, regarding her with disappointment. He sighed. "Did you leave a charm with everyone, Abigail?"

"I gave him the anchor after we became friends. He carried it in his pocket. I sewed it closed for him so he would never lose it." There was a note of hesitation in Abigail's voice now, elusive and guarded. "I was only trying to help, Father. I was only trying to lead him along the path to God."

Abraham listened. He nodded his head. "And the others?"

She hung her head, ashamed. "It seemed like a small thing to do to help their souls on their journey to judgment."

Kali spoke into the silence that followed, revolted by all that she had heard. "Do you know about the legends of monsters on Lāna'i, Abraham?" said Kali, in an effort to distract him from his tray of knives. "The old stories say that evil was banished from the island, but that's your true power—you brought all that evil back." She took a deep breath as a new wave of dizziness swept over her. "And now you've brought it here, to Maui."

There was the sound of a door opening and closing, and Ruth Waters stepped into the pool of light near Abraham, accompanied by another woman. They were dressed similarly to Abigail, their blue skirts brushing the floor. Ruth's hair was pulled back into a knot, but the other woman's hair flowed freely across her shoulders, snowy white and still thick despite her age.

"You're Linda Bragden," said Kali, her breath labored. "You were on the ferryboat."

The woman looked at her. "Linda *Waters*," she said, correcting Kali. "Yes. I saw that mark on your arm." She smiled at Abraham.

"What are you doing here with these people?" asked Kali, attempting to appeal to the woman's reason, if she still possessed any. "Is it because of your daughter? You couldn't save her, so you felt a need to punish yourself? Or did Abraham help you punish Matthew Greene instead?"

Linda looked directly at her, but Kali couldn't read her expression. The woman seemed to have blocked out her words. She said nothing, only took Ruth's hand and moved closer to her. Ruth's presence seemed to comfort her.

"I'm so glad we got here in time to witness this salvation," said Ruth. Her voice still carried some of the snarl that had been present when she'd shouted at the police station. She gazed at Abraham with adoration. "Truly we are blessed."

"Did you move the vehicle?" asked Abraham.

"We sent two of the girls to bring it here. They should be back any moment now."

Kali looked around the room. There was a row of three narrow windows close to the ceiling. The walls were covered in cheap wood paneling, and she had the impression that the space she was in had been built partially underground. One end of the room held a wooden platform and what appeared to be an altar in front of it. Folding chairs had been stacked along one wall. There was something scraping the glass of one of the windows, as though shrubs were growing close enough for the branches to reach it. She thought about the buildings she'd seen on her visit to Abraham's Maui address. Basements weren't typical in Hawai'i, and she tried to picture which building she was being held in, deciding that she must be on the lower level of either Abraham's house or Abigail's.

Then she realized it didn't matter. There was little chance of reaching the windows, or making her way to the door. She tensed her arm and leg muscles and released them, doing her best to wake them up fully. Abraham didn't seem to notice. Stepping toward the steel cart, he chose a pair of surgical gloves and slipped them on, then lifted a small knife with a thin blade. Kali felt her heart race as she watched him examine the edge of the blade.

"Killing me isn't going to help your cause, Abraham." Her voice sounded shaky, even to her own ears.

He turned to her, eyebrows raised. "Kill you? I'm not going to kill you. I'm going to remove your tattoo and give you the opportunity to repent, to choose the path of righteousness." He lifted the bottle of alcohol and a cotton pad, and walked to her chair. He gestured to Nathan, who stood beside her. Nathan held up her sleeve as Abraham poured alcohol onto the pad and began to rub her arm where her tattoo snaked across the flesh of her deltoid.

"What's the point of sterilizing my skin? If you cut away that much skin, I'll bleed to death and you know it. You may not be a good surgeon, but I'll bet you learned at least that much in medical school."

He smiled at her. *He looks like a crocodile prepared to devour something small and meaningless*, she thought.

"If you bleed to death, it is nothing to do with me," he said. "It is simply God's will. I suggest you begin to pray and to ask for His forgiveness."

"That's the same excuse every religious fanatic uses to explain their choice to commit evil," said Kali. She knew she should be quiet, but she couldn't help herself. Whatever they were planning to do to her was likely to end badly on her side, and she felt an urgency to let Abraham and Ruth and Abigail know that she was aware of what they had done. She struggled to recall the facts she'd learned while discussing cults with Hara. "Let's see—off the top of my head, the history books have Theodore Rinaldo in Washington State, arrested for rape of a minor; religious leaders William Kamm, Warren Jeffs, and Wayne Bent, who all raped children—Bent through the auspices of his Lord Our Righteousness Church; Graham Capil, who headed up the Christian Heritage Party, and who went down for sexually abusing little girls who hadn't even reached their twelfth birthdays; plus . . ."

Nathan stepped forward. He was no longer calm. His eyes blazed with wrath. "Enough!" he shouted. He raised his hand to strike her again. She braced herself, feeling the skin of her lip split wider as his hand met her cheek, the force of the blow making her swoon. The taste of salty blood filled her mouth again, and she spat on the floor.

"And then, of course," she said, blocking out the pain, enunciating each word clearly as she spoke directly to Nathan, "there's your mother, who was raped by her own father when she was thirteen." She turned toward Abraham." Isn't that right, Abraham? Or maybe you've already told your grandson the truth?"

Abigail's eyes met Kali's, then darted away. She twisted her hands anxiously. Beside her, Nathan smiled. Kali looked at the two of them, standing side by side, and suddenly knew the truth. The stocky, broad-shouldered man with the round, freckled face and dark, curling hair reaching toward his short neck. The tall, narrow woman with the pronounced forehead and the blue eyes. The photos of Helen Stafford and Reggie McCartney flashed before her eyes, and she felt the missing pieces fall into place like bits of broken glass drawn back into shape by some invisible, magnetic force.

"You don't look much like your mother, do you, Nathan?" she said.

Abigail looked up sharply.

Kali met her eyes. "This is not your son," she said. "Your child died at birth. You stole this boy and his life, and you left your dead infant lying next to another woman in an old field of fruit. What will your God have to say about that, I wonder?"

"Do you know the meaning of the name 'Nathan'?" asked Abraham. His voice was unnervingly calm. "It means 'gift from God,' and that is exactly what he was to us and our family. When Abigail's child was born without the breath of life, Ruth and I knew at once that Helen's child was meant to be hers. It was so clear."

"Helen was disobedient and willful," said Ruth. "She slept with her friend and became pregnant when she knew her duty was to carry Abraham's child."

Abraham waved his hand in the air, the knife flashing against the light. "Enough of this," he said. "Let us begin."

"Hallelujah!" said Nathan. He looked at Abraham, ecstatic. "You've saved so many souls from damnation, Grandfather. Today I will do my part to share God's love!"

Nathan began to sing. Kali knew it was a hymn, though she didn't recognize the words. His voice rose and fell, and Ruth and Linda joined in. As they bowed their heads, Kali could see that their eyes were closed. The singing was beautiful and trancelike, and she had to shake herself from falling under its spell.

Abraham signaled to Nathan, who stepped forward and grasped her arm firmly just above her elbow. Abigail backed away, against the wall. Kali tried to keep the desperation from her voice. She took another breath and spoke again.

"Nathan! In my pocket! The official report, the autopsy report that proves you are not Abigail's son!"

He didn't seem to hear her. She felt the deep, piercing cut of the knife slice into her flesh, striking the bone of her upper arm. The room spun around her. She heard herself scream as the blood poured down her arm. There was a roar like the walls collapsing as she threw herself backward with all her might, and her chair tipped over, slamming to the hard floor. She was dimly aware of a door crashing open and a man's voice shouting in words she didn't understand. The cart with the surgical equipment hurtled through the air, the clash of knives and the metal shelves loudly ringing as they struck the wall. The prayerful singing reached a wailing pitch. Then came more screaming. Only it wasn't hers. One man's voice thundered above the others, and she imagined that she recognized it. Then the light was extinguished, and she remembered thinking how odd it was that her last thought on earth would be a blurred vision of Elvar's face.

"Stay still."

Then she heard Elvar's voice, but it made no sense. *I'm hallucinating again*, she told herself. She dreamed she was being lifted into the air as the outline of everything receded and the edges dissolved into black.

CHAPTER 32

Kali cautiously fingered the edges of the wound where the sutures had grown stiff with dried blood, wincing as a tidal surge of pain washed through her arm and up her neck, landing with a spectacular burst in her head. From the angle of sunlight illuminating a stretch of the scratched floorboards, she concluded that it was early afternoon, and that she'd successfully slept away most of the day.

"About time you rejoined us," said Walter. He leaned back in the old armchair in the corner of her living room, his hands dangling off the ends of the armrests. He'd pulled the coffee table close, resting his feet on its surface.

"Get your feet off my table," she said.

He snorted. "Don't give me housekeeping lectures." He swung his feet to the floor. "This chair I'm sitting in has enough dog hair on it to build a whole new dog. Nina's going to make me sleep in the garage when she sees the back of my shirt."

"I'm constantly surprised she doesn't make you sleep there every night," said Kali. She winced as she pushed herself into an upright position on the sofa, looking around. "Why am I out here and not in bed?"

"That's as far as your boyfriend wanted to carry you. He said this is where you sleep most of the time anyway." Walter looked at her inquisitively. "Is that true?"

She shrugged. "It's closer to the coffeepot. And he's not my boyfriend."

Walter observed her carefully, noting the bruises on her face, the black eye, the sutures on one arm, the rooster scratches on the other. "You're a real mess," he said. "I think you may be carrying the whole battle-scar-collection mission a little too far. At least lay off the roosters. And put some fresh ice on those bruises."

She stood up, feeling shaky. "What are you doing here anyway? I don't need a babysitter." She looked around. "And where's Hilo?"

Walter regarded her, a half smile on his face. "You were pretty out of it after the painkillers. The medics and the emergency room team sewed you back together. Hilo's with your neighbors. The sister stopped by a little while ago and left you a big salad and some banana bread. Oh, and some fish stew, which was excellent."

"You ate it?"

"Didn't know when you'd wake up. Fish stew doesn't keep forever, you know." He patted his stomach. "Besides, keeping you safe is hard work."

"So fill me in," she said. "But first let me get a slice of that banana bread." He rose to get it for her, but she shook her head, gesturing for him to stay put. She walked slowly to the kitchen counter, her body aching, and made a pot of coffee while Walter gave her the details that had been gathered during the arrest of Abraham Waters and his family. She poured a mug for each of them, and Walter came to carry the coffee and plates holding the bread back into the living room.

"Do we finally have a name for the pineapple man?" she

asked, as she settled back down onto the sofa and Walter made himself comfortable in the armchair.

"We do. Joey Manu. He was only eighteen years old when Abraham murdered him. His parents are still alive, and are very happy to know that their son has finally been found." He took a bite of bread. "According to Abigail, and a follow-up call Hara made with Manuel Raso, she and Joey became friends pretty quickly when they met at the plantation. She was still pretty young, being dragged around by Ruth. Joey and Abigail eventually planted a giant sunflower garden together near the office building at the plantation where'd they play, and everyone used to tease them about being sweethearts. Joey was four years older, though—plus he was gay. Abigail didn't care. They were best friends, and they stayed friends even after the plantation shut down. When Joey found out that Abigail was pregnant, and then witnessed some of the interchanges between her and her father, he suspected who the father of the child was and urged her to tell the authorities."

Walter went on to say that when Abigail refused, Joey became increasingly concerned, saying he was going to report his suspicions himself.

"He went out to Eden's River to confront Abraham first, and that's when he was killed. The refrigerator had already been pulled out of the kitchen in the break room back at the plantation, along with everything else, and Abraham used it to hide the body in the field. Because the plantation was pretty empty by then and was so close to the commune, no one saw anything."

Kali listened, nibbling her bread and sipping from her mug. "Must have been tough to move."

"Abraham had enough of a following by then. There were probably plenty of people at the commune to help move an old refrigerator without ever knowing what was inside. We don't know yet who those people were or what they knew, but everyone who can be tracked down is being rounded up for questioning. That woman you met on Lānaʻi—Anita—is supplying names. Hiding the other bodies didn't require any help. Abraham, Ruth, and Linda Bragden could have handled that themselves."

"And Matthew Greene? Was Linda Bragden part of that?"

"Not according to her statement, but that will be for a jury to decide." He finished the last of his banana bread. "Damn. That woman next door—what's her name? Birta?—is a really good cook. She'd make a great sister-in-law. And that Elvar is something else. He clocked both Ruth and Abraham, and managed to knock out the grandson while he was at it. And that's before carrying you up the stairs and out of the house."

Kali caught the sideways look he gave her, but she didn't respond. She finished her slice of bread and took another sip of coffee. Walter watched her, his concern plain.

"You got whacked pretty hard, you know. You need to take it easy. In fact, that's a direct order from a superior officer." He shook his head, slightly amazed. "Your skull must be made of cast iron. I really don't understand how you came out of this whole thing without a major concussion."

"Well, people have been telling me my whole life how hardheaded I am," she said, attempting a small smile. Her head throbbed, but she didn't want Walter to leave. The guest bedroom door was propped open, so she went into the room, reaching for the cheerful stuffed horse sitting on the bed where she'd left it. She lifted it and carried it back to the living room.

Walter watched her as she sat back down on the sofa. She tossed the horse to him. He caught it, a look of surprise on his face.

"For me? Thanks, but I don't remember asking for one."

"Maybe one of the girls would like it? I bought it for Makena. You know, as a baby gift. I'd rather not see it around, but it's kind of cute, and I don't want to just throw it away."

"Sure," he said. "Suki will love it. She's obsessed with horses. She keeps hinting at riding lessons. And she's always eating carrots. She says it's because horses like them." He chuckled. "As though that's going to convince either Nina or me that we need to add pony club to everything else we already have on our schedules. Suki gets her way a lot, being the youngest, but I'm playing the tough guy on this one."

They sat together for a while, discussing the upcoming cultural festival, and the role each had to play. Walter was far more excited about the ukulele competition than she was about the hula demonstration.

"Hara got out of the drumming, didn't he?" she asked.

"He lucked out, you mean. Turns out there was a family birthday party on the same day, so that took precedence." Walter looked at her arm, then lifted his gaze to her face. "You're going to scare the hell out of the audience with your bruises and cuts," he said, matter-of-factly. "Parents are going to warn their kids that hula is dangerous."

She was going to agree that this was true, but only if there happened to be a cult leader around who thought there was something wrong with being Hawaiian. Her hand reached for her hip, and she lightly pressed the spot where her other, private tattoo lay safely hidden. If Abraham had discovered that one, she might have had a real excuse to duck out of the festival showcase. *We like to think we're so different, so evolved, with our computers and cathedrals, our art and our philosophy*, she thought to herself. *But are we? We plunder the earth and destroy what is beautiful and necessary; when we kill, it's not just for food and territory, but too often for reasons that are selfish and spiteful and small.*

Walter's phone buzzed. He answered it, then looked at Kali. "Yes, she's awake. She looks like she was thrown off a bridge onto a slab of concrete, but here she is." He passed the phone to her, and she glanced at the screen as she took it, surprised to see that the caller was Stitches.

"Hello, Detective. Glad to hear you're all right. The price we pay, yes?"

"I suppose it is," said Kali. "Tangle with killers, and you might get killed, or something like that."

"Yes. However, I'm glad you're on the mend, and hope that there's some satisfaction to be had knowing each of our nameless people has at last been identified."

Kali frowned. "Well . . . we're still missing a head," she said. Walter looked at her, then shrugged.

"Unlikely that it will be found unless one of those cult people decides to be generous and tell us where it is," said Stitches. "Well, I must get back to work. Feel better, Detective."

The line went dead. "Is Abigail Waters being held in Wailuku?" Kali asked Walter.

"For the moment." He folded his hands. "She's not going to tell you anything, you know. She still doesn't truly understand that her father did anything wrong, and talking to you just implicates her further."

"She was a child."

"She's been an adult for a long time, sitting on the knowledge of four deliberate deaths and one stolen identity. I don't think you're going to get a confession out of her that she knows anything about anything."

"That's okay," said Kali. "I don't think we need it. Can you call Tomas and have a team go back to the plantation? Specifically to the building that was used as an office with the break room. Find out from Manuel Raso where Abigail and Joey planted their sunflower garden, and have a search team check the ground there. Tell them to be thorough. I think Abigail buried the head there."

* * *

After Walter had left, Kali fell asleep again on the sofa, drifting in and out of slumber until Tomas called her. Her hunch had been correct. Joey Manu's skull had been found buried in the old sunflower garden he'd created with his friend Abigail Waters. It, too, had been smashed in. Kali felt a sense of completion, and fell into a deep, untroubled sleep.

In the morning, she put more ice on her swollen face, surveying the damage in her bathroom mirror. The festival was two days away, and Walter was right. She was likely to scare anyone who got a good look at her. She sighed and changed her clothes, putting on her shoes. She needed to go next door to thank Birta for the food—and Elvar for saving her life.

CHAPTER 33

The turnout was far better than anticipated. The grounds of the park where the Fire Garden Cultural Festival was being held were packed. *No one*, thought Kali, *not even people like Abigail and Abraham, had been able to quell the spirit of Hawai'i.* She smiled wryly, acknowledging to herself that now even the legacy of battles and darkness, of zealous missionaries and intoxicated tourists and horrendous traffic, were part of the story of the islands, woven indelibly into the fabric of her own personal history. *Less beautiful or gratifying than brilliant sunsets and tales of goddesses, perhaps; but still chapters in a much longer tale.*

She looked around, admiring the displays, savoring the scent of the foods that had been prepared as part of the celebration. Carrying a cloth bag that held the dress she'd given to Makena, she found her way to the seating area in front of the stage. She wasn't sure why she'd brought it. She reminded herself that Makena had never actually promised to come.

The cheerful music of a ukulele band on the main festival stage was augmented by a larger soundtrack made up of laughter and chatter. The night was filled with the joy of locals participating in a beloved festival that celebrated their culture, mingled with the happy voices of visitors on a much-anticipated holiday, each of them reveling in the air of the warm, fragrant island night.

She glanced at her phone, checking the time, then searched the crowd with her eyes. There was no sign of Makena. She tried not to feel anything, but as the minutes ticked by and she failed to appear, Kali was startled at the level of disappointment that washed over her, both sudden and unexpected. Of course she hadn't shown up. Disappearing, after all, was one of Makena's most highly developed skills.

Near a display of handcrafted wood art, she caught sight of Elvar's tall figure. He was examining a bowl created from a single piece of koa wood, turned by a skilled artist who had revealed the patterns swirling through the grain in a contrast of gold and a deeper brown, and who had celebrated the wood's small imperfections in a live edge along one side.

"Nice," she said, standing beside him. "That would look beautiful on your dining room table."

"Yes," he said, running a finger gently along the bowl's rim. "I am thinking of buying it for Birta as a gift. Her birthday is next week."

"I didn't know," she said, thinking that she should. Birta had been her neighbor for years, and it seemed a simple thing to know about her. She looked up at Elvar. "I don't know your birthday, either, come to think of it."

"March first. I'm a Pisces. What about you?"

"July sixth," she said.

"Ah. That makes you a Cancer, and both of us water signs." He smiled. "Very compatible, according to the zodiac."

His observation was followed by an awkward silence.

"Good to know," she said, her words coming in a sudden rush. "I wouldn't want to be at odds with Hilo's favorite babysitter."

Elvar looked down at the bowl in his hands, and Kali mentally kicked herself. She had meant to say something more personal, but words had failed her.

"No, we can't have that," he said. He looked at her, his gaze steady. "I must not keep you from getting ready. Walter told me you are performing a traditional dance tonight. I look forward to seeing it. Birta should be here soon as well, and I know we will both enjoy your performance."

She took a deep breath, not knowing exactly how to put into words all the things she wanted to say. "Elvar, I know I've already said thank you, but I hope you know how much . . . how much I appreciate what you did for me."

He looked into her eyes. "I am just grateful you are safe and on the mend." He smiled again, wider this time. "And I have no doubt that you would do the same for me."

She stood, trying with all her heart to come up with better words. He waited, but she looked away, and he turned to speak to the wood artist. Kali stepped back into the path that had been created between the tables and displays, again feeling as though an important moment had been lost. As she approached the stage area, she saw Tua standing by the backstage steps. He was holding a clipboard, waving to her as she drew closer.

"They roped you in as well, I see," she said.

He shrugged. "I don't mind. I've helped out before, and enjoy the energy of the festival. At least," he said, looking meaningfully at her, "no one got *me* to agree to dance."

"But you *do* dance," she protested. "Quite beautifully, too."

He bowed slightly. "That's very kind of you. But my hula practice isn't for general public consumption. I get a little nervous when too many people are watching."

She looked up at the stage. A trio of drummers dressed in brightly patterned sarongs was performing, and the delighted crowd had been mesmerized into silence.

"Am I next?"

"Almost. I'm going to offer a chant, and then the musicians will begin your song. You can walk on as I walk off."

"Okay. Just a warning: I haven't danced onstage since I was a kid, and my teacher at the *hālau* hula volunteered our class to perform at a wedding."

"You'll be fine!" His eyes twinkled. "But just to add a little pressure, you should know that Walter won the ukulele solo competition."

She laughed. "Oh dear. Guess I'd better get my game on for the glory of the department."

The drummers had finished, and Tua put down his clipboard and walked out onto the center of the stage. The cheering crowd quieted. In the sky, the full moon shone brightly. The torchlights flickered, and Tua bowed his head. Then the deep, resonant sound of his voice filled the air as he offered a traditional *mele ʻāina* that told of the Hawaiian people's deep and respectful connection to the land.

Next to the stage, Kali listened, her heart filled with his words and the images they evoked. She adjusted her dress. The skirt of the sea-green silk material lightly skimmed her body, falling to her upper calves. There was a lei of soft, fresh plumeria flowers around her neck. Her hair was loose, and she wore a single white plumeria blossom tucked behind her right ear. She had hesitated before placing it, as the position of the flower indicated that she was an available single woman, but had decided at the last minute that it was appropriate.

Tua finished his chant, and the band moved back into position. She made one final search for Makena in the crowd, then allowed herself to accept the simple truth that she was alone. Taking a deep breath, she stepped onto the wooden boards of the stage in her bare feet. The song she had chosen to dance to was one she had listened to countless times. It told a melancholy story of loss, but ended with the promise of renewal. It was a fitting choice, she felt, given her mood of late. The crowd in front of her grew silent, watching in appreciation as she swayed and moved across the stage. She smiled as she danced, but it was a humble smile, not one that would challenge or tempt any jealous gods or goddesses who might be lingering in the shadows.

She could see Walter in the front row. He was standing next to Birta and Elvar, who was smiling. Their gazes were fixed upon her. She let herself slip more deeply into her dance. There was optimism in the words of the song as it approached its end. *What is it that I hope for?* she asked herself. And then, as she caught another glimpse of Elvar, *Who is it that I'm dancing for?* She stepped sideways in a *kâholo* movement to the right, moving closer to the space where he stood. *Is it for the past, or am I dancing toward the future, a different future from the one I once dreamed of?*

She felt her heart racing in confusion as the last notes of the song faded and the audience applauded. Before she had time to leave the stage, Walter climbed the steps to stand beside her, already strumming his ukulele. He waved to the crowd, and launched into a brisk, upbeat tune. He pointed at Kali and the crowd applauded again.

"Who wants to keep our detective dancing?" Walter called out, grinning. The crowd clapped enthusiastically. Several of her colleagues called out in encouragement. Walter played faster, a familiar tune, and Kali fell into step, beginning a new dance. Other dancers who had already performed joined her, their smiles all filled with delight. There was no more melancholy—just simple joy in the movement and the music. She looked toward Elvar. He was smiling, too. He waved to her as their eyes met, and she laughed.

She left the stage as Walter was joined by several other musicians, and the festival continued. Standing against the trees in an area where tables laden with food and gifts had been set out, she watched as the red and gold flames of the tiki torches erected around the audience area flickered in their own kind of ballet.

The musicians played for a while, taking turns to mingle with festivalgoers and to enjoy the abundant food and drink. She could see people surrounding Walter as he came down from the stage, congratulating him on his trophy, and heard the deep, familiar tones of his voice as he made everyone around him feel as though they had won as well.

A couple, arm in arm, passed her on their way into the clearing in front of the stage, eager to join in the festivities. She watched them for a moment and was about to walk away when Walter looked up and around, his eyes searching the crowd for her. He waved when he spotted her. She smiled and blew him a kiss, then made the shaka *no worries* sign with her right hand.

No worries. At least not for tonight, while the moonlight spread a glow across the island-scape, and a fleeting sense of camaraderie and well-being emanated from the crowd. She gathered up the cloth bag with the dress that had gone unworn, hoping that Makena was somewhere safe. Then she stepped back beneath the trees, turning toward the parking area. She slipped away into the night before anyone else might realize she'd ever really been there in the first place— before Elvar found her and she had to think too hard about how true it was that nothing good ever seemed to last quite long enough.

If you enjoyed THE BONE FIELD, be sure not to miss
Kali's first investigation:

THE FIRE THIEF

**The scenery may be beautiful, but dangerous secrets are
buried beneath paradise in this first thriller featuring
Maui detective Kali Māhoe.**

Under a promising morning sky, police captain Walter
Alaka'i makes a tragic discovery: the body of a teenage
surfer bobbing among the lava rocks of Maui's southeastern
shore. It appears to be an ill-fated accident, but closer in-
spection reveals something far more sinister than the results
of a savage wave gone wrong. Now that Alaka'i is looking
at a homicide, he solicits the help of his niece, Detective
Kali Māhoe.

The granddaughter of one of Hawaii's most respected
spiritual leaders, and on the transcendent path to becoming a
kahu herself, Kali sees evidence of a strange ritual murder.
The suspicion is reinforced by a rash of sightings of a
noppera-bō—a faceless and malicious spirit many believe to
be more than superstition. When a grisly sacrifice is left on
the doorstep of a local, and another body washes ashore,
Kali fears that the deadly secret ceremonies on Maui are just
beginning.

To uncover a motive and find the killer, Kali leans on her
skills at logic and detection. But she must also draw on her
own personal history with the uncanny legends of the islands. Now, as the skies above Maui grow darker, and as she
balances reason and superstition, Kali can only wonder:
Who'll be the next to die? And who—or what—is she even
on the trail of?

On sale now wherever books are sold.

CHAPTER 1

Police captain Walter Alaka'i struggled for footing in the warm, waist-deep water. In front of him, revealed by the morning light, the body of seventeen-year-old Kekipi Smith bobbed back and forth with the current, no longer encumbered by the constraints of will or desire. The deep gash in his skull had long since ceased to bleed, washed clean by lonely hours spent drifting along the ragged beach beneath the last shard of February moon. The boy's eyes were half open, as though he were struggling, out of politeness, to stay awake.

Walter braced himself as a wave crashed in, then drew away, tugged by the invisible force of the tide. The naupaka blossoms in the dense coastal bushes caught his eye—fresh, gentle, wrenchingly out of place this morning. He backed carefully toward the dense mangrove roots behind him in the shallow cove of water that had pooled between the scissory lava rocks along Maui's southeastern shore. With his right hand, he grasped one of Kekipi's ankles, and did his best to keep the body from jolting against the rocks and gnarled labyrinth of twisted tree roots as each incoming wave lifted it and pushed it forward.

There was a thud, thud, thud of running footsteps beating against the heavy sand along the shore, followed by a soft splash as Officer David Hara slid into the water behind him. Hara averted his eyes from the face staring up from the sea to the cloudless sky, and Walter noted how he kept just out of reach of the floating arm that stirred with the moving current.

"Reinforcements here?"

Hara nodded. "Coming down the hill now, sir, with the stretcher. Photographer's with them, but the coroner says she's about a half hour out if she gets on the road before the tourists. She said to go ahead and pull him out when we're through, since it's an accident." He hesitated. "And that old fisherman who called it in is waiting for you at the top of the hill path."

"Okay. Tell him to stay put until I've had a chance to talk to him. Surfboard's just past the entrance to the cove, washed up in some kiawe roots," said Walter. "I'll stay here with the body. Be sure they get photos of the board."

The tip of an orange surfboard jutted from a clump of thick brush about fifty feet away. Walter's eyes locked on the board, and he calculated the facts at hand. The entire scene clearly implied the savage results of a wave gone wrong—an innocent surfing expedition turned fatal. Walter shook his head. It was not the first surfing death he'd seen over the years, and he was fully aware that it was unlikely to be the last.

He braced for the next wave as Hara scrambled past him, using the snarl of roots and branches to pull himself onto higher ground. The current from the receding wave tugged at the body. From the shore, there was the sound of movement, then voices. The branches were pushed aside, and hands reached out. Walter kept his hold on one ankle as the police photographer recorded the morning's unfortunate discovery, not letting go until the medics had taken over and had hauled both the sodden body and Walter from the sea.

The sky above was regrettably blue, given the events occurring below. The boy was wearing swim trunks, and his brown, tanned torso and feet were bare. Walter watched, dejected, as the slender remains were maneuvered onto a stretcher waiting on a patch of thick grass, then covered over with a thin sheet.

Along the water's edge, the police photographer moved away from the spot where the surfboard had been jammed. He paused briefly as he passed Walter. "All yours, brah."

Walter grumbled. He looked back to where Hara was waiting next to the stretcher, then to the spot where the medics stood. They had walked away, down the beach, and Walter was aware that they were deliberately avoiding making eye contact with him. "You expect me to pull that damn thing out of the water?"

The photographer shrugged. "Not like you're going to get any wetter, you know? Give the rest of us a break."

Walter sighed. It was true. There wasn't a dry inch of him to be found. He edged himself back into the sea, then took a deep breath and ducked beneath the surface and came up with the board resting on one shoulder. He struggled over the sharp rocks, scraping his arms and legs, his bulky frame not designed for this much physical activity, especially not this early in the day.

He carried the board to where Hara stood, shifting nervously from one foot to the other. Walter ignored him, doing his best not to be bothered by Hara's persistent discomfort in his presence. Every junior officer who had ever worked for him had exhibited the same nervous response, and though Hara had been under Walter's supervision for nearly four months, he was clearly not going to be an exception.

No practical experience, but clearly eager to learn, thought

Walter. Maybe too eager. At twenty-three, Hara was an absolute pain in the ass. And, in Walter's estimation, he was far too good-looking to be a cop. Wherever he went, it seemed that a small parade of women magically appeared in his wake. Walter had just enough sense of self to admit that he found this to be more exasperating than anything else.

"Captain, there's something . . . well, something you should take a look at in here. What I mean is, sir, I think you might want to—"

Walter held up an impatient hand. "What is it, Hara?"

"The body, sir."

Walter sighed. "Just spit it out, please."

"Well," Hara began, confused. "The head wound . . ."

Walter walked past him without saying anything more.

The body lay silent, the legs slightly splayed out, permanently stilled. Hara moved to the top of the stretcher, then pulled the sheet aside and pointed to the wound. "Looks like the bone around the cut is crushed, sir."

Walter frowned. He stared in silence, considering the inference. "And? He hit those lava rocks and split his skull open with the impact of coming off the board, most likely."

"Except for this, sir." Hara stepped to the side, pointed at the gash. Walter bent closer and peered at the wound. There was something there, embedded in the edge—something shiny and white caught in the flesh.

Walter glanced at the medics, now standing at the edge of the water engaged in conversation, their sensitivity dulled through necessity and long years of recovering drowning victims. He pulled a pair of wet gloves from deep in his back pocket and slipped them on.

"Flashlight," he said, his voice terse.

Hara fumbled at his belt and removed a small, powerful penlight.

"Angle it right here . . . no, more to the left."

Walter studied the uneven opening in the skin, probing gently at the edges, speaking to himself. Hara stood beside him, still fidgeting.

Walter shook his head in confusion. "Well, I'll be damned. If I'm not mistaken, that's a *manō* tooth."

"That's what I thought, too, sir. But what's a shark's tooth doing in his head? That wound isn't a bite. If he cracked his head open on the lava rocks while he was surfing, why would there be a tooth in the flesh? And wouldn't a shark have, well, eaten some of him? Wasn't—"

Walter held up his hand again, muting a vexed Hara. "Calm down, Hara." Walter peered off toward the distant haze of horizon. "That's all true, but it makes no sense."

Hara took a deep breath, then gestured to the surfboard lying nearby. "And the surf leash is still connected to the board but not fastened to his ankle."

Frowning, Walter squinted more closely at the wound. Were his powers of observation slipping? Hara had made a good point about the surf leash, not that Walter saw any good reason to acknowledge it immediately. The fact that the leash's Velcro collar hadn't been secured around the boy's ankle was odd, as the cost of surfboards made leashes a practical necessity for recovering one after a fall. If he was correct about his unofficial identification of the body as local surfer Kekipi Smith, he knew that the family included five children and that a good surfboard had likely been a luxury.

Something stirred in Walter, and his voice lost its edge of sternness. "Right, then," he said. "Something here isn't adding up." He turned to Hara and nodded. "Good observation, Hara. Time for Detective Māhoe to get her tattooed-warrior ass over here. Let me have your cell phone. Mine's over there on the beach somewhere. You can look for it while I'm talking."

Hara handed over his phone and stepped toward the edge of land that fell away to the cove where the body had been found. Walter punched in his niece's familiar number, beginning the climb up the steep path leading from the sea to the parking area above. She needed to see the body in the full context of its surroundings, before it was taken away, while the boy's *'uhane*, or spirit, was still lingering in the place where he had died.

"And tape off this area," Walter yelled after Hara's retreating back. "We might have a crime scene on our hands."

CHAPTER 2

Detective Kali Māhoe stretched her fingers down as far as possible, her lean, muscled legs wrapped around the thick lower branch of the old mango tree in her yard in the small village of Nu'u, near Hana. She could almost touch the ground with the tips of her middle fingers, where the ends of her long ebony hair mingled with the thick grass at the tree's base. From her upside-down position, the horizon was reversed, and she watched as a bug labored through the green blades toward the edge of ocean-sky.

Kali had spent a lot of time in this tree when she was a child, dreaming of the day when she'd be tall enough to reach the ground, and being warned by her grandmother from the front porch that not only was tree climbing unladylike, but it was also a guarantee of broken bones. She smiled to herself. Her thirty-fifth birthday had just passed, and she'd yet to break anything.

Being outside, hanging from the tree, was far preferable to being indoors, sitting at the wooden kitchen table, which doubled as her desk. She'd been up for hours, and things were not progressing well with the presentation she'd been working on, which was to be given in conjunction with an adult night course the following spring at the University of Hawaii's Maui College. Besides her detective status with the Maui Police Department, she held a degree in cultural anthropology and was a recognized specialist in the cultural and spiritual traditions of Hawaii—a unique insight and perspective that often proved useful in her role as a detective.

Her grandmother, the renowned author and historian Pualani Pali, had left her this house and, by extension, the mango tree. It was also Pualani who had identified Kali as her community's next *kahu*, a spiritual leadership role traditionally handed down from grandparent to grandchild, which had been revealed to the older *kahu* by subtle signs that included Kali's natural interest in plants, her rapport with animals, and her dreams and visions, which were often layered. Pualani had confirmed Kali as her family's next *kahu* when she was five years old, after Kali had insisted that a sea turtle had warned her of a coming tsunami, which had indeed arrived soon after, with deadly flooding.

She pulled herself upright, grasping an upper branch, and dropped gracefully to the ground. The movement caused her dog, Hilo—the enormous offspring of a Weimaraner and a Great Dane—to raise his head briefly from his stretched-out position in a patch of sunshine.

The water beyond the lawn was tinged with grayish green. Bobbing gently on its surface was an old fishing boat badly in need of a new coat of paint. The name *Gingerfish* could just be made out along the length of the stern, and Kali felt a familiar sense of relief to see the boat still at anchor where she'd left it. Walter had purchased it from a friend moving to the mainland, and Kali had offered to let him keep it at the rickety dock at the edge of her property. Walter spent a great deal of his free time aboard in a comfortable deck chair, plucking away at a vintage ukulele, while she continued to point out the need to replace the aging anchor chain. So far, the only measurable progress was the amount of rust that had accumulated along its length.

The dog trotted beside her as she walked across the lawn to the cluster of papaya trees that separated her three-acre property from the neighbor's yard. She reached for a ripe fruit, then twisted it slightly until it came loose in her hand. There was a *hālau* partially obscured by the papaya trees' branches. The small shelter, with its roof of dried palm fronds, offered minimal protection to the unfinished canoe resting on sawhorses beneath it, caught forever in its half-carved form, unlikely ever to be completed.

Kali looked away from it, afraid of stirring up the memories it carried of her late fiancé, Mike Shirai. She took the papaya inside, placed it on the kitchen counter, then opened the refrigerator door and gazed idly inside. There was some rice and shrimp from yesterday's dinner and a bowl of limp sliced pineapple that should have already been eaten.

The papaya, she decided, would have to do for breakfast. While coffee brewed, she cut open the fruit. The soft orange-hued interior was filled with dark seeds that ran the length of its center, and she scraped these from their nest. The juice trickled onto the counter as she placed the halves on a plate.

Plate in one hand and coffee mug in the other, she passsed the kitchen table where her computer hummed, and pushed open the screen door. She made her way out onto the lanai, which ran along the front and one side of the small house. The sky was growing lighter as the morning progressed. She walked softly along the wide porch and settled into the threadbare cushions on a wooden deck chair, her legs tucked beneath her, then scooped up the sweet flesh of the papaya fruit with a spoon.

The sea spread out before her. The calls of gulls and the wash of waves against the shore were usually soothing, but this morning the sounds failed to relieve the sense of restlessness that troubled her. She hadn't slept well, having woken during the dark early hours that had yet to give birth to the dawn. Something was out of balance, and she knew it as surely as she knew the cloudless morning sky would be filled with rain clouds before evening arrived. Just as she had felt the approaching tsunami when she was five years old.

Kali sighed, adjusting her legs beneath her on the cushion. She had just eaten the last of the papaya when her phone rang, harsh and intrusive. Still holding the plate, she went inside and located the phone on the small table next to her sofa. As she lifted the phone, it slipped between her fingers, skittered across the wooden floor, and landed between a ceremonial drum and a spear gifted to her years before by a visiting New Zealand elder. She bent over, careful to avoid knocking over the spear, and retrieved the phone. As she pressed the button to accept the call, the plate fell from her other hand and broke into pieces as it struck the floor. She looked around the small room uneasily.

The voice on the other end of the phone was familiar—the deep, resonant tones of her uncle, Walter. "Aloha, Kali. You okay? Sounds like you're throwing things around."

Kali took a deep breath. Walter sounded oddly strained. "Not yet, but it's still early in the day. What's up?"

There was a tense pause on the line. "Well, I hate to drag you away from whatever it is you're not doing, but we've got a body down here on the beach. No positive ID yet, but I'm pretty certain it's Kekipi Smith, Anna Smith's eldest son. She made a call last night to say he hadn't come home, and it looks like he drowned down there off the cliffs near Haleakalā National Park, probably sometime late yesterday. Surfboard washed up nearby, so it appeared to be an accident."

Kali frowned, tightening her grip on the phone. "Appeared?"

Walter's voice was carefully noncommittal. "Well, seemed that way to begin with. But now something's turned up that doesn't make any sense." His voice wavered, but just for a second. "Can you get over here and have a look before we send him off?"

Kali's eyes darted back to the sea, just visible through the window. A dull malaise fluttered behind the bones of her chest.

Walter spoke into her silence. "I'm not feeling good about this. I'll explain when you get here, but we're treating it as a suspicious death. There are elements that put it right in your wheelhouse."

She closed her eyes and felt a shadow leaping into the darkness.

"Okay. I'm on my way."

She picked up her keys and headed out into the sunlight. Hilo followed, pushing the screen door open with his nose. He jogged close beside her, his long body bumping against her legs. She reached down with one hand, patted his head briefly, already lost in the story she was about to hear.